"No good deed goes unpunished."
- Morris Quint

"'Things are seldom what they seem; skimmed milk masquerades as cream.'"
- Abigail Critchley

"I actually liked this one."
- The author's mother

Cover illustration via Leonardo.ai
Cover design by Bespoke Designs,
Yelverton, Devonshire

ISBN: 9798884380066

The Cardinal's Legacy

by Michael Reidy

Volume IV of the *Unvarnished Truths* series

Lattimer & Co.

PHILADELPHIA • PARIS

2024

A Cristina
la bellissima redattrice di Milano

It's an odd thing but when you tell someone the true facts of a mythical tale they are indignant not with the teller but with you. They don't want to have their ideas upset.

Josephine Tey
The Daughter of Time

Foreword

Sophie's facetious comment at the end of *Bickering* suggesting that Sir Nigel go to Rome to reinvent himself as a religious painter seems to have been too big a challenge for him to resist.

Most people can point to several stages in their lives when they made key decisions that changed – or could have changed – things forever. External factors can force changes, too – like the death of Sir Nigel's young wife. Other choices are wholly deliberate.

While Rome was not unknown to him, Sir Nigel knew no one there. There were a few people he knew who could possibly turn up, but he made no attempt to contact them in advance or after he arrived. He had Sophie with him, and when they left London, they fully expected to return together.

☙

The Cardinal's Legacy began life as a short story variously called "Letters from Rome" and, for a short time, "Busman's Roman Holiday."

I didn't think enough people would remember what a busman's holiday was. Sadly, many wouldn't know *Roman Holiday*, either.

The idea was that the story would be the final one in the collection in development, and that it would neatly draw the adventures of the painter and the actress to a close. However, Sir Nigel and Sophie had other ideas, the tale grew beyond short story length, and I now find I've written a series of novels about the actress and the artist rather than the one-off I had expected when I finished *On the Edge of Dreams and Nightmares*.

January 2024
London

Part One

Chapter I

After yet another less than comfortable escapade at Bickering Place and upsetting various friends in the London art world, Sophie suggested that I have a break and get away from England for a few weeks.

"We could go to Rome and you could reinvent yourself as a religious painter," she had said. [1]

As this was her counter to my declaration that I thought I'd retire, I took the suggestion only semi-seriously. Over the next few days, I toyed with the idea, balancing the exciting prospect of going to Rome again with the palaver of modern travel.

London had gone damp and grey at the beginning of September and the weather in Rome, the internet assured me, was bright and warm. Still, the pleasure of the daydream outweighed the idea of check-in lines and endless airport corridors.

That was before Sophie banged on my door, no doubt having heard me drop ice into my glass for a gin and tonic from her set across Rope Walk.

"Are you packed yet?" she asked, when I let her in.

I poured her a drink and sat down.

---

[1] *Bickering,* 2023

She remained standing.

"Are you?" she demanded, glancing around the room.

She stared at me.

"You haven't accepted a commission, have you?"

I shook my head.

"If you haven't begun to pack, you'd better get started," she said. "You won't need much, we can buy you new clothes when we get there. All you really need are your bank card and passport, but I expect you'll want a few dozen pencils and a sketch pad – no forget that, you can get them there. I've listened to you go on about Italian paper for years."

"It's very tempting," I began. "I've even mentioned it to a few friends who thought it an amusing idea."

"It's more than that," she said, loudly, after taking a mouthful of gin. "The train is at eleven-ten tomorrow."

She took another drink while I glared at her.

"Don't worry. It's all taken care of. A car will be here at nine-thirty."

"Are you – ?"

"I told you. I only have until mid-October before I start rehearsals."

℘

She was right. The circumstances were perfect. I needed a break; I had no urgent commissions; my passport was still current, and it wouldn't take me more than half an hour to pack.

All right, forty-five minutes counting the artist's materials.

After I'd got things in order, I headed out to my club to say goodbye to friends and gloat a little, but I didn't get that far. As I approached Burlington House, I saw Alex Josephson exiting the forecourt and stepping into Piccadilly. He saw me and waited for me to catch up.

Sir Alexander Josephson was a former president of the Royal Academy and a prolific and versatile artist. He had the gift of making a few lines take life and define an object, a face or place, and with a bit of colour or shading, an atmosphere.

Alex was more a colleague than a friend. We got on well enough, but I suspected he still considered me a lucky amateur. He was a high-flyer who moved on a different plane to me. He enjoyed society. I did not. He was no sycophant, but he was adept at fund-raising and had done much to consolidate the finances of the RA. He also defended it and maintained its reputation in some difficult situations.

"I hear you're headed to Rome," he said, demonstrating just how tight and gossipy the art world is. "No doubt to paint a few cardinals and maybe His Holiness?"

I laughed.

"I leave tomorrow, but with a different objective," I said.

"I'm going to the Arts Club. Come with me," he said.

We said little until we were seated with our drinks. There were many friends to greet. Alex knew everyone, but I held my own.

"So, is this just a Roman holiday?" he asked, affably.

"More of a busman's holiday," I said. "Sophie thinks I should get out of my ruts, away from London and exit my comfort zones."

"Daring at your age," Alex said.

"She tempted me with the idea of doing some religious paintings."

Sir Alex froze. His eyebrows lifted and he fixed me with an uncharacteristic stare.

"That is very astute," he said. "She knows you very well. It's a very good idea – no, a transformative one."

It was my turn to stare.

"There hasn't been really great religious art in a very long time," he continued, with increasing gravitas. "One problem is that the talented people haven't attempted it. Another problem is that there is precious little market for it – even showing it is difficult.

"However, the real problem is that fewer and fewer people know the stories and symbols."

He looked me straight in the eye and paused until he was content that he had my full attention.

"You and I – Catholic and Jew – are heirs to some of the greatest stories the world has known, but as artists, for the last century, we've been silent about them."

I shifted in my chair to face him more squarely.

"I've thought about this since Sophie proposed it," I said. "I keep asking myself, does the world need another Nativity, Martyrdom of Saint Sebastian, or Moses in the Bullrushes?"

Alex gave the hint of a smile, understanding me perfectly.

"You would have thought that there would be a generation of amazing Jewish art after the Holocaust," he said. "There has been some great art by Jews in that time, but nothing to approach *Guernica*. *I* certainly haven't done anything. Not even a Jewish wedding."

"Come on, Alex," I protested. "Your Jerusalem water-colour series is wonderful – and popular."

He shook his head.

"Painting a Jewish place is not painting the Jewish story – though some Zionists might argue otherwise."

"We paint what we paint," I said.

"And how selfish is that?" he countered. "Together, we have wonderful rituals, philosophies, and traditions – and you stole half of ours," he added, smiling. "When you get back, we should have a meal and a good discussion. We owe that to our forefathers, and you can show me what you learned in Rome."

I nodded.

"I'd like that, Alex."

"Your Catholicism is more visible than my Jewishness. I don't hide it, but I don't get into the newspapers by falling over outside Farm Street Church," he laughed, then grew more serious. "I observe the rituals at home, but keeping Shabbat as the PRA was impossible. I tried to do events after sundown, but. . ."

He paused, then brightened up.

"If not nativities and St Sebastian, what do you have in mind?"

"Absolutely nothing," I said, shaking my head. "It's not well-known, but Andy Warhol did a lot of religious pictures, especially towards the end of his life. The critics never talk about them – probably because they don't understand what they mean. I think only Catholic magazines print pictures of them."

Alex looked surprised.

"He went to Mass every day," I continued. "He never spoke about what he believed, but a requiem Mass was said for him at St Patrick's Cathedral in New York."

Alex glanced at his watch.

"I'm afraid I have another appointment, Nigel," he said, "but promise me two things: meet me when you get back so we can discuss this further."

I nodded.

"And?"

"Have a go at an Old Testament subject."

୫

I reflected on the conversation with Alex as I packed, and later the next morning as we rode to St Pancras and boarded the train. Sophie knew something was on my mind as we chatted, but she knew not to ask.

Despite my ruminations, it was with excitement that we began our journey and installed ourselves in our comfortable Club Duo seats, and soon, we were having lunch and enjoying a few glasses of acceptable cabernet sauvignon as we slid into the channel tunnel.

Sophie had made all the arrangements but frustratingly didn't tell me what they were. I had no doubt she had done it all herself. She wasn't a helpless celebrity who needed everything done for her. While she did have an agent, she set her own terms, paid her own bills and balanced her chequebook.

(How she did this last task, I'm not sure as she once asked me to rip out a cheque for her, and I saw that the stubs all had addresses, emails, telephone numbers and recipes written on them. Sophie liked writing cheques, as did I, but for her it was a game whether it would be deposited or kept for her autograph.)

At the Gare du Nord, we queued for a taxi which took us to the Hôtel des Grandes Écoles.

I looked at her curiously once we were settled in the car.

"I thought you liked it," she said, as if there were a doubt.

We had stayed there before on a not-entirely success-ful weekend, though I painted one of my favourite pictures while there. [2] I was surprised that she risked a repeat performance.

Somehow, she had managed to book the same rooms overlooking the garden, and I wondered if this trip had been as spontaneous as she led me to believe.

It was barely mid-afternoon, so after unpacking a few things and freshening up, we walked up to the Café Souf-flot for a few glasses of wine and a mixed *charcuterie et fromage* board.

Sophie sat back in her chair with such abandon that I was afraid she'd slosh wine all over herself.

"Oh, it's lovely to get out of London!" she sighed. "I love it, and variety keeps one young."

I agreed. Getting this far had been painless, and my French was good enough to feel comfortable.

"What's planned for tonight?" I asked. "Maxim's followed by Crazy Horse until the early hours?"

"The Musée d'Orsay is open tonight," she said, ignoring my facetiousness. "We can do a turn around the Luxembourg after this, then have a short rest, go to the museum and have dinner afterwards."

Did she have the whole expedition planned?

———

[2] *On the Edge of Dreams and Nightmares*, 2018

"I'm fine with the first parts, but I have no desire to go to a museum."

Sophie put her glass down.

"You are turning down a visit to the Impressionists?!" she exclaimed, almost accusingly.

"Isn't this supposed to be a break?" I asked, forking another piece of sausage.

She tried to recover.

"Then, what would you like to do?"

I thought a moment.

"I think I'd like to go to a bistro or café on a very busy corner, have a good steak and watch the crowds."

Sophie shook her head in despair.

"And have you selected such a place?"

I shrugged, getting into French mode.

"The choice can be serendipitous," I replied, grandly. "Place Saint Michele, Place du Châtelet, Les Halles, Place des Voges. Anywhere busy."

"Do you want noisy and dirty, too?"

"Sounds delightful."

☙

For those not following our curious relationship, the best way to describe it is that we are anchors for each other. We've never been lovers, and, indeed, we were barely aware of each other for decades, until Sophie, as Ligeia Gordon, her stage name, asked me to paint her portrait.

During the sittings, she revealed that we'd met when she was fourteen and I nearly thirty. For her, I was someone who knew her in her innocent days. For me, she was someone whose company I could enjoy without the expectation of anything more than drinks, meals, conversation and companionship.

We were also each other's secret-keepers.

I wanted little more since I was still in love with – or in mourning for – my dead wife. As an award-winning actress, Sophie needed someone with whom she could feign a normal relationship. In reality, she could not stand to be touched.

She managed well enough on stage and in films when she was playing someone else, but as herself, hugs were brief and air kisses the norm. On rare occasions, like on a train, she'd doze with her head on my shoulder. Sometimes, she could even hold my hand for nearly three minutes. Putting her arm through mine was the only nearly physical contact she could sustain.

Our togetherness was one of separateness; she yearned for normality. She would flirt with witty conversation and her RADA-learned looks, glances, carefully crafted head turns and tilts. Anyone watching would be taken in by the performance and see a couple devoted to each other.

It didn't take long after I began to paint Sophie that I realised this lady needed help. She revealed that she had been abused by her uncle and it had changed her life.

So did murdering him.

She never told me how, and his death was never regarded as suspicious. Although I was possibly, technically an accessory after the fact, there wasn't a shred of evidence that a crime had been committed, and more than forty-five years had passed.

So, Sophie never sought help, and I never said a word, and that is why we are as we are today.

☙

Our brief walk through the Jardin du Luxembourg was remarkably refreshing. We watched the fountains, strolled the avenues of carefully manicured trees, and wandered aimlessly in the Romantic sections before heading back to the hotel.

I realised after my shower that I had become so absorbed in Paris that I'd forgotten that our destination was Rome. I also realised that I had no idea when we'd get there or how.

Sophie knocked on my door shortly after seven and we made a leisurely walk to Gare Austerlitz where we took the Metro to Place de la Bastille. It had been our intention to head to Place des Voges, but on crossing the treacherous intersection, I spotted the Café Français and it offered the busy and noisy ambience I sought.

We read the menu and inspected the rows of tables and chairs along the pavement. Sophie liked the menu as the desserts were listed on the first page. There was an excellent selection of meat and pasta dishes and the *modern Art Deco* design had an honesty about it that was refreshing.

The automobile traffic wasn't too bad, and the crowds of people who passed seemed eager to start the weekend.

We ordered drinks and perused the menu.

"Are you looking forward to Rome?" Sophie asked.

"Is it a symptom of age that getting out the door is the hardest part of travelling?" I asked. "Once I sat down in the Eurostar, I felt twenty years younger. So, yes, I'm looking forward to getting to Rome, but I'm enjoying being here."

Sophie caught my inflection.

"But. . .?"

I laughed.

"Not really a but. I'm curious what you've arranged for the rest of our journey."

Our wine arrived.

"To a holiday for us, a rest for me, a profitable excursion into new artworks for you, and maybe even an adventure," Sophie toasted.

"I'm not sure about the adventure, but I'll drink to the other things."

I'd chosen a Burgundy, mostly because I tended not to drink it in England (for no good reason). This one had good body and more complexity than I expected from a wine simply labelled "Burgundy" on the list.

"Don't you want another adventure?"

I thought about this.

"As long as it doesn't include people as bonkers as April and Marissa," I said.

"Oh, don't get pompous!" Sophie chided. "You know there was great affection there. For all your protests, you wouldn't have painted her like you did if you didn't feel something for her."

"Fortunately, my Italian isn't good enough to get caught up in a similar domestic intrigue."

The waiter appeared. Sophie ordered a *filet de bar*, while I chose my sautéed *steak au poivre avec frites maison*. One is in Paris.

We watched the crowds and enjoyed the wine and bread as we waited.

I was musing on the continued popularity of shades of gold in French women's clothes. It was as perennial as red, white and blue, and I noted it on the first visit to Paris with Sophie.

"Of course, that other bit was another story," Sophie suddenly said.

"Bit of what?" I asked, yanked out of my daydream. "Something else you wanted to order?"

The look I got wasn't one of Sophie's patient ones.

"Bit of fluff," she said.

I could tell she was irritated, so I refilled her wine glass.

"The dead one?"

Now it was Sophie's turn to look blank.

"Whose dead?"

"The singer."

"The dead singer."

I remembered her name, of course, but winding Sophie up with feigned vagueness was the best way to deal with her bouts of synthetic jealousy.

I was comfortably settled back in my chair which I knew would be a further irritant. I could see her trying to think of who I was talking about.

"The American?"

"That's her," I said. "Fletcher."

She nodded.

"Fletcher Bailey. You took up with her when you were cross with me."

At the end of the refrain, thrust home.

"See, you *do* remember," I said.

"She's dead?"

"Car accident last summer. You were up at April's," I said.

She considered this.

"That's very sad," Sophie said. "You didn't think she was very happy."

"No, I don't think she was," I said. "I did do the little secret picture for her which seemed to please her."

Sophie thought about this and was still doing so when our meals were delivered. We made appreciative comments, and she immediately stole several of my frites, before turning to her sea bass.

She had swallowed the first piece when she realised she hadn't finished teasing me about the bit of fluff.

"You're getting too good at manoeuvring me off the point," she said, as I emptied the bottle into her glass.

"Same again, or something different?"

"That was good," she said. "Another would be fine."

I asked for another bottle and turned to my steak.

"You're not serious about Miss Rawding, are you?" I asked, correctly guessing that she'd lost interest in the tease.

"She was sweet," she said. "Being widowed at such a young age can't have been easy. I suppose that's why you two got along. You had real empathy."

"If that was the reason, it was unspoken," I said.

The painting of Rachel Rawding - *The Yellow Frock* – was one of the last portraits I'd done, and I had only recently shipped it to Lincolnshire. Its success – winning three prizes at the Royal Academy Summer Exhibition – was one of the reasons I'd decided to retire. Sophie and I had visited the Academy with Rachel, and I had sensed more empathy between Sophie and Rachel than between Rachel and me.

Sophie now moved on to talk about the plans for the next day.

"We can have a lie in and a late breakfast – either at the hotel or somewhere else," she said. "We can leave the bags at the hotel until we're ready to leave, so we can do what we like with the day. Any ideas?"

"I expect you'll want to visit Galeries Lafayette," I said.

"And you will haunt the bookstalls and art shops," Sophie countered.

Somehow, we managed to find room for dessert: *crème brulée* for Sophie, *îles flotante* for me, then several cups of coffee.

"Brandy?" I asked.

She shook her head.

"I just might have something in my room back at the hotel."

Chapter II

Friday went as orchestrated by Sophie. We walked up Boulevard Saint Germain to the café at the Hotel l'Abbatial where we had coffee and various pastries and decided to walk to Saint Michel and over to the city to see if we could see anything of the Notre Dame restoration.

While Sophie didn't get to Galeries Lafayette, she was able to shop, and so was I. On our first trip to Paris, I had treated myself to a sable watercolour brush which I brought with me on this trip; this time, I acquired another by the same maker in a different size.

We looked through the massive shopping centre in Les Halles – the second since the original markets were destroyed – where I picked up a light murder mystery and a book on the mathematics of the Greeks. Sophie picked up a number of accessories which I couldn't begin to name.

Passing through Place Vendôme, Sophie suddenly stopped outside a gallery and peered in.

"Is that a Roger Fry?" she asked.

We went in.

It was an excellent spot by Sophie. There aren't many known street scenes of Paris by Fry. This was in the style of *Le Sacré-Coeur, Montmartre* with its bright light, sharp contrasts and imperfect perspective. This painting was smaller and in a portrait orientation. It had the same bright light and strong shadows and was a pastiche of every contemporary French artist he'd ever seen.

I looked at Sophie as she read the label.

"*Rue Norvins*, 1920."

"*C'est charmant, n'est pas?*" the gallery chap said.

"*Le charme est le grand fléau anglais. Il tache et tue tout ce qu'il touche,*" I replied, nearly quoting from a favourite book.

"You don't like it?" he asked in English.

"It's decorative."

Sophie retreated to look at a sculpture of a fish made of bottles and cans at the far end of the gallery. Whether this was to conceal laughter or embarrassment, I didn't know at the time.

"Fry's portraits were fine, if derivative," I said. "But, he was the only one of the group who could paint."

The man was about to open his mouth, but I interrupted.

"Now *this* – "

And I moved to a small pointillist painting of a harbour.

" – is beautiful."

Happy to agree, the man told me about the picture, who had painted it, where, and who had owned it. I asked the price, and he wrote the details on a card for me.

"What was all that nonsense about charm?" Sophie demanded. "You were very rude about the painting."

"It wasn't very good."

"Really? I liked it," she said.

"It's pleasing, no doubt," I said. "I doubt I'd have recognised it as a Fry. I really only think of him as a portrait painter – when I think of him at all."

"And the others?"

Well aware that I'd been sounding pompous.

"The next time you see paintings by the Bloomsbury crowd, imagine you're seeing them in a GCSE or A-level art class exhibition and ask yourself if they belong there or in the best museums of the world."

We walked up rue de la Paix and took the Metro back to the hotel to collect our bags. Sophie asked at the desk for a taxi.

When it came and our bags were loaded, I expected that we'd be dropped at the RER station that would take us to the airport.

"*Gare de Lyon, s'il vous plaît.*"

In the back seat, I looked at her and she gave a smug grin.

Our luggage was unloaded, and we headed into the station. Sophie glanced at the clock.

"Good. We've got time to get something to eat."

We'd gone a long way on some croissant and *torsades*, and I was hungry. Sophie's careful planning had ensured we had time for the next leg of the trip, and we made our way into Le Train Bleu.

While the main restaurant was closed, the bar offered equal elegance and memorable dishes and some cold Chablis that would hold us until a late dinner.

"All right, I give up," I said, after we'd ordered. "Tell me how you recognised the Roger Fry picture."

"Do I have to? A girl likes to have some secrets," Sophie replied.

"Very well," I said, taking a drink. "This place and the Opera Garnier must be – "

"If you must know," Sophie interrupted, "I once narrated a dreadful ballet for some charity event. The dancers were in their final year of ballet school and were excellent, but the ballet was based on Maupassant's supernatural tale, 'Le Horla.' The backdrop for the ballet was the Roger Fry painting of Sacre Coeur. It was supposed to show the bleakness and loneliness of life."

"Sounds enchanting."

"The music was by Constant Lambert, who no one remembers, and I narrated the whole thing in French, which was pointless since there were sur-titles in English," she said with a mixture of amusement and embarrassment.

"Not a West End hit, I gather."

"I was contracted for three performances, but the choreographer and librettist hoped it would be taken up," she said. "I think there were thirty people in the audience on the third night. Still, the main event was full and raised the needed money.

"I felt sorry for the dancers who were wonderful and lovely people."

Our food came and we enjoyed it, unrushed, in our opulent surroundings.

"Have you given any thought yet as to what you might do in Rome?" she asked. "I expect at least one good painting to be taking shape by the time we leave."

I had given a lot of thought to the subject. I had done so for decades.

Once having considered going into the priesthood, when I found myself painting portraits, I considered bringing my desire for a vocation together with my new interest in painting. The state of religious art of the fifties, sixties and seventies was pretty dire, but there was still the impulse among a small number of painters and sculptors to pick up religious themes.

"Knowing where to start is the hard part," I began. "Painting the major figures, Christ, the Blessed Virgin, the apostles, and saints is too close to portraiture to be the break from it that I need.

"There are endless Biblical subjects, but most have been done – and done magnificently," I said. "I've been thinking of doing small architectural drawings. The bits I did at Bickering showed me what I needed to learn. I can also do details of some of the major works and try something new like icon painting."

Sophie smiled but said nothing. She didn't have to, I had told her what she wanted to know: I *had* thought about it and *did* have some plans.

Eventually, she asked if I knew how to set about doing all that.

"I have my campaign all mapped out," I said. "I'll tell you about it when we get to Rome."

A man likes to have some secrets, too.

଼ଠ

With less than an hour until our departure shortly after seven, Sophie told me we'd be taking the sleeper, arriving in Rome shortly after midday. We used the time to buy some water, a few packs of biscuits (savoury and sweet), and a few magazines.

The sleek train with its mix of red and white, and green and white liveries was curious, but overall, it was a tribute to modern European railways. The shadows and perspectives were fascinating.

Sophie moved me out of my daydream (again) and guided me towards our carriage. While we had adjacent compartments, they did not connect. Shortly after dropping my bag, I knocked on her door.

"This is amazing!" I exclaimed. "A private loo and a shower! I hope you've got that, too."

She assured me she did.

"Come for me at eight and we'll go to the dining car," she said, shutting her door.

My bed was made up, but there was a seat I could comfortably use. I could see that an upper berth was folded against the bulkhead to accommodate another person. At least it didn't occur to Sophie to put me up there.

Sleeper train accommodation could be very much like that on shipboard. Junior naval officers would share staterooms and while storage was pretty good, there was barely room for two people to stand up at the same time. On shipboard, the orientation of berths was dictated by the operational mechanical demands of the ship, which made them a tertiary or quaternary priority. An American I painted expressed surprise at the configuration of European train berths at ninety degrees to the direction of travel rather than along the direction of travel. The fact that you could sleep more people in a car with the European orientation never occurred to him. The American imagination isn't confined by space.

A change in the lighting made me look up from my sketchbook to see that we were moving. For those of us of an age who remember trains starting with a lurch, the way that modern trains glide into motion remains a source of wonder.

When my mind stopped considering the geometry of *waggon lits*, I spent the time continuing to make quick sketches of what I'd seen in Le Train Bleu and of our train, the platforms, crowds, cast iron columns and the double pitched shed. I could visualise a painting in oil, but not in watercolour.

File it away; it's not what I'm on this trip to do, I thought, remembering my intention to focus on religious paintings. Perhaps I should go to America where they used to have Catholic chapels at the large stations often called "Our Lady of the Railways," which struck me as a very American concept.

It was about a minute to eight when I glanced at my watch. I hastily put my things away, tidied myself up and knocked on Sophie's compartment.

There was an extraordinary amount of rustling, doors and drawers closing, switch clicking and coat hanger clinking before the door opened.

"Are you all right?" I asked. "It sounded like you were fighting off griffins and harpies."

"How can you lose something in less than two square metres of space in less than an hour?" she asked, clearly fed up with herself.

I looked her up and down.

"You don't appear to have misplaced anything."

"I was looking for the water we bought in the station," she said, sounding exasperated.

"You gave it to me," I said as neutrally as possible.

"Well, *why* didn't you *tell* me?"

"Would you like me to get it?"

"You can buy me something stronger in the restaurant," she snapped, as she stomped to the door at the end of the carriage and punched the button to open it.

She'd regained her composure by the time we were seated, and she had a glass of Bordeaux in her hand.

We watched the darkness close in as our meal arrived. Unusually, we'd ordered the same things: *foie gras* with fig preserve, chicken breast on creamy mushroom *tagliatelle* with spinach and pine nuts followed by *tiramisu* and *espresso*.

Sophie was now relaxed, and I thanked her for making all of the arrangements.

"I just hope you like the hotel in Rome," she said. "It was difficult to know where to be," she said. "Near the Forum, the Vatican, the river, the Pantheon, the Spanish Steps – "

"I'm sure whatever you booked will be fine, Sophie. It's Rome."

Without normal relationships, Sophie's phases of wanting to feel affectionate, useful and normal had curious manifestations that could become obsessive. She clearly cared how this holiday would work out and I couldn't hurt her.

"I gave the agency a list of things we wanted for our rooms. I specified with a decent dining room or near a variety of restaurants. I specified a roof terrace – with or without a bar, and to be near a Metro station. I wanted an old building, not a modern egg-crate."

"Did you ask for *aqua minerale gassata* on tap in every room?" I asked.

"I just wanted to get it right, Nigel," she said, then she brightened. "They came back with a suggestion that met my demands, but said it was a little eccentric because it was family-run, but clean, and friendly. It's got four stars, but apparently, just barely. The rooms are apt to be small."

"As long as we have access to the roof terrace and the sparkling water, we'll be fine," I said, with a smile that Sophie returned.

It was now dark outside. When we finished our espressos, we went back through the carriages to our sleeping car.

"Thank you, Sophie," I said, at her door. "I'm sure everything will be splendid. Neither of us is that hard to please."

She giggled.

"I hope we can get some sleep."

The bed had been made up, but I was still able to sit up and read for a few minutes before drowsiness made me get ready for bed. I debated whether to close the curtain. I didn't mind getting up with the sun nor did I worry about being seen asleep in Dijon or Bologna, though I might be awake by the time we got to Florence.

Seeing lights flash around the compartment was something unusual to be indulged as a pleasure. Once in bed, I resumed reading for another few minutes before giving up and switching out the light.

ↃⱰ

Some people can't sleep on trains, no matter how luxurious the accommodation. I can sleep nearly anywhere. Boarding school noise, shipboard rocking and machinery sounds and open windows in London all taught me to seize the opportunity to sleep when I wanted to and ignore other people's noise: if you're not responsible for it, then don't let it bother you.

I woke up shortly after five, debated whether to pull down the blind or just put on my eye mask. (Noise is one thing, flashing light is another.) I opted for the mask and went back to sleep not waking up until nearly seven-thirty. Presumably, we'd stopped in Florence and were now streaking through the Tuscan countryside and heading to Lazio and Roma.

Being able to shower was a luxury and there was plenty of hot water remaining for a good shave. It was a considerably more pleasant experience than the Royal Navy provided.

I was just about ready for the day when Sophie banged on my door.

ⱰↃ

Breakfast in the dining car was a perfect prelude to the day. The bright light on the countryside increased the anticipation of arrival. After several cups of coffee, we adjourned to Sophie's compartment which had been restored to its daytime configuration. We went there since she somehow had far more to pack than I did.

As we approached Rome, with Sophie still packing, we went through what seemed to be a continuous succession of tunnels, long and short, before slowing into the great fishhook leading into Roma Termini.

Chapter III

The chaos of getting a taxi at a busy Italian station will be known by anyone who has attempted it, but it cannot be described.

Our hotel was, as Sophie hoped, central, convenient, family run (why is shouting amusing in a foreign language but irritating when you can understand what's being said?), and with a comfortable dining room with a good menu. The rooms weren't as small as I expected. The light was good, there was a desk, chair and armchair. The furnishings were the sort that would be found in a good guest house seventy years ago and, while worn, everything was clean, and the bed was comfortable.

Some would object because there was no television or USB port, and a very basic telephone service that still went through a switchboard at reception. The roof terrace, however, made up for it. There were tables and comfortable chairs, and the views were magnificent. There was no bar, but because there was a lift all the way up, staff didn't mind delivering drinks as it got them into the daylight, albeit briefly.

After dropping our bags and having a look around, we set out, partly to get some exercise and partly to get some lunch. We cut through the narrow streets to the Pantheon where we found an *osteria*. I had an excellent *gnocchi* with an outstanding *parmigiana*, and Sophie opted for a spaghetti with smoked salmon. There was rustic bread and a country wine that slid down far too easily.

"Isn't it lovely how different this feels from Paris and London," Sophie said. "It's hard to describe, but there is a certain something in Italy that is distinctive."

"Everything is an opera," I said.

"That's what I missed in Paris," Sophie said, waving a piece of bread.

"The chaos?"

"No. It would have been nice to go to the opera. Can we see if anything's on?"

"I don't expect the season to have started yet, but we can see."

Animated conversation and banging of pans and plates could be heard from the kitchen, but they were sounds of busyness and not anger, and we continued our meal enjoying the beginning of something new.

❧

After lunch, we aimlessly followed the narrow lanes to the river and looked across to the Castel Sant'Angelo and the bridge, but were surprised that from where we were, we couldn't see St Peter's. We walked down the embankment and onto the bridge. Sophie stopped me when we got to the middle.

"We're here for two weeks," she said. "We can do that another day."

I had no objection and was content watching the artists painting the scene and selling paintings to tourists. On the half of the bridge and its approach that we saw, there were more than a dozen mostly young artists bravely taking on a scene that many masters struggled with.

The variety was impressive, from small, beautifully detailed water colours, sketches and pastels to large semi-abstract oils with exaggerated colours. Should anyone wonder about the next generation of painters, if what I saw was any indication, the world of art was secure. Of course, not everyone was talented – and amongst the crowd, the bad ones really stood out – fully two thirds of them deserved wall space somewhere and one or two would almost certainly become highly collectable.

Sophie appeared less impressed and stood at the stone and bronze parapet wall looking at the river.

After exchanging some comments with a few of the painters – who were only willing to chat if you were willing to buy – (that's mean; I don't see anyone until a commission is in the bag) – I joined her and watched the slow flow.

"It's so quiet," she said.

I looked at her, not understanding as the noise of automobile horns and general traffic noise were at the normal Roman levels.

"The river," she said, looking back at it. "In London or Paris, there would be a continuous flow up and down. Only one tourist boat has gone by since I've been standing here. Nothing else."

We crossed to the other side to look upriver, but it was just as quiet. We turned back to the city and walked along the river to the next bridge where Sophie picked a bus stop.

"Let's go sit in the Forum," she said, then laughed. "I always wanted to say that."

She'd obviously done a lot of homework because, in time, a bus to her liking came along, she produced two passes and we found seats. I made no comment about her organisation – and wouldn't until we'd reached our intended destination.

At Piazza Venezia we negotiated a change and not too long later arrived at Colosseo and entered the Forum. Anticipating a comment, Sophie turned to me.

"I expect you've been here in a former life," I said.

"Most recently on my sixth form grand tour."

"And before that?"

She laughed.

"Who would be most appropriate? Take your pick: Portia, Livia? Calpurnia?"

"All patricians, I see," I said.

"But of course! One knows one's place!"

We were up the via Sacra and turned left to the Temple of Vesta. There was a stone bench and Sophie sat down. From there we could look further up the via Sacra to the Temple of Concord and the old senate.

"The one thing I remember about visiting here on my grand tour was a recognition that this was *real*," she said. "I'd seen the movies, read some history and the odd bit of literature in Latin classes, but to *be* here and realise that those events and those *people* were all real sparked the beginnings of a – I don't know what the word is – *appreciation* is too weak – it's like an *absorption* of the truth of reality. I'm saying this badly."

"No, you aren't," I said. "The words have just been debased over time. *Imbued* with a sense of the history is what I think you're driving at."

Sophie nodded and smiled.

"Permeated."

"Exactly!" I said. "Have you ever read Gibbon? I read a few hundred pages of it while on shipboard, but his sense of atmosphere and his ability to create visual pictures is extraordinary."

She shook her head.

"I probably read a few passages. Nothing I remember."

"He sat here in the Forum with his notes and a few sources and wrote – *en plein air* as it were – and the prose is amazing."

We sat in silence until the chill of the granite bench made us get up and continue our walk.

Sophie took my arm and leaned close.

"I played Cleopatra once – not in Shakespeare but in *All for Love*," she said. "To think that she walked, rode or was carried right along this street is quite a thought. It's really rather narrow for a grand procession."

"Two chariots wide and no place to park."

"After Antony and Cleopatra were dead, their surviving children were brought back to Rome and brought up by Antony's Roman wife, Octavia, Augustus' sister."

"Even today, that would be considered pretty unusual," I said. "What happened to them?"

"That's unusual, too," Sophie replied. "Apparently, they integrated into Roman society. Their son became a civil servant or something."

"You couldn't make it up."

"That's the really amazing thing: you couldn't make *any* of it up. And, as odd as it all might seem, it all rings true, but what amazing people they must have been."

It wasn't until we'd left the Forum and took a bus back towards the hotel that I considered that it must have been unusual in the age of the smartphone, that neither of us took any pictures, and even during the times we were sitting, it didn't occur to me to make any sketches.

I was thinking of what I hoped to do in the next week in a semi-daze sitting on the bus, but Sophie was looking about and seemed agitated.

We left the bus shortly after Venezia and walked to the hotel.

"Did you notice the man in dark glasses and a hat?" she asked.

"On the bus?"

"No. In the forum."

"Most men in the Forum seemed to be wearing dark glasses and hats of some description. Ball cap? Fedora? Stetson?"

Sophie's expression turned to her normal exasperation with me. She appeared to be about to drop the subject.

"What was he wearing? Jumper? Jeans? Jacket?"

"I thought he was following us."

She looked around.

"I guess not," she smiled.

When we reached the hotel door, I reckoned there was just enough time to get to the art shop I'd seen on the next street.

"Will you be all right?" I asked her.

"Of course. I'm going to have a wash, lie down and try to learn some of my lines," she said.

"What time do you want to eat, and where?"

"Knock on the door at seven-thirty," she said. "I thought we could have Sunday lunch here tomorrow and go out tonight. Somewhere not too touristy."

૬ઝ

As I walked to where I thought I'd seen the art supply shop, I continued thinking about Sophie's comment in the Forum. On the bus, I had been considering that, too: those people who had thronged the streets of the Forum two thousand years ago were real. They did their shopping, bought clothes and food, tidied their houses or rooms, brought up their children and worried about how they would survive in their changing world – if they were aware that it was changing.

I realised that considering past lives was what I did when I visited galleries – indeed, I did it while I worked.

Looking at the faces and into the eyes of people in paintings could reveal a lot if the painter was good. Part of the portrait painter's craft is to give subtle hints of his own opinion of the sitter without the sitter recognising them.

I remembered coming across what I thought was an astute observation in a mystery story I'd read when I first began my career as a painter. At the time, I had no confidence that it would end up better than my career as a naval officer, but the lines gave me an inkling of what might be accomplished.

The character, a bed-ridden police inspector, had considered the face in a portrait and, not knowing who it was, made the following deductions:

> *Someone used to great responsibility, and responsible in his authority. . . A candidate for gastric ulcer. Someone, too, who had suffered ill health as a child. He had that incommunicable, that indescribable look that childhood suffering leaves behind it; less positive than the look on a cripple's face, but as inescapable. This artist had both understood and translated into terms of paint. . . the old-man look in a young face.*

From then, I tried to make that level of under-standing part of my craft. I didn't always succeed, of course, and my many trips to look at old portraits revealed that I was not the only painter who failed.

The art shop, I found, would be open for another forty minutes. I had brought brushes and the small jars I used for water as well as a small palette, but I needed a larger pad of paper and some colours.

I had found the limited palette I used for the paintings of the dig in Bickering satisfactory and would try using them in Rome. While the brands were different, I was able to buy the colours I needed: alizarin crimson, lemon yellow, ultramarine, and ivory black. Given the number of fountains in Rome, I also bought some masking fluid.

The successful result of my shopping was of no interest to Sophie when I told her as we set off for dinner. It was a small measure better than, "That's nice, dear," but it was clearly what she meant.

"Chiara at the desk says there's a reasonable neighbourhood trattoria just around the corner. She said it's used more by locals than tourists who think it looks boring," she said.

"Good camouflage," I said.

"I thought so. How hungry are you?"

"I think it will depend what's on offer," I replied, after considering it for a moment.

"Well, I'm starving."

Chapter IV

A lthough very busy, the Trattoria della Pigna found a table for us against an ancient stone wall. The restaurant comprised three barrel-vaulted rooms connected with several small archways.

It was old-fashioned in that there were white table-cloths, the waiters were in black and white, and the menu was traditional and without concessions to culinary trends. It was cosmopolitan in that it had dishes from all over Italy, but the wine list was strictly Italian.

When Sophie opened with a *tonnarelli cacia e pepe,* I knew we were in for some serious eating. I ordered a *tonnarelli carbonara* and a *cotoletta panata* and Sophie a *pollo alla Romana* which was cooked with pepperoni. She also chose a *Nero di Troia Passera Scopaiola* as recommended by the *cameriere* who'd been flirting with her since he handed her the menu. He was nearer her age than I was and perhaps fancied his chances. However, Tonio, when we came to know him over the next two weeks, was just being charming and was a dedicated family man with a hoard of children, the oldest of whom, Fabrizia, also worked in the Trattoria, and no doubt kept an eye on her father.

The wine arrived quickly with the basket of coarse bread. We'd learned at lunch to be careful about indulging in too much of that.

The noise level wasn't as high as I expected with the stone walls and floor but would occasionally peak with laughter or a few boisterous shouts. While busy, the staff were in good humour and used to working with each other.

Sophie and I would sometimes play a game in busy restaurants to identify the pecking order of the waiters and waitresses. In London, the order was male-dominated, but here, it appeared that the young Fabrizia wielded most of the power.

"She doesn't abuse it," Sophie observed. "She asks rather than tells. Her hand movements are encouraging and gentle."

We watched her throughout the evening. We noticed that she was the one to deliver coffee and digestifs to all the customers and to chat with them for a few minutes. Nothing she said or did was rushed.

Our *tonnarelli* arrived and our conversation and speculations ceased.

Sophie and I had outgrown facile comments about our food unless it was remarkable in some way. Tonnarelli isn't commonly found in our London haunts, but it made a superior alternative for more prosaic pastas. It was distinguished by its rougher surfaces that held the sauce, its square profile and lightness.

Sophie put her fork down and glanced around.

"You know, you could do worse than to paint this busy interior," she said. "There's lots of action, good geometric structure and plenty of people."

I laughed, perhaps too loudly.

"Do you want me to throw the *minerale* at you?" I said. "Have you forgotten already why I came here?"

Although surprised by my reaction, she laughed, too.

"I just don't want you to spend all your time painting disappointed looking Madonnas," she replied. "It wouldn't be good for you."

I was about to reply that there were several painters who painted cafés and restaurants more brilliantly than I ever could when I saw how I could stop her wind up.

"Now that you mention it, I think there's a good possibility for a full portrait of the lovely Fabrizia here," I teased. "The square canvas could take in the whole archway, the till, and maybe a diner or two in the background. You wouldn't like to make a cameo appearance, would you?"

The demonstrative rebuttal was defused with the arrival of our main courses.

Sophie was trying to recover dominance of the conversation, but I got in first.

"*Buon appetito.*"

I met Sophie on the roof the next morning shortly after nine. I asked if I could bring up a coffee and some pastries, but they brought it up for me. When it arrived, there was a large pot, extra pastries and another cup.

"Signorina Sophie asked for a call to be put through to your room as soon as you stepped into the *ascensore*," Angelina said. "She will be joining you in *un momento*."

I thanked her, but wondered if the odd Italian word was thrown in for local colour, or just to remind me that I was in *her* country.

The sky was clear, and the temperature was about thirteen degrees and promised to be warmer. Later, I would bring up my pencils and sketch book and see what I could do with the view.

I had just poured my coffee when Sophie arrived. She was more warmly dressed than I. Whose anticipation of the weather would be more accurate would be proved by who took off a coat or put one on first.

"I thought you'd be out looking for a church and doing your roaming Catholic thing," she said, sitting at the small table and contemplating the *pasticcini*.

"Been there, done that."

She looked up suspiciously.

"There was an eight o'clock Mass at Chiesa del Gesù," I replied, smugly.

"Do the Jesuits implant a magnet in children's brains?" she countered, looking even more smug and showing she'd done her homework, too. Chiesa del Gesù was the mother church of the Society of Jesus.

"No," I said, laughing. "They just tie an invisible thread to you."

I poured her coffee, and she sat back and sighed.

"I didn't think I'd ever want to eat again after last night's dinner. What time did we get back?"

"Not that late. You hadn't turned into a pumpkin."

For one of the few times since I'd known her, Sophie looked embarrassed.

"I remember very little after leaving the restaurant," she confessed.

"You have nothing to worry about," I said, but she was not reassured.

Not only was she trying to remember, but she was also trying to decide whether I was telling her the truth.

"Was I able to walk?"

"The second *limoncello* might have introduced a challenge, but you actually wanted to walk," I said. "It was a lovely night."

She drank some coffee.

"You're going to make me work for this, aren't you?"

I said nothing, but looked at her affectionately, and with just a touch of pity.

She took a deep breath.

"Tell me this – and only this: why were my shoes and tights wet?"

"We walked to the Piazza Navona. We walked all around it. Then, you wanted to sit down for a minute. You said your feet – or shoes – were hurting.

"We sat on the guard rail, and you took a shoe off to rub your foot."

She put her hand over her mouth.

"That was unladylike," she said. "Did I drop it?"

I hesitated.

"No, you put it back on, swivelled around, stood up and stepped into the fountain."

Her eyes opened wide as if to ask if that were true.

"You did it," I said, gently.

"And you made no attempt to stop me?"

"I didn't want to get my shoes wet. Anyway, I was looking around for the police."

"I suppose that was gallant," she conceded.

"Not really. I was going to ask them to help me get you out."

Sophie was now beyond words, so I continued.

"I thought 'BAFTA Award-winning Dame Ligeia Gordon Arrested in Rome for Jumping into a Fountain' had a nice ring to it. Not many sixty-two-year-olds would be so daring."

"Sixty-*one*," she corrected, sharply.

46

"Ah, you see? You're more upset about someone getting your age wrong than any fear of publicity for fountain jumping."

Finally, she laughed.

"Bastard! You really had me going," she said. "I must have been away with the fairies, though."

"I'm going to get my drawing paraphernalia," I said. "If someone comes up, could you ask for more coffee."

I was nearly at the door when Sophie called to me. I stopped and turned to her.

"So how did my shoes *really* get wet?"

ରେ

After our dishes were collected, Sophie pulled out her script and a pencil and opened it somewhere in the middle.

"I'm not sure this play is going to be successful," she said. "It's a good thing that I know several of the other actors; we can play off each other and sculpt the lines to achieve various effects, but the director and playwright must let us."

"Is that likely?"

"No idea, I'm afraid. I've never worked with either of them," she said, sounding uncertain.

"But it's the National," I said. "They're not in the business of producing flops."

"No, but with new writers and directors, you never really know what's going to happen," she replied. "They could be geniuses, or they could be *poseurs*. The best to be hoped for is one of each. Get two of either and you have a certain flop.

"Anyway, could you try these lines with me?" she asked. "I can't tell how they're supposed to be said. There are minimal stage directions."

"Like Shakespeare, you mean?"

I got her black look, and she pointed to a line.

"From here."

"*We can't afford for you to lose another job,*" I read.

"*I can't stay there. It's a dead end. I'm better than that.*"

"*Are you?*"

"*Oh, thanks a lot!*"

"*I'm serious. Why do you want to keep a job that you hate? It doesn't even pay well.*"

"*Lobster.*"

"'Lobster'? Is that a typo?!" I asked, "What's that supposed to mean? Is all this pointless?"

"*Nouvelle vérité,*" Sophie said.

"*Ancienne eau de cale,* more like – and what's Gérard de Nerval have to do with anything?"

"Just read, darling," Sophie said, patiently.

I looked back at the script.

"*Are you capable of a rational discussion?*"

"*Arbitrage.*"

I rolled my eyes.

"*You used to care. What's changed?*"

48

"That's good," Sophie said. "Now, where can we give this some colour? If I try – "

"Wait a moment, old thing. What kind of play is this? Is it drama? A comedy? A tragedy?"

Sophie turned from the script and looked at me.

"You know, I've read this play four times now, and I couldn't tell you."

"So, what happens if the cast want to play it comic, but the director thinks it's some deep psychological tragedy."

Sophie smiled.

"With this cast – which has half a millennium experience – I think I know who'll win," she said. "If we don't, we'll just get fired one by one. It will be great publicity for the play, like *Lady Chatterley* being banned. No one would have looked at it otherwise."

"You won't just do as you're told?"

"Actors aren't the prostitutes we once were," she laughed. "Do your first line again, but don't sound desperate this time."

We tried the section a few different ways, but Sophie didn't feel she had it yet, though by the end, we'd both memorised the lines which made it more spontaneous.

"It's not good writing, is it?" I asked. "It has neither rhythm nor euphony."

She closed the script.

"No, it doesn't," she agreed. "I'm going to get my book to read. You can do some drawing."

We went down to our floor together. I fetched some pencils and one of the tablets I had bought the previous evening. When I returned to the roof, Sophie hadn't returned. I set up near the edge where I could fit a portion of the dome of St Peter's into the frame.

Its shape surprises every time. It's a building that you can recognise instantly, but when you look at it closely, it's not quite what you think. On a previous visit, I observed that the façade is like a French railway station, complete with clocks. Until you see the cross held by Christ on the top of the building, the apostles (and St John the Baptist), the figures could be anyone, and the rest of the façade is positively puritan compared to the great English cathedrals. Not an angel in sight.

For an hour, I drew little more than doodles. I tried the interior of the trattoria from memory, the view from where we sat in the Forum (I had a tourist leaflet to cheat from) and was about to try the buildings across the street when Sophie rushed onto the roof.

"He's here!" she exclaimed, in a near panic.

"Who?" I asked, sitting up.

"The man, who was following me," she panted. "He's in the lobby."

I put my hand on her arm and gently guided her into a chair.

"Breathe, Sophie. Breathe," I said, softly. "Have you forgotten everything you learned at drama school?"

For a moment I expected my next thoughts would be considering the sensation of being hurled from the roof, but she gave the germ of a smile.

"Tell me what happened?"

She breathed a few more times.

"Well, nothing happened," she admitted, "but I went to the desk to confirm our reservation for lunch, and he was standing at the desk, chatting easily with Chiara."

"What did you say?"

"Nothing, of course. I don't accost strange men," she replied, offended by the suggestion.

I stood up and walked toward the lift.

"Don't hit him!" Sophie called.

I could have used more time in the lift to consider the twists of her thinking.

When I entered the lobby, a man of theatrical good looks in his mid-to-late forties, was chatting to Chiara. It didn't look romantic to me, and it certainly wasn't threatening, as both were laughing easily.

On seeing me, Chiara put on her professional face and turned from the man.

"How can I help you, Sir Nigel?" she asked.

"It's more about helping Miss Gregg," I said. I turned to the man. "I'm afraid that this is about you."

Chiara's eyes widened, and the man reacted with innocent surprise, stepping back with a big smile on his face.

"*Io? Cosa ho fatto?*"

I smiled back.

"I don't think you've done anything, but Miss Gregg thought she saw you at the Forum yesterday, then on the bus, and later that evening around the hotel," I explained. "I think it unnerved her."

The man was still smiling but lost for words.

"Perhaps I can help," Chiara said.

The man and I glanced at each other.

"*Sir Nigel è un maestro ritrattista e il tutore di Miss Gregg,*" Chiara explained to the man. "Gaetano is – what's the English? - *un cugino di secondo grado* – "

She looked at both of us for help.

"A second cousin," I offered.

"Si, second cousin," they said, simultaneously and laughed.

"I think I am beginning to understand," Gaetano said. "Like most Romans, I haven't been into the Forum in a long time, but sometimes I go there to think and *rinnovare l'esperienza dell'essere romano.*"

Chiara began to translate, but I raised my hand to indicate I'd understood.

Gaetano continued.

"I thought I recognised Miss Gregg," he said, "so I came by Uncle Angelo's hotel when I saw where you'd come.

"Is Miss Gregg not Dame Ligeia Gordon?"

"She is."

"Do you think it might be possible to speak with her," Gaetano asked. "You see, we have friends in common."

ༀ

Before leaving the lobby, I asked for more coffee to be sent up.

On the roof, Sophie was in the chair where I left her, now wearing dark glasses with the script in her lap and a pencil in her hand. I watched her for a moment as she read a bit, tipped her head back, mouthed the lines a few times, then made a note.

I resumed my place.

"Well, I think I resolved that for you," I said.

"What did you say? What did he do?"

"I can assure you that you are not about to be carted off by a demented fan, nor kidnapped and held for an extravagant ransom. *Si può dormire facilmente*."

"I'm not worried about sleeping easily," she snapped, betraying an understanding of Italian she had not admitted hitherto. "Did you talk to the stalker?"

"I did."

"What did you say?"

"I invited him to lunch."

Chapter V

Sophie thought I was joking and it took some time to convince her that the man she'd seen wasn't a stalker, wasn't dangerous, and was actually someone she wanted to speak to. Gaetano had asked me not to tell her more. I knew Sophie would resist, but it might be fun.

It took an extra few minutes to get her to the dining room where Gaetano was deliberately seated to face away from the door, so we couldn't see his face.

The room was comfortably full, and the smell of food was wonderful. I led Sophie around the table to the seat facing him. During the process, she refused to look at him, but when there was no longer a choice, she looked up and gave a gracious smile – which quickly disappeared and turned an expression of astonishment.

"*Gaetano Minetti*?!" she exclaimed.

He stood and gave a slight bow.

She turned to me.

"Why didn't you tell me?" she demanded.

"Lobster."

"The fault is mine," Gaetano said, as we sat down. "I asked Sir Nigel not to tell you."

"Nigel, *do you know who this is*?"

"Yes, it's Gaetano, Chiara's second cousin."

"Gaetano is one of Italy's finest actors and directors," she said, enthusiastically. "He's been called the Italian Truffaut."

"In another universe, Truffaut is called the French Minetti," he said.

"You saw *Effetto Vertigine*. That's Signor Minetti's."

"Ah, the film within the film," I said, not noting that it was a clear homage to *La Nuit Americain*. Many critics failed to call it an homage but labelled it an imitation.

"Please call me Gaetano, Dame Ligeia. I am, as Sir Nigel says, only Chiara's second cousin."

We went through the ritual of inviting the use of our familiar names by which time we were asked for our lunch order. Gaetano asked for wine and some bread while we got down to the serious business of deciding what to eat.

Once we had decided and ordered, Sophie made a few comments about *Effetto Vertigine* – which we had both enjoyed.

"Alas, I have made some other films," Gaetano said, a little sadly. "Unfortunately, it is always the early success that gets the most attention."

Sophie laughed.

"I can identify with that," she said. "I wonder what I've done with my life when people tell me how much they loved me in a production I did thirty years ago."

"You are not working now?"

She explained how we were on holiday, and she was preparing for the play.

"Perhaps I could tempt you with something," he said, but we'd have to wait until after lunch to find out what he had in mind.

Over our very good meals, they talked about mutual friends in the theatre, who they like working with, and some very funny stories about pranks, mishaps and other things that film industry people found amusing.

By the time we got to coffee, Sophie's curiosity could not be contained, but she would never ask, so I did.

"So, what proposition do you have for Sophie?"

He wiped his mouth, folded his napkin and placed it on the table.

"It was just a thought I had when I saw you in the Forum," he began. "And it is much less a proposition for you, but a favour that might be fun.

"I am currently making a film very loosely based on Massenet's one act opera, *The Portrait of Manon*. It is set in the twenties with the fast set of flappers and jazz. There's also a bit of *La Traviata* thrown in."

Sophie was nodding her approval.

"It's a very simple story, but rather than confined in the one room, takes in the whole picture of society and contrasts it with pre-war elegance," he continued. "The des Grieux character spends much of the time remembering his lost love."

In all those recollections, the belle dame does not appear, but when Gaetano saw Sophie, he had the idea of one filmy appearance for their final kiss to give the daydream a firmer foundation.

"If you are agreeable, I can set it up and you can come to Cinecittà and we can do the shoot in half a day," he said, then looked at me. "It's what Americans call a cameo appearance."

"Which means no pay and no credit," I replied.

Sophie looked mortified.

"Ah, a film fan," Gaetano said, with an easy laugh.

"That was just my observation," I added. "I am not Sophie's agent."

Sophie put on her professional look.

"I will have to check with my agent to make sure that there aren't any residual exclusivity clauses. I certainly don't remember any," she said. "It sounds like good fun. Just one question, though."

Gaetano looked a little concerned but nodded.

"What age am I supposed to be?"

Gaetano considered this, no doubt thinking of additional costs for CGI or other effects, and Sophie began to look concerned.

Gaetano then smiled.

"Shall we say thirty-nine?"

ରଡ଼

From that point, things began to feel distinctly Italian.

Gaetano was happy and called for a bottle of champagne, which I later pointed out was the only payment Sophie would receive.

Since Gaetano was working all week, he asked Sophie to give Chiara her answer as soon as she spoke to her agent, and things would be arranged from there.

Gaetano disappeared when the champagne did, and I thought Sophie could do with some fresh air, so we joined the Sunday crowds in the Pantheon.

"I thought you'd take me back to Piazza Navona," she said.

"I will, but next time it will be before a meal, not after."

We walked in silence and shuffled around under the oculus before coming out into the Piazza della Rotunda. The sky had clouded over and the temperature dropped. We could sense rain.

"Can we go back to the hotel?" Sophie asked.

When we ascended to the corridor with our rooms, she looked up at me.

"I've got rather a lot to think about," she said. "I think I was more frightened than I thought, too. I have to call my agent – and that play – well, I could do with a rest."

She fiddled with my lapel which was something she did when feeling vulnerable.

"I expect you'd like some time to yourself, too," she said.

৪০

I sat in the comfortable chair by the window, my paper and pencils within reach, and began reading a book on modern religious art. After Sophie had suggested going to Rome, I had downloaded a number of articles and videos about modern Christian art and contemporary Catholic art.

While I had no illusions about breaking new ground with any paintings, I didn't want to simply repeat what had been done before in brighter colours or sharper lines. There was a lot more material than I'd supposed and some young commentators – who were neither experts in art or experts in Christianity – had some striking perceptions.

One of the more provocative commentators was by a young chap who noted that in earlier times art was used to communicate Christianity to illiterate societies but that it was now needed to communicate Christianity to a religiously illiterate culture.

The depth of the ignorance of Christianity, the historical role and contribution of the Church, and the seismic impact it had – and still has, despite deniers – on European culture never ceases to astound. This ignorance is not usually the fault of the individual, but of those who failed to teach them, and once that continues for a few generations – combined with an ignorance of secular history – the outlook for civilisation starts to look grim.

However, one of the basic teachings of the Catholic church is that it will survive, and more than one pope has recorded that it is that thought that kept him from petrifying into inaction.

It's not my purpose to lament the state of things, but finding a base on which to begin is part of my process.

How is one to approach painting the Blessed Virgin in the twenty-first century? There is something of the mediaeval myth about virgins today causing them to be regarded with the same incredibility as dragons or unicorns. How do you make sense of a virgin who is also the mother of God incarnate?

Murillo came close. His depictions of Mary were profoundly reverent, but she was a real woman of her time with just a touch of grubbiness on her feet, hands, and cheek – most of which has been edited out in the endless chocolate box and Christmas card reproductions – but see the originals, and you are looking at a flesh and blood woman.

Do that today you'd be thought to be defiling her or making some vaguely sexist social comment.

The same problems arise with painting the key scenes in both the Old and New Testaments: you'd either belittle the event with an archaeologically accurate picture, or be accused of painting a wide-screen Hollywood spectacular and sensational work. Scale it back and end up with little more than a children's book illustration.

I made a list of possible scenes to paint but soon found I had no appetite for a nativity, transfiguration, walking on water, feeding five thousand, crucifixion, resurrection, or ascension.

What kind of painter did that make me? What kind of Catholic?

I was not disheartened, just tired. I knew there would be something that would appeal, some lesser known improbable incident, a minor figure. I don't deceive myself that I'll discover something new, rather that I might see something different in an old scene.

That presented another dilemma: do I look at lots of art first, or do I home in on a handful of ideas?

It didn't look like two weeks would be nearly long enough to come to grips with this.

◌

I knocked on Sophie's door at seven. She was ready and suggested we find another local restaurant.

"Somewhere that I can remember what I did after eating there."

We didn't have far to go. We crossed the via del Corso and connected to the Via di S. Marcello where, just of the Piazza dell'Oratorio on the Via dell'Umiltà we found a place that seemed to be between an osteria and a pizzeria. The smells were enticing.

"I think I'm hungrier than I thought I was," Sophie giggled.

It was busy with people at the tables squeezed into every conceivable place, but we found places where it wasn't too cramped.

We were given menus that showed the breadth of the offering and were scanning the selection as the basket of bread and a litre of purply red wine were placed before us. As in such places in France, the wine glasses were small juice glasses.

As we looked around, an antipasto platter went by.

"Yum!" said Sophie. "Shall we get one of those? If we're still hungry, we can split a pizza."

I poured the wine which looked very purple when Sophie attempted a swirl.

"It looks like it was made yesterday," she said, before tasting it.

"It's really good!"

I filled my glass and toasted:

"To the soon-to-be sensation of the Italian cinema!"

Sophie smiled.

"I can't drink to that," she said, and countered, "to new paintings."

The *antipasto* was comprehensive with salami, pepperoni, ham, prosciutto, three cheeses, black and green olives, some peppers and basil leaves.

We took our time and were amazed that we could still successfully split an anchovy and mushroom pizza.

"I'll have to rely on CGI to keep me looking thin," Sophie joked.

"So, you *are* going to do it?"

"I emailed my agent. I should hear from him tomorrow. I've never been in an Italian film," she said, affecting a twenty-something would-be starlet.

"Have you done any cameos?" I asked.

"Yes, several. They were all while I was filming something else and the other productions were at the same studio," she explained. "Most of them for television. Once, I actually forgot I had done one and didn't see it when it was first broadcast. I was shocked when I saw myself in a re-broadcast years later."

It was good to see that Sophie had relaxed after her brush with supposed danger. Her whole manner was less self-conscious; it even came through in her voice.

The empty platter was cleared and while we waited for the pizza to be delivered, Sophie asked how I'd progressed in thinking about my new painting.

I told her my feelings about painting the major subjects which I felt would be the best to attract a little attention. She questioned me about the problems I anticipated, then just as the pizza arrived, she made her suggestion.

"Forget the Holy Family," she said. "I can see that you can't jump in with a Last Supper or Resurrection, but what about the saints? There are thousands to choose from, each with a unique story," she said, enthusiastically. "Some may not have specific symbols associated with them. You could raise awareness of them. They're still making saints, aren't they? You could choose a modern one if you wanted to weave in some social commentary."

I ordered coffee but declined limoncello, Strega and others on the recited litany.

Sophie said nothing, but her look suggested that she still wanted to know if my narrative of the previous night was accurate.

"Why not think of them as portraits of saints rather than as something iconographic or devotional," she suggested. "Let that come later."

This was an interesting thought.

"Later in my painting, or later in the picture's life?"

"Does it matter?"

Chapter VI

On Monday morning, I woke about seven. It was dark and raining hard, so I rolled over and went back to sleep. I'd have to rethink my day, but that could wait. Although it hadn't been late when we returned from the restaurant, Sophie's relief had made her tired and she said she was going straight to bed. I read a novel for about an hour before turning out the light. It was warm enough to have the window open and the city noises, different from London and Paris, were no distraction.

It was just after eight when I got up. I forgave my sloth, telling myself that I was still on London time. Once dressed, I took my copy of the *Journal of the London Mathematical Society* and went to a bar I'd seen around the corner for breakfast.

While it is common to stand at the bar, there was a small table available. I did not expect to be served and was surveying the scene to see what was being eaten, but a waiter came. I ordered a cappuccino to buy some time and settled on a cornetto, a few granola biscotti, and a slice of what I would have called a cheese and vegetable quiche.

With the *Journal*, I was able to eat slowly, and when I finished, I asked for another cappuccino. The waiter suggested a small bowl of fresh fruit which rounded things off nicely.

The ambiance was pleasant, if ordinary in the extreme. It was essentially a shop front in a modern building and as featureless as such places anywhere in the world. Its name was basic, too, Bar 43 – the street number – but it was clearly a place for locals with lots of coming and going, greetings, banter and business.

After breakfast, I returned to the hotel and checked the roof to see if Sophie were there. Not seeing her, I collected my pad and pencils and walked to the Palazzo di Venezia, a fifteenth century palace with large lights and exquisitely designed rooms. Largely unfurnished, the palace lets the spaces speak for themselves, whether carved stone or ornate *trompe l'oeil* architectural and design features.

I wasn't trying to produce finished pictures, merely to practise quick sketching and experimenting with suggesting detail without being fussy or spending too much time on it.

There were few places to sit, and I was asked to get off the floor, but I managed to find perches near the features I wanted to capture.

Since it was still relatively early, there weren't many people there, so it was easy to have a good look around before I settled down to work. What the building did produce was a succession of internal and external vistas that were exceptional for such a building in the heart of the city. Allegedly, the palazzo contains one of the largest rooms in Rome.

You would think that someone who has been painting continuously for more than forty years wouldn't need to practise perspective. Well, in most cases, you'd be right, but my formal training in painting was limited, and while many of my paintings contain architectural features (and have won awards for them), it is not my bread and butter. So, if I am to hare off in some new direction, I don't want to embarrass myself.

Many artists do a surprising amount of additional training during their careers. Most of it is informal: painting with other artists in the studio or on outings, setting each other challenges, or enthusiastically passing on new tricks. Curiously, this happens more frequently as one progresses in one's career. A lot of these are art school tricks, but we all didn't go to the same school – if we went at all.

I once painted the eminent conductor of one of London's premier orchestras. One day, his protégé and soon-to-be successor at the orchestra came to pick him up and was in my studio for about twenty minutes. As the old maestro had changed from the top-half of his white-tie and tails and was tying his normal tie, he and the younger man were discussing how to get the maximum volume from the end of a piece. Apparently, it is easy to reach the maximum volume (without damaging tone or rupturing the wind players) too soon.

"There's an old trick that John Philip Sousa used with his bands," the maestro said. "If the *stringendo* has got out of control, about four bars from the end, have the slightest *rallentando*. It is short enough to maintain the excitement and give the illusion of the volume continuing to increase."

If conductors do it, I've never been able to detect it, but that, I suppose, is the point.

Another way that artists share techniques is when in galleries together. It can be a modern picture or an Old Master. Comments like, "Can you see the scumbling?" or, "How many glazes do you think there are there?"

Art restoration videos on the internet have given away most of the tricks and techniques that artists use. Yet, the truth is, we artists seldom add new tricks to our bags. We use the ones that have worked for us. While we may occasionally experiment with something new, it's rare that it enters our repertoire permanently; it's there if we need it, but we seldom do.

Like novelists, playwrights, and singers, we perform for our own audiences. Everyone sees paintings differently. We're drawn to different colours, styles, textures, forms, subjects, and in the case of portraiture, people.

Artists suffer in a way that literary novelists, for example, do not. Everyone thinks they have a valid opinion about art, but few are willing to think enough about a literary work to dare to express an opinion. You never hear an instant reaction, "What rubbish" to an Umberto Eco novel, or even to a modern piece of music. In the case of the latter people generally have the sense to realise they don't know what they're talking about and keep silent, or they say they'd like to hear it again.

If viewers invested the same amount of time and thought looking at a picture as they did reading an Umberto Eco novel, they might not utter such nonsense.

Mind you, with a lot of art, the instant reaction is the same as the considered one.

∽

When beginning my painting career in my early thirties, I spent a lot of time going to galleries and looking at portraits.

My feelings of inadequacy were enormous, but so was my sense of excitement. Here was something that had no links with my late wife. Going to art museums except randomly wasn't something we did. We knew the Fitzwilliam, of course, and sections of the BM, the V&A and the various science museums. The Soane, the Hunterian, the Royal Observatory, the Wellcome Collection, the Faraday Museum, and the now defunct, Museum of Mankind. (This last one's home is now occupied by the Royal Academy of Arts.)

We liked scientific bookshops, and Charing Cross Road used to have a number of second-hand shops specialising in the sciences.

I wasn't illiterate in art, but when surrounded by roomfuls of faces staring down at me, I had to keep my nerve; after all, I had several commissions to fulfil.

One of the strategies I applied was one from mathematics, and that was to see how others reached their conclusions. The way I found of doing this was to rely on books. I looked at hundreds of paintings of the Queen, and Winston Churchill – who seemed to have been painted by more people than most.

I also looked at portraits of Somerset Maugham and Dame Edith Sitwell. These names are little known today, but Maugham had more plays running simultaneously in the West End than anyone achieved again until Alan Ayckbourn in the 1970s – and then only if you counted *The Norman Conquests* as three plays in simultaneous production even though they were performed on successive evenings at the National Theatre.

Maugham had trained as a medical doctor before writing a novel and becoming a playwright. I read most of his books and stories while on shipboard. The plays and novels are very dated, but the short stories capture aspects of human nature quite vividly. The old Hollywood productions of *Rain* and *The Letter* are still gripping and prove the point.

Maugham was drawn and painted by half a dozen or so artists. I am an admirer of the Graham Sutherland portrait in the Tate but find a good deal more interest in the cubist picture by Édouard MacAvoy.

While some of Sir Gerald Kelly's work holds its own today, his portrait of Maugham looks merely comical. Perhaps it did in 1899, too. In the 1970s, a Kelly sketch of Maugham came up for auction at one of the big houses and I went along to see if I could pick it up. I didn't have much free cash in those days but could have just managed the estimated price of £125. In the event, it shot past that figure almost instantly, and I was never really tempted to buy at auction again.

That didn't mean I didn't go. Auctions offer the chance to see works that haven't been seen for decades – often for more than a hundred years – and feel the excitement of acquisition. For many, it's a good way of picking up neglected pieces of art for not a lot of money; for others, it's about the vanity of winning and owning, and for an increasing number, it's about money-laundering.

Looking at how others paint the same people continues to fascinate me. It's all the same person – perhaps a little younger or older – but the same person, and each artist sees – or pretends to see – something different. This, as I have mentioned before, is what Wilde talks about when he says that the painting is one of the painter, not the subject.

There can be few people who provoked such contrasting reactions as Edith Sitwell. I always liked her poems with their uncompromising freshness and oblique observations. I also admired Osbert's writing about his youth, especially in the Great War.

The portraits of Dame Edith are even more extraordinary than those of Maugham. Painted in her teens by Sargent, then by Roger Fry, Percy Wyndham Lewis, Rex Whistler, Christopher Nevinson, William Palin and a dozen others. Even her photographic portraits are extraordinary.

Spend as much time with a painting as you do with a book and it's remarkable what you can learn.

That is the curse of being a portrait painter. If you're lucky, your work gets two minutes. These days, it's probably closer to twenty seconds.

That is why sitting here on a cold stone bench trying to draw an empty room is so revealing. In a few hours, I have filled my sketchbook, worn down my pencils and learned about creating beauty through light, perspective, proportion, texture and colour.

These ramblings tell me it's time to pack up and maybe put my feet up for an hour before it's time for an *aperitif*.

◌

Alas, even on this "holiday," there are things to be done.

Before going back to the hotel, I went to the art shop to collect a new sketch book. I also found an inexpensive A6 notebook with 320 pages of paper with a decent finish. I could carry it easily and draw quick impressions, architectural details and *aides memoire*.

Opposite the art store there was a small shop with some nice shirts. Impossible to resist. There were some other nice clothes, too, they could wait. I'd have to convince Sophie that I'd brought these with me.

It was after five when I returned to the hotel. I knocked on Sophie's door at seven to see if she were interested in finding a place for dinner. She would have a more interesting day to talk about, I'm sure.

I was perfectly satisfied with what I'd done, but knew it was procrastination and that I'd have to look at some pictures and decide what I wanted to do. Sophie's suggestion of personalising lesser-known saints was a good one, but vanity was tempting me to attempt the standard pieces.

The last time that had been done by British artists was by the Pre-Raphaelites.

Chapter VII

O n Tuesday morning, I was up early (very early) to watch Sophie get into an enormous sleek, black six-door Mercedes limousine. A uniformed driver held the door open for her and she blew me a kiss in the event anyone was taking a photo.

She was off to do her thirty-second shot at Cinecittà and make her mark on the Italian film industry. While she treated it as a joke, at dinner the previous evening, she could hardly contain her excitement.

"You appear to be more chuffed with this than with your major awards," I said, over some excellent gnocchi.

"Silly, isn't it," she said, with a giggle. "I think it's partly because of the way it happened. It was so – "

"Italian?"

She laughed.

"I was going to say random."

"Close enough."

She had spent the day shopping but had only bought a very long, colourful silk scarf.

"I'll take it with me," she said. "Perhaps it could be a prop."

"Haven't you moved beyond security blankets?" I asked.

Rather than throw her piece of *pane Tuscano* at me, she considered the comment.

"I don't think it's as much that as having something distinctive," she said.

"A talking point?"

"If you like."

When Sophie was preparing for a part, she'd go into a thoughtful mode where it was best not to disturb her. In this case, I suspected old fears were making themselves felt. For this performance, she had no script. It would be a nostalgic dumb-show and she'd be completely in the hands of the director. Without the assurance of a script, she'd feel at a loss.

One of the ways this manifested itself was that over dinner, she did most of the talking, and it was mostly about herself. Normally, she'd ask how I spent my day but there was none of that.

We didn't always tell each other everything; our lives simply weren't that interesting. She'd have rehearsals, a public appearance, a prize-giving at a school, discussions about forthcoming work, or a performance. I'd walk to the studio, paint someone, go to a gallery or a talk somewhere, have a drink and maybe dinner at my club and come home. People who think our work glamorous see only a fraction of it.

I was gratified to see that it was a confident and happy Sophie who climbed into the back of the Mercedes and hoped she would be equally happy when she returned.

ℰつ

Sophie had left so early that I went back to sleep for two hours before going to Bar 43 for breakfast. One of the waiters remembered me from the day before and recommended smoked salmon scrambled eggs. Several indulgent pastries and cups of cappuccino later, I collected my new sketchbook and took a taxi to the Galleria Borghese.

It was amusing to thread the way through the morning traffic. Somehow, there seemed to be less than on previous visits. While the Vespas aren't around in the numbers they once were, there are electric scooters, mopeds, and small electric cars aplenty to make the white-gloved traffic controller's job continue to be stimulating.

The Galleria Borghese boasts the largest number of Caravaggio paintings in the world, and I hoped to revisit all six as well as its other treasures. What I was looking for were deviations from the expected portrayals of religious subjects. Perhaps the near-misses of art.

Michael Caine, on learning of the remake of the 1966 film, *Gambit*, asked why good films needed to be remade. Certainly, the better candidates for re-making were the ones that had – despite their merits – just missed.

It was Sophie, of course, who told me this anecdote, but it made a lot of sense, and I had for a long time wondered if and how it could be applied to art. Could you copy a design but change it, make improvements, re-imagine it as today's vernacular puts it?

Re-making a film opens myriad legal problems, but would a new version of Murillo's *Immaculate Conception*, or any traditional re-interpretation of a religious work?

Apart from the Caravaggios, I wasn't sure what I'd encounter at the Galleria Borghese. Art and life are full of surprises, but I don't want to get ahead of myself.

I sought out the Caravaggios with the intention of returning to the rest of the collection. I started with *Bacchus Malatato*. I think I've only seen this in books before and seeing it close up in reality did nothing to improve my opinion of it. Without the Caravaggio name and the belief that it's a self-portrait in character, this would be an indifferent picture. As if to support my view, more appears to have been written about the medical diagnoses of the artist from the symptoms depicted than commentary on the subject of a sick Bacchus.

It begs the question, "Would Bacchus be Bacchus if he could have an upset stomach or a hangover?"

I concede that the peaches and grapes look tempting enough to pick up, but there's not a bottle of wine in sight.

One lecture I attended many years ago noted about Caravaggio that there is always at least one disturbance in his paintings. While not unique, the idea gives one something to look for in a picture, which is always a good idea. In this case, I reckon it's the end of the knot of his cincture that rests on the table. In reproductions, the colour of this material varies from burgundy to brown. In reality, it is a rich, dark chocolate.

I went to the next profane (old meaning) painting, *Giovane con Canestra di Frutta* (more mundanely, *The Boy with the Basket of Fruit*). Painted just after *Bacchus Malatato*, it is, again, the fruit that dominates the painting. The arm of the boy is clearly carrying weight: the fruit has solid mass. It is as if he is holding its nourishing beauty close to him. We don't mind that much of the figure is outlined in black; we don't care that the neck is disproportionate or that he seems to have very narrow shoulders: we are seduced both by the fruit and beauty of the face. The musculature is all wrong and the folds of the toga undistinguished: details, details. What matters is the impact, and the brightest light is on the *fruit*.

We have become afraid of *looking* at great paintings critically. We are intimidated by the names and the preponderance of fawning opinion.

The boy (thought to be the artist Mario Minniti) is unimportant: it's the fruit that matters. Shape, colour, texture, mass are all there. Bursting with freshness, all that's missing is the smell.

Next on my list was *St Jerome Writing*. St Jerome is almost always portrayed reading or writing, such was the impact of his major work, the first Latin Bible translated from Hebrew, the *Biblia Vulgata*, commonly known as the *Latin Vulgate*.

There is huge irony about this work. As the name implies, it was the Bible in the "common language." Today, Latin is hardly common, but the real irony was that the Catholic Church has been traditionally cagy about ordinary folk reading the Bible. When I was occupied with such things, I learned that while one could *study* any Bible, one – as a Catholic – could only *read* a Catholic Bible. (Maybe it was the other way round; it's rather long ago.)

The *Vulgate* was an important development because it provided a version that was accepted and used for more than a thousand years. Today, Biblical scholars have found older sources than the Hebrew, so the controversy smoulders on. Growing up in England, it was impossible to avoid the King James version with its magnificent and memorable language.

From the perspective of an ordinary Catholic – and apart from the missing books – there are few theological objections to the King James version though its ancestry is considered illegitimate.

St Jerome is depicted as an old man who had been robust but now has the spectre of death near him in the form of a skull. Caravaggio's saint is in that pattern.

Just as the comparative paintings of the Queen, Churchill, Maugham and Edith Sitwell enabled me to conceive my approach to portraiture, so a comparison of the representations of St Jerome can help one infer the character of the saint. (My own favourite painting of St Jerome is the one by Joos van Cleve which puts the saint into a cosy Dutch house. Well deserved in his old age, I think.)

There was much more to consider on this painting. In the decade since the painting of *Bacchus Malatato* and *The Boy with the Basket of Fruit*, and St *Jerome Writing*, Caravaggio's mastery had blossomed. The richness of the drapery, the refinement of the texture and tones of the skin, all speak of greater maturity.

Caravaggio returned to the subject a few years later, in Malta, where he painted another *St Jerome Writing*, but this is of a younger man with more hair and flesh. Was there something in this saint that spoke to Caravaggio, or was it simply a commissioned painting with the subject dictated by the customer?

So, where's the disturbance in this painting? The whole picture is disturbing enough. Works like this create a completely false impression of how people in earlier times lived. Jerome was born around 345 A.D., and few have any real idea what life was like then. (This is why I like the van Cleve painting as it brings him into an environment frame that can be recognised. Another Dutch painting of him even has a clock on the wall.)

Scholars probably didn't have skulls sitting on their

desks – especially Christian ones who would have had greater respect for the dead. Medical scholars would have been the exception, but that wasn't Jerome who was a priest, historian and translator. It's also unlikely that he would have worked in the way depicted.

What we have in the painting is solidity. The strong man, the robust table, the heavy tomes. This sturdiness is reinforced by the legs of the table which are like pillars. Even the garments have weight, and we suspect they are wool. The red and white textiles (symbolic of life, death, purity and blood/passion) hang to balance the composition and – not by accident – create the structure of a pediment that gives a nod to the Trinity. And then, there is the skull. Solid enough to survive the grave, yet a symbol of mortality. The deceptive simplicity of the composition is seductive and gives us a figure to contemplate, to emulate.

I went to the next gallery to find a bench to sit down before seeking my next Caravaggio.

The problem of painting the ineffable was settling on me. St Jerome had made me keenly aware of all the levels I'd have to be thinking of while painting. For my usual subjects, this was natural: I was working with mere mortals in my own time period. This was different. Either I'd have to re-create a credible period setting, or an anachronistic context in which to place any saint I painted.

Painting the Holy Family or the Trinity was too big a first step.

When putting paints into my suitcase, none of this had occurred to me and the implications were making me want to get on the next train back to London. Facing judges, general and minor royals were as nothing compared to this folly.

I'd leave this mad idea here and return to the sunshine of today, have a good lunch, sit on the roof and sketch buildings for a while before having a late afternoon *riposo*. I looked at my watch and found it was nearly lunchtime, stood and looked around for the nearest way out.

"Is that you, Sir Nigel!" a female voice with a trans-atlantic accent called loudly. "I thought it was! It must be fate!"

More like fatal.

Chapter VIII

An ordinary looking business woman of about forty walked, then accelerated, towards me, and looked about to embrace me. I had no idea who this was. Portrait painters don't have crazed fans; indeed, they seldom have fans at all.

She was well-dressed in a classic grey suit, white shirt, court shoes and medium length greying dark hair. What I noticed most of all was that she wasn't smiling, and that told me who she was.

"Miss Baker!"

"Why was I so sure that you'd remember me," she asked, abandoning the threat to embrace me and taking my hand.

"Probably best not to go there," I said.

My plan to escape Rome was never more appealing.

I had painted Francine Baker about twenty years before when as a British-Canadian celebrity she was in London. At the time, I had little idea why she was a celebrity and still don't. Somehow, she had got into the best parties, been seen at the best restaurants, gone to the best clubs, was photographed with the best people, went to the best receptions, and jumped into the best fountains. This got her face – and other parts of her anatomy – in the papers, but, alas, not the best.

Someone pointed her to me as the (hopefully best) person to paint her. What should have taken three weeks at most and one week at least to paint her had taken six months. I became sick of her excuses which were no better than, "My dog ate my homework." Forgot, last minute party/trip/shopping/interview, etc.

Francine Baker was the one responsible for my institution of a missed appointment fee.

"Still so proper, Sir Nigel," she said.

Lines like that when delivered with a smile form enjoyable banter. Delivered without a smile, they can be sinister. At least her eyes assured me that her mockery was harmless, if not affectionate.

"I suppose I should be pleased you remember me," she said, "but that should really be your line, shouldn't it?"

My old friend, Bill Warren, the retired Scotland Yard inspector, often noted that a good detective can tell a lot from a face. I fancied that I could, too, and Francine's had a lot to tell. Most of it unhappy.

"Shall we get a drink?" she suggested.

"There's one more Caravaggio I want to see while I'm here," I said, and began moving toward the next gallery.

She followed, easily.

"I don't expect I was very nice the last time you saw me," she said.

I looked at her.

"It's not then that I'm concerned about."

She looked sad and considered the remark.

"No. I can see that," she said. "I won't tell you that I've changed. You'll have to discover that for yourself."

I found the gallery with *David with the Head of Goliath* and began to look at it. The pale, almost green, tinge to Caravaggio's living flesh has always made me wonder if it was deliberate, or a chemical reaction with the under-painting, or a breakdown in the chemical composition. Curators and art historians like to feel that what we see is just how Caravaggio painted it and the technical teams don't like to argue or disappoint them.

"I'll wait for you by the exit," Francine said, pausing to look at something more pleasant on her way out.

David's expression captures what must have gone through the young boy's mind at the time. Pride, humility, disbelief in what he had just done, and maybe some sadness at the loss of innocence. He grasps the hair resolutely: there is no regret in that grip. And the head – though not visibly – is truly severed and makes the viewer check the floor for gouts of blood.

The lighting is masterful, shining on David with just enough falling on his trophy to give it its mortal horror.

Here, unlike in *St Jerome Writing*, is a straight-forward statement. There are no tricks, no symbols, no hints of anything else going on. This is plain and simple death.

I found Francine outside sitting on the steps of the galleria. At least it wasn't in a fountain.

"Thank you for waiting, Miss Baker," I said, moving a few steps below her and facing her.

In spite of the sun, she didn't wear dark glasses and the pupils of her grey-blue eyes were sharply defined. That was one of the only enjoyable things about painting her: the clarity and intensity of her eyes. It took a while to match the colour, but once I had it, it was almost easy.

She extended her hand which I gripped and pulled her to her feet.

"Actually, I'm not Miss Baker anymore," she said, but not unkindly. "Nor am I Francine. I am Francesca, Contessa Polidori."

She affected an Italian accent as she said it.

I smiled.

"You were born for that name," I said, and received the nearest thing to a smile I'd seen her give.

"Have you had lunch? I haven't. Let's see what we can find."

She had not let go of my hand and continued to hold it until we were out of the park.

Francesca – I suppose I'll have to get used to that – didn't know the area either, but we happened on a trattoria. It was busy, but we found a place.

Sitting opposite her, I was able to look at her properly. My immediate impression was that at twenty-years younger than Sophie, she looked older. Sophie had the advantage of her face being her fortune, as it were, and that its care and maintenance were part of her profession. (I wondered if all her beauty products were tax deductible as business expenses.)

Francesca's face was one of experience. Still very attractive, it was a face of one who had to fend for herself.

A basket of bread and carafe of wine were brought, and we were directed to the board where today's food was posted. I chose a meaty pasta dish while Francesca chose poached fish with fried potatoes and salad.

"*Santé*," she said, raising a glass. "Old friends."

I raised my glass but said nothing.

"All right, old acquaintances," she conceded.

Her eyes were sparkling, but she was still not smiling.

"Why are you in Italy?" she asked. "Are you painting?"

"Knowing how you became the Contessa Polidori sounds much more interesting," I said, but didn't want to bully her. "I needed a break from portrait painting. A friend suggested I come to Rome and consider trying religious painting."

She looked at me, thinking.

"There's a lot of life to catch up on," she said. "If you want to."

I smiled.

"At least a lunchtime's worth," I replied.

She gave the hint of a smile.

"You painted me half a lifetime ago," she said. "Literally. I was twenty-two, now I'm forty-four. Why has your God crossed our paths again, I wonder."

"Don't blame this on Him."

"My daughter just turned twenty-one," she said. Without emotion. Without pride. "I was pregnant when you painted me, though I didn't know it. I still have the painting, by the way. It's hanging in the castle."

"What's your daughter doing now?"

Francesca looked up from her bread and directly into my eyes. I suspected it was because I didn't respond to "castle."

"That's why I'm here. For her birthday."

"And where do you usually live?" I ventured.

We were interrupted by the *cameriere* placing the appropriate cutlery then refilling our glasses.

"Some place that sounds idyllic but isn't," she said. "You might think that appropriate. I had the feeling that you thought I didn't know what I wanted – or what was good for me."

"And Count Polidori?" I asked, trying to keep the conversation on track.

"He's across the street from the castle," she said, off-handedly. "Next to the church. In the graveyard. With his first wife and his ancestors. I expect he's very content."

"And on your side of the street?"

Our meals arrived, smelling as good as they looked.

"I tell you what," she began. "I'm having dinner tomorrow with Carrie and the new Count and Contessa Polidori – Giorgio's son by his first marriage. It's at our apartment here."

She tasted her fish and nodded approvingly.

"Do you have someone you can bring to leaven the atmosphere? I'm not particularly popular with the younger generation."

I smiled inwardly. This would demonstrate to Sophie that I was well out of my comfort zone.

☙

I survived lunch, obtained the details necessary for Sophie to know what she should wear, but I learned little more about Francesca's life between the last time I saw her and now, and nothing about her late husband or the other Polidoris.

Only slightly later than I'd hoped did I get back to the hotel and take my place on the roof for an hour. It was chilly, but Chiara had found a mug for me which was not only good for tea, but for keeping my hand warm. I only needed my right hand unencumbered, so I had a warm glove on my left.

I had now drawn the same scene four times since my arrival and could finally see some progress. The lines were more fluid, less fussy, and more accurate.

My mind did wander to Francine/Francesca. I was trying to picture the portrait, but while her face was clear, the rest of the setting was not. I had no recollection of what she wore, the background or any objects that had been included. The portrait was never shown, so there were no press photographs popping up from time to time, though I did have a good studio shot in my files.

My endurance of the chill and the light lasted about the same length of time, and I went to my room.

Sophie knocked on my door at seven and we went out for an *aperitif*. She was full of her day at Cinecittà, and I was happy to postpone talking about Francesca.

"It was a fantastic place and though it had the latest equipment, it had the feel of a traditional studio," she said, in wonder. "Today, so many 'studios' are just warehouses with hired equipment moved in and out by the day or week. This felt like it had been there for decades. History seeped through everything."

I laughed.

"Old and grubby?"

She gave me the warning look.

"It was wonderful, and everyone was charming," she continued. "I think Gaetano told everyone to pretend that they knew who I was."

She told me about going in for makeup and costume selection and fitting.

"Then we went onto the simple set, and he just looked at me for about ten minutes – from every angle," she said. "I was used to that thirty years ago, but it felt odd today."

There was no way I was going to reply to that.

"Finally, I broke his silence. 'Something missing?' I asked. He said, 'Si,' in a way that showed he didn't know what. 'I think I can help,' I said, and went back to my dressing room, threw the scarf around me and walked back to my place.

"In a good story, he would have said, '*Perfetto!*' and we would have done the shot, but he said, 'No. It's wrong,' then added, 'but it's the right idea.'

"He sent for the wardrobe mistress who then brought out about two dozen silk scarves, and I wrapped each one around myself and they both tweaked them this way and that."

"Gaetano had the lighting softened, then made more twilight blue, then back to where it had been. He'd then hand one scarf back and give me another. All this was taking time, and I watched helplessly as my own scarf was buried deeper in the *costumista's* arms.

"Eventually, Gaetano demanded to look through the lot himself while the lighting crew adjusted the lamps yet again.

"'Try this one,'" he said, finally selecting one. The *costumista* put down the others and tied it elegantly for me. The lights came up, and I took my place.

95

"'*Brava! È perfetto!*' he exclaimed, 'Are you happy?' he asked. I said I was, and so was the *costumista*.

"'*Fantastico*. Let us continue,' he said, and I had to keep a straight face for the rest of the shooting."

"It was your scarf."

Sophie nodded and burst out laughing.

"You said it would be perfect," I said. "Did he ever catch on?"

"No – and at the end, he proceeded to give it to me as a memento of our work together," she said, giggling. "At this point, the *costumista* couldn't take it anymore and ran from the set."

"I see why you don't like making films," I said, when we finally stopped laughing.

"And the actual shooting?" I asked. "To be honest, I didn't expect to see you until nearly midnight."

"We had a good lunch with the scriptwriter, an assistant director and clever wardrobe mistress, but it was a very early start, and the lunch was just to fill in the time so we could look at the different takes."

"How many did you do?"

"Twelve," she laughed. "At least I had no lines to flub. It was just changes to angles, lighting and the type of shot. From the movement standpoint, he was satisfied with what we'd both done on the first take.

"I was pretty tired by then and nearly fell asleep while watching the seventh take. Gaetano and the photographer began discussing taking a clip from this take and sticking it into that one, and I simply excused myself, found the driver in the canteen and came back to the hotel.

"How did *your* day go?"

ଈ

As we'd both had big lunches, we went to a small *tavola calda*. These snack bars are usually only open at lunch time, but in neighbourhoods where there are shift workers, they can be open almost anytime. They are self-service, akin to a cafeteria, but the food is fresh and plentiful. With neither of us up to any more fuss, it suited us perfectly – though we managed to get through a full litre of red wine.

Sophie was most amused by my encounter with my old subject and laughed freely at my unease.

"Poor Nigel, just when everything was looking so peaceful," she teased, still laughing. "I'm sure she wants to see you again," she added, enjoying the situation. "Does she want you to meet the family, too?"

It was barely possible for her to cut into to her *melanzane alla parmigiana* she was laughing so hard.

"As a matter of fact, she does."

An explosion of mirth.

"Tomorrow."

Another.

"She wants you to come, too."

The rest, as they say, was silence.

Chapter IX

S ophie could protest as much and as vociferously as she
wanted, but I knew she'd come. She wouldn't miss it
for anything. To see me surrounded by people I didn't
know and made uncomfortable by the one I did, wasn't
something she was going to miss.

She wanted to know who would be there, what she
should wear, who these people were.

The fact that I could not satisfactorily explain much
about Francesca/Francine herself didn't help.

"All I have to do is paint people," I protested. "I don't
have to know their history, love life, or financial situation."

"I don't know anything about Polidori *pere* or *fils*. I
don't know who Carrie's father is. I don't know about the
son or step-daughter-in-law."

"Hopeless man!" she exclaimed on the way back to the
hotel. "You were with her for three hours. What did you
talk about?"

"I gather Carrie is at one of the universities," I said,
feebly.

"Reading what? Does she have a boyfriend? Will he be
there?"

This last exchange was in stage whispers outside her
door.

"I promise you, Dame Ligeia, by this time tomorrow, you will have all the answers."

℘

If only it had been that simple.

Sophie hadn't surfaced in the morning when I went to Bar 43 for breakfast. Over another excellent breakfast, I made notes on how I wanted to spend my day. I knew how Sophie would spend hers: she'd shop for something to wear to dinner. I warned her that if it were just family, they'd be apt to all be in jeans.

I had seen enough art in the past few days to need some time to digest it. I'd also done enough sketching to be satisfied that I could meet the basic needs.

What I decided to do was to return to the Palazzo Venezia which also housed the National Institute of Archaeology and the History of Art library. They were open from eight-thirty to seven-thirty and would provide a good thinking and working area – if I could keep from being distracted.

A public library, entrance was easy. Wearing a jacket and tie and carrying a small document case, no one gave me a second look. When I entered the main room for the art books, there were already scholars and students hard at work.

One of the other things I had done when beginning as a portrait painter was to look for things in portraits that added interest. These are simple features like doors, windows, staircases, a choice piece of furniture. The working surroundings of subjects also make strong points of interest: tools, papers, books, machinery, views from their offices – I've used all these but with enough variation that only other portrait painters recognise what I'm doing.

Painting saints or the Holy Family in the twenty-first century is a lot different to painting them in the fourteen, fifteen or sixteen hundreds. In the first place, there was considerable demand for them, then. Today, commissions for such things are rare. Very few of the new churches bother with statues and paintings but opt for the badminton court look with exposed frame works and white walls.

This was today's challenge: look at the hurdles and explore ways of overcoming them.

Painting the ineffable for believers would be hard enough, but for those who only had the faintest idea who – or what – any of the saints were, the ability to connect or communicate anything on a spiritual or even temporal level was remote.

The traditional symbols and emblems mean little or nothing. Once the language of love and belief was common to civilised men across Europe, they are now all discarded images. The wheel, the gridiron, the tower, the tree, the scallop shell, bees, a dog, an anchor, anvil or bell: all these spoke loudly of faith, integrity, courage, and often martyrdom.

What would be the point of painting these today?

For each of these thoughts, I leafed through an art book, idly looking at the pictures. More were unfamiliar than familiar, but that's to be expected. I'm not an art historian. I don't see the hundreds of pictures daily that dealers do. I can tell whether something is well or badly composed and painted, but I couldn't tell you if a picture was a good free copy or an original.

A "free copy" (there are a variety of other terms) is a copy of a painting that doesn't slavishly follow each brushstroke but copies the picture. While free copies lose the precision of the original, they avoid the static, dead nature of the precise copy. This sort of painting is excellent practice for a beginning portraitist.

On one of my metre square canvases, I have a dozen copies of Sargent and Sorolla hands, eyes and mouths. On another, pieces from Norman Blamey, David Hockney or William Coldstream. I also liked some Americans and copied them, too: F W Benson, Warren Prosperi and Jamie Wyeth.

I suppose it says something about my pusillanimous nature that I never dared to copy Rembrandt, Rubens or Caravaggio from whom I may have learned the most.

My next observation was that I would have to decide whether – and how – to re-interpret or re-imagine, as the current phrase had it, Biblical stories or saints' lives with miracles and martyrdoms.

They had all been done so brilliantly already. How could you paint St George and the Dragon today? How could you make it make sense to anyone? No doubt it would be criticised as another twitch of a white upper middle-class male refusing to let the British Empire die and encouraging the far-right supremacists.

Painting Jean d'Arc would probably provoke the same reaction. Or Don Beotti here in Italy.

Would it not be colossal vanity to tackle these subjects?

More arrogant would be to try to make these images relevant. Isn't the whole point of faith that its relevance is of no matter?

The final thought I had, as I returned the books for reshelving, was that I would have to paint these from the imagination or hire models. For that, I'd need a studio.

This was becoming more complicated than I'd hoped. I was content that I'd identified the major problems, but what to do about them would require more thought.

I finished making my notes and glanced at my watch. It was already after two.

Enough. Time to move.

∽

The air was chilly and the sunlight fading as I walked up Via del Corso. The pavements were crowded and the traffic at its normal Italian volume. My intention was to stretch my legs, blow out the cobwebs and go back to the hotel via a longer route.

On the way, I came to a small shirt shop. I stopped to look in the window and see if I could deduce how outrageous the prices were. It looked ordinary, so I went in.

The man behind the counter looked up, smiled and nodded, and went back to his paperwork. I liked that. I also liked the visibility of the prices. There were a few brands I recognised and many more that I did not.

But it was a tie I was after, not more shirts.

Ties were in several areas: hanging in cellophane sleeves on a rack, fanned out in a large circle on a table, and smartly rolled in a glass cabinet.

The trouble with buying a tie is that you instantly know what you like and don't like, and nothing will persuade you otherwise. If it costs anything less than a new car, you have to have it – the ascetic life be damned.

Married friends tell me that for the right tie, you'll risk upsetting your wife for a week.

The right tie signals to you from across the room and the moment you see it, it has to be yours. That's all there is to it. Some men feel that way about cars, others about fountain pens, and some about women.

You don't need insurance for a tie, it won't leak on your shirt, and it won't go on at you until you're close to murder or suicide.

Yes, there it was. It was silk and handsome, and I'd wear it tonight.

With that major decision made and paid for, I continued on my way, turned left and found myself on the steps of the Chiesa di Sant Ignazio di Loyola. I knew it was there, of course. It was just not in my present conscious, but after looking at all those paintings, I recognised a sign when I saw it and went in.

I'd been there before: the principal Jesuit church in Rome. Its architectural and artistic magnificence isn't foreshadowed by its restrained façade. But today, I wasn't there to bask in beauty. I was there to reflect and pray.

Primarily, I was there to reflect on all I'd seen and been thinking. Secondly, I was there to do what I always do: pray that I had done the right thing with my life; that I had used my greatest gift and not squandered it painting.

I sat in a quiet area towards the back, closed my eyes and listened to the silence. It was far enough from the main roads, so the ordinary traffic noise didn't come through, but there was a soft rumble that distracted me. As I listened, it seemed to have a periodicity; it gently rose and fell.

The idea struck me that the building was breathing, and my eyes flashed open to find the noise grew louder.

More signs?

Not this time. It was my own breathing that had penetrated a brief doze, and it was difficult not to laugh out loud.

Yet, in that momentary drift from the world, I knew what had enabled hundreds of years of painters to rise to the challenge of painting the ineffable; to paint what had been painted before; imagine new ways of telling the same story the people already knew. Obvious, really.

It was a leap of faith.

ଓ

I sat there for another twenty minutes or so, filling with conviction and certainty, and as I did so the germ of an idea began to form.

There was nothing to put words to, but – as happens in dreams – there was an *impression* of something, and you knew what it was, but the thing that gave you that strong impression had nothing to do with the ultimate something. Not looks, not shape, nor smell, nor sound – but it was unmistakeable.

I think psychologists call this pre-conscious thought. Others might call it inspiration. I never tried to name it. Recognising it was hard enough.

At this point, all I could "see" was a room. I couldn't tell you where it was, its colour, or size. As of yet there was no one in it.

Of course, there would be someone in it.

I'm a portrait painter after all.

ଓ

All the thinking had made me tired. Nodding off in the church on my own is better than nodding off at dinner.

Francesca had said seven o'clock. A bit early for aristocrats, but it was a weeknight.

After a dreamless *riposo*, I prepared for the evening and put on one of my new shirts and my new tie.

I went down to the lobby and asked Angelo to call a taxi for us.

"You must plan to have dinner here on Thursday," he said. "Thursday is the day we serve fresh fish and other seafood."

"I'll tell Sophie," I said, noncommittally.

"It's the same fish that the other restaurants serve on Friday as fresh fish!" he said, giving a great laugh.

Sophie made a stage entrance for me through the lift doors. She had struck the perfect note between casual and elegant. Her hair and makeup were perfectly pitched to look like what you'd see ladies wearing in a smart department store, yet every detail had been deliberate.

"Did you have a good day, darling?" she asked, approaching me.

"Very productive."

She looked me up and down.

"I like the shirt but take off the tie. Too formal," she said. "I didn't know you brought that one with you."

Chapter X

I gave the address to the taxi driver who set off without a word. We lurched and wound through the evening traffic, making spontaneous turns to avoid road works. While I knew where we were going, Sophie had no idea and nothing we passed along the way offered much in the way of clues.

We arrived at our destination just after seven, and I thought I could take a few more minutes to show Sophie where we were.

"Just don't ask me to find this place again," she said, as the taxi rolled off.

We were in a large, cobbled square that opened even further revealing a large obelisk. As we approached it, Sophie displayed no recognition of the location until I led her to the left and approached the edge of the piazza.

She looked at the view, then quickly turned to look behind her, then back towards the city and down at the broad steps leading up to us.

From where we stood, the dome of San Carlo al Corso dominated the view, but I led her further along and the dome of St Peter's appeared.

"I had no idea!" she exclaimed, with a laugh. "Your friend lives near the Spanish steps?!"

We walked back to where the taxi had dropped us. Sandwiched between two grand palazzos was a much thinner building with a restaurant on the ground floor. A small, anonymous doorway gave access to the apartments above.

The floor above the restaurant was used by it while the Polidoris occupied the top two floors.

I stopped outside the door.

"Ready for this?" I asked Sophie.

"I'm just a spectator," she replied, mischievously. "This is your party."

The door was opened by a man of about forty who flashed a big smile.

"Sir Nigel and Dame Ligeia!"

He stood back and with a grand gesture ushered us into the apartment.

"I am Stephano and very glad to see you," he continued, shaking my hand. "I am surrounded by women, and it is good to have another man to talk sense to."

Sophie was about to offer a comment, but he turned and headed into the sitting room.

While the building had looked small from the outside between the two massive structures, the apartment now looked impressively large.

Francesca came forward to greet us.

"I was just welcoming our English visitors to the home of an Italian family living next to a French church by the Spanish steps," Stephano said, and we all laughed.

"One day, I'll get to say that first," Francesca said, and Stephano looked at me, alluding to his earlier comment.

He had an easy manner and a good, strong face. He looked physically fit, and no doubt could be a tough businessman, but is eyes were kind. He was not the sort of man to let pain show – and that thought sparked something else in my brain – but it would have to wait.

We introduced each other for the next few minutes. The *contessa*, Laura (the digraph is pronounced "ow"), was tall, thin and elegant. She had long light brown hair with blonde highlights. She had a strong jaw, narrow lips and a model's neck. There was an Audrey Hepburn aspect to her thinness, and I wondered if she'd suffered from anorexia at one time. By the end of the evening, Sophie would be able to tell me.

She was welcoming and superficially friendly, but wary. Was this general, or did she have an instinctive dislike for any of Francesca's friends?

As soon as I thought this, I realised that Francesca and Stephano were nearly the same age.

We then met their daughter. She had remained on the sofa looking at a magazine until she was called to meet us. She was fifteen going on thirty and had made no attempt to dress up a little or be social. Most teenagers would at least go through the motions, in my experience.

Sophie said it better when we got back to the hotel: "Spoiled, skinny, sulky, slutty and possibly sick." She'd obviously worked on that description all evening.

With encouragement, the girl slinked up to Sophie and held out a limp hand.

"I'm Alegra," she said, in heavily accented English. "Alegra Maria Assunta.

She then turned to me.

"Are you one of Francesca's many lovers come back to haunt her?"

"Sorry to disappoint you," I said, as nonchalantly as I could. "I only did some work for her once."

The *contessa* was mortified and was instantly puce. Francesca, for once, was lost for words.

"If you can't behave, go to your room!" the *contessa* spat.

"*Il tuo desiderio è il mio commando,*" Alegra replied.

"Alegra. . ." her father warned.

And she disappeared.

"*Si droga di nuovo?*" Francesca asked, *sotto voce*.

The *contessa* gave a shrug of helplessness.

"Why don't you ask Carrie down," Stephano suggested. "She might enjoy a drink and some conversation after studying all day."

Francesca headed upstairs. I just hoped that she wouldn't encounter Alegra. We'd hear it if she did.

Meanwhile, Sophie was having a lively conversation with Laura, and I chatted to Stephano as he opened a bottle of Franciacorta.

"This grows very near my home," he said, removing the *coiffe* and *muselet*.

"Predore."

He gave a surprised look but said nothing and popped the cork.

"Unlike Prosecco, Franciacorta has its second fermentation in the bottle."

"Like Champagne."

This time, he smiled.

"I can see that we will get on well."

He stopped and listened for any exchanges upstairs.

"I apologise for Alegra," he said, quietly. "She has had a hard time and – as Francesca impolitely observed – she has had problems with drugs. It's one of the reasons we are in Rome. It's away from her old friends and there are good clinics here."

I nodded.

"There is no need to say any more," I said. "I'll tell Sophie if the *contessa* isn't doing that now."

He looked sad.

"We both spoiled the girl, but it has made Laura ill, as – as a portrait painter – you will have observed."

Something else flashed briefly in my head.

"But now," Stephano said. "Let us enjoy our drink. I hear the ladies arriving."

The sound of six high heels on marble stairs was hard to miss. All three were laughing, and Stephano and I began to hand out drinks.

"Nigel, I'd like to introduce you to my daughter, Carrie," Francesca said. "I feel you've known her as long as I have."

Carrie didn't flinch and extended her hand. She gave me a solid handshake and looked me in the eye. It was hard to believe this was Francesca's daughter. She had an athletic freshness and confident modesty that her mother never did. What marked them as most different was the ease with which Carrie laughed and smiled.

"I have loved your portrait of my mother since I was a little girl old enough to notice it," she said.

"She was about your age when I painted her," I said. "I am sure she has told you about our sittings. You are at university?"

"At La Sapienza."

"She studies all the time," Francesca said. "And, still, look how happy she is."

"Do you live here?" I asked.

"This apartment has made being here possible," Carrie replied. "I'm not sure how I would cope with the full student scene."

I glanced at Francesca, who was listening proudly to her daughter.

"And there are so many fountains," she said, with regret.

I laughed hard and wondered what Carrie knew about her mother's youth.

"It must have been tempting," Carrie teased.

"I'd grown up by then," Francesca said. "I was the Contessa Polidori and couldn't disgrace my husband or his family."

Carrie smiled.

"She was twenty-seven when she married."

Stephano refilled our glasses.

"I see you are getting to know my stepsister," he said, with his charming smile. "Carrie was about four when Father married Francesca, so I didn't know her very well when she was growing up. I was at school, at university, in the army, and then I got married."

"You were in the army?"

It was obvious when I looked at him again.

"He was one of the Alpini," Laura said, with obvious pride.

"The Alpini is the oldest mountain infantry in the world," she said, before he could reply.

He smiled at her. There was obvious affection and I noted that the two watched, smiled and touched hands throughout our visit.

"I was an engineer," he said. "It was tough, but I enjoyed being in the mountains. The teamwork was amazing. You have two enemies," he joked. "The real enemy who shoots at you, and the terrain that also tries to kill you."

"It nearly did, Stephano," Carrie said, looking up at Laura who approached.

"Not really," he replied. "My life wasn't in danger, but when a path gave way and I slid down the mountain, it broke a bone or two."

"Collar bone, clavicle, top arm bone, lower arm bone, wrist. . ." Laura recited. "Tibia – "

"Laura worked in the hospital," Carrie chimed in, again.

"Stephano had so much wrong with him that the military hospital couldn't deal with it and sent him to me," Laura said. "When I first saw him, he was drugged to the eyeballs because when he arrived, we cut off all the plaster casts to do our own imaging."

"Laura is trained in X-rays, MRI and CAT scans," Stephano said.

"And he needed a lot of them," she smiled. "We had so many problems with the machines that week. I kept having to have him brought down."

Through the doorway beyond the staircase, I could see lights going on and off. Laura saw me looking.

"Dinner must be nearly ready," she said, and went into what I presumed was the dining room.

"We're ready, Stephano," she called.

"I'll get Alegra," he said and went upstairs.

"Come," said Carrie, touching Sophie's and my elbows.

With five women and two men, the seating wasn't going to be perfect. Stephano and Laura would be at either end while Sophie was on his left and I was on Laura's left. Carrie sat opposite me and Alegra opposite Sophie, and Francesca was between Alegra and me.

I was a little surprised when the Polidoris all waited for Stephano to say grace. Not often does one see that simple ritual. And then the food started to arrive. Soup, *Zucca Mantovana* ravioli, veal marsala, vegetables, salads, desserts, limoncello and on and on.

The conversation was remarkably good. Sophie managed to get a few words out of Alegra, then Laura began asking Sophie about her work. Neither Alegra nor Carrie had heard Stephano call Sophie Ligeia, though I suspect Carrie knew. However, both were open-mouthed as Sophie described the previous day's filming with Gaetano.

I was talking to Stephano about his time in the army and his subsequent engineering career, and he was curious about my time with the Royal Navy.

Sophie later said that she felt like visiting grand-parents to all of them, but their welcome was sincere.

Salad plates were being collected and dessert delivered when Sophie turned to Carrie.

"What are you reading at university?"

"Mathematics," she replied.

Sophie sighed audibly and turned away from Carrie.

Carrie looked confused and a little offended, then Sophie turned back.

"I was hoping to have a nice conversation with you," she said, "but now, I won't be able to get a word in edgewise."

I chuckled.

"I'll keep quiet," I said. "You go on."

Sophie shook her head.

"No. You never get the chance. She's all yours."

Laura and Stephano were watching this with interest, but Carrie now looked nervous.

"Don't worry, Carrie. You're safe enough," Sophie said. "However, Nigel is going to monopolise you for the rest of the evening: he has a PhD in mathematics from Cambridge."

Carrie's face lit up.

"Seriously?"

I nodded.

The next ten minutes were spent seeing where our interests overlapped. I liked the basic things: linear algebra, geometry, numerical analysis, topology, cosmology. She liked strings, mathematical biology, dynamics and relativity, but we shared an interest in number theory, algebraic topology and linear analysis.

Halfway through our discussion, Laura changed seats with Carrie so we could talk, and she could chat with Sophie.

Carrie and I talked through dessert and coffee and only stopped when we were offered brandy or limoncello.

Carrie giggled and apologised to everyone. I spoke to Francesca saying how proud she must be of Carrie, for her passion for the subject was great.

"She does seem to enjoy it," Francesca said. "She's hoping to continue and do the next two years."

"I'm sorry I monopolised her."

"That was wonderful for me to hear," Francesca said, seriously. "I didn't understand a word but hearing that – that joy – was a special moment."

Before I could reply, I heard Sophie gasp.

Francesca and I looked over to her.

"It's after midnight! These lovely people have to work tomorrow," she said.

They protested, but what Sophie said was true. Alegra and Carrie had classes to go to, Stephano would have meetings, and Sophie would be able to fill me in on what Laura and Francesca did with their time.

"Let me call you a taxi," Stephano said.

"It's safe enough to walk, isn't it?" Sophie asked.

"The bars and restaurants will still be open," Stephano said. "There will be crowds on the main streets."

"We're staying near the Palazzo Venezia," I said. "Down the Via dei Condotti to Via del Corso?"

"*Perfetto!*" he said. "It's about twenty minutes."

We kissed everyone goodnight and were nearly to the top of the steps when Alegra looked at Sophie.

"Are you his mistress?"

Sophie must have done an instant search of the scripts of all the plays she'd been in and came up with:

"I am whatever it pleases you to believe I am."

ॐ

I was furious, and with my Catholic guilt, felt that I was the one who'd been compromised in the exchange, but then, I had said nothing.

Sophie laughed it off.

"We should be flattered you know," she said. "Don't let it spoil a memorable evening."

Our walk back was quick. As Stephano had said, there were lots of people about: standing in the piazza looking at the city, sitting on the steps, milling around at the foot of them, and window shopping along the Via dei Condotti. The Via del Corso wasn't as busy, but there were people about and plenty of vehicular traffic.

Chiara was at the desk when we entered. They usually locked the door at midnight, but she knew we weren't back and that we wouldn't be too late.

She asked about our evening then handed me an envelope.

"This was just delivered by a taxi driver five minutes ago."

Sophie looked over my shoulder as I looked at it.

The cream envelope had an embossed "P" on the flap.

In fact, there were two notes inside. The first was from Laura and was to Sophie. I passed it to her.

"'I pray that you can forgive Alegra, Sophie,'" she read. "'I cannot make excuses for her behaviour but hope you will visit us again. We all enjoyed your company. Fondly, Laura Polidori.' What does yours say?"

"'Apart from the obvious, a delightful evening. Carrie would welcome the opportunity of another conversation and asked if you'd be prepared to answer some questions.

"'To that end, I may have a solution: would you be prepared to paint her? She's the age I was when you painted me, and it would be very special to have pictures of the two of us by the same great artist. Love, Francesca.'

"There's also a Hoare's cheque for five thousand pounds as a down payment."

Part Two

Chapter XI

Sophie tried to get me to talk about the note that night, but I needed to think about it first. I'd never mastered the knack of fully understanding her, and usually saying, "Tomorrow," or "In the morning," was enough to get her to stop pressuring me to talk. I think part of the matter was that Alegra had upset her and not just by what she had said.

Around seven next morning, I went down to the lobby and left a message with Chiara for Sophie.

"Could you please tell Dame Ligeia that I'll be back around one for lunch."

"*Certo*. Have a wonderful morning."

I headed out to join my friends at the Bar 43. I always liked things with prime numbers, and 43 had a number of special features. It's a twin prime (a number two or less from another prime, in this case, 41), a repdigit in base 6, and the numerologists consider it a "highly spiritual" number, and don't get me started on "angel numbers."

Most people think that mathematics is boring, complicated, "out there," and a number of other pejorative things, and for many, this is true.

The conversation with Carrie was of the sort I used to have every day but haven't had in more than forty years.

Her bright enthusiasm connected that interest that has been nearly dormant. Mathematics has moved on a lot since I wrote my papers and finished my doctorate. Today, at a university, I'd be an old fool, one of yesterday's men. Yet, the possibility of a few hours' conversation with a clever undergraduate would refresh the brain.

I read the newspaper over breakfast and didn't rush the delicious food. Having been there all of three times, I was getting a *buon giorno* from the *propietàrio* and the odd customer. They saw I was reading English and didn't try to extend the conversation.

My first item of business was to post Francesca's check to my bank. Sophie would be furious and possibly even hurt that I was deviating from the religious painting plan, but that was not really the case. I was beginning to see a way to do both.

After my visit to the post office, near Bar 43 in the Via della Scrofa, I wanted to think and returned to Chiesa di Sant Ignazio.

The previous evening had dumped a huge bucket of experiences on me: seeing Francesca with her daughter; meeting her stepson and his family; the extraordinary behaviour of Alegra, and the wonderful food and wine. Heady stuff for an old man.

I took Francesca's note out of my pocket and read it again. There were two surprising elements to it (three, if you counted the cheque). The Francesca I first knew would not have asked me to paint her daughter; she would have instructed me to. Secondly, she didn't mention Sophie at all. How many times did one have dinner with an award-winning actress who had just done a scene with one of Italy's major actor-directors?

Sophie had been on very good form, too. She engaged with everyone, asked them about their interests and told stories. I looked forward to hearing what she said about everyone – if she were still talking to me.

It wasn't warm in the back of the church, but I hoped that would help me think.

I had two things to consider. First was the commission to paint Carrie. It had been a long time since I was asked to paint someone so young and vivacious. She would be an easy subject and readily share ideas on how it should be done. Then, I wondered, if Francesca had discussed the matter with her. It would not have occurred to Francine/Francesca to do so. Next, there were the matters of where I could paint, and if I could acquire an easel. I had a few brushes with me and wouldn't need to buy too many more. I'd seen metre square canvases at the art store I visited, so that would not be an issue.

Francesca had called her cheque a down payment. I wondered how much more she was planning on paying. I don't remember what she paid twenty-two years ago, but I do recall pushing up the final price because of her no-shows, cancellations, lateness and general faffing around.

I wondered if any of my colleagues from the Royal Academy or the Royal Society of Portrait Painters were in Rome from whom I could cadge some equipment. I'd send some emails after lunch.

I took out my little pocket notebook and began to sketch one of the capitals of a nearby pilaster. I've always found the Baroque overwhelming, like a too rich meal, but the artistry and craftsmanship cannot be faulted.

As I drew, I moved to the second thing to consider.

I had been very much moved by Stephano Polidori. Throughout the evening, I kept waiting for the hint of a dark side. He had faced pain and injury, he had a step-mother his own age, a delinquent daughter and seemingly exemplary niece.

He and Laura interacted naturally with each other, and she was obviously devoted to him. Alegra even held his arm as we'd walk to the door to say goodbye.

He seemed comfortable with all of them – though it was obvious he was waiting for Alegra to grow up. There was no hint of conflict or resentment between Laura and Francesca, either. I'm sure they were not totally happy, but they appeared to accept each other for what they were.

There were all sorts of reasons why this might be the case. For example, the terms of the late count's will might insist on them sharing use of the properties in order to benefit from any income. Or, they may have just worked out a way of surviving comfortably together.

Stephano did not immediately strike me as a patient man, yet that is what I saw.

What struck me the moment he had opened the door was that he had a face I wanted to paint, and as the evening went on, how I wanted to paint it took form. This wouldn't be a commissioned picture, but one that could begin my new career.

The germ of the idea I'd sensed the day before was taking shape. It happens as it does in animated cartoons: a few wisps swirl around and a cloud forms and spins and pulsates until something solid comes together. Often, I find, that during the process, creative flashes pierce through like angels' eyes in the Apocalypse and accelerate the process.

After lunch, I'd go back to the library and do some research, but my first saint's painting was gestating.

I drew a few more pilasters and groynes and put away my materials. On leaving the pew, I genuflected, turned and came face to face with a Jesuit walking up the aisle.

"*Chiedo scusa, Padre,*" I said, and stepped out of his way.

"Have a good afternoon," he replied.

I turned to speak to my obvious countryman, but he had not waited and was approaching the altar.

Out in the fresh air, I realised that I would need to contact Carrie and Francesca, but I had neither phone numbers nor emails for them.

I entered the hotel a few minutes before one and saw Sophie in an armchair in the lobby holding a glass of wine. At least she wouldn't shout at me in public.

"How hungry are you?" I asked.

"Moderately," she replied. "That was a rare feast last night."

"Shall we go back to the *tavola calda*, or do you want something more civilised? We could eat here."

"We can do that tonight," she said. "Let's go to the *trattoria*. We don't have to eat a lot."

That's what we always say.

Fabrizia welcomed us and showed us to a table and gave us menus. Confronted with the seductive smells and colourful dishes, we ate more than anticipated.

Sophie had spent the morning studying her script.

"I've got a week left and am only certain of about a third of the lines," she said.

"You will still know more than anyone else on the first day," I said.

"That's true, but not good enough," she said.

"Do you want me to read with you again, or did that not help?"

"It helps the most when the ambiguities are greatest," she replied. "I'm making a list of them we can work on."

Over dessert, Sophie finally said what had been on her mind.

"I thought you were taking a break from portraits to try religious painting."

She was obviously using all her control not to sound put out.

"I'm working on a scheme to do both," I said, and Sophie looked up.

"Really?"

I explained how I wanted to use Stephano's face as that of a saint, and that I wanted to find some way of getting him to agree without him thinking it was an impertinence.

"He should be flattered," she said. "As for painting Carrie – "

"I was going to try to explain that," I began.

"No need," she laughed. "You will both love the experience, and I have no doubt it will be another prize-winner. Actually, I wouldn't be surprised if you ran off with her."

༄

It was hard to concentrate in the library after that.

I began to do some research on my idea which was to paint Stephano as Sir Thomas More in his cell. The features I'd seen in his face had almost instantly brought that saint to mind and my earlier vague idea about a dark space with a solitary figure fit with More.

There are a number of contemporary portraits of More: at least four by Hans Holbein the Younger survive. One by Peter Paul Rubens (c. 1630) is based on Holbein,

Antoine Caron's *The Arrest and Supplication of Sir Thomas More in 1535* is a sensational imagining, painted after the fact. Following his execution, More became even more of a hero in England. Few spoke of it in public, but Shakespeare pays tribute to him in *Henry VIII* – which would have popularity with the groundlings, if not the Queen.

Holbein's group portrait of More and his family was destroyed in an eighteenth-century fire, but Rowland Lockey, in the late sixteenth century, painted several versions of it based on Holbein's sketch. Copies and variations on the Holbein portraits exist in the thousands.

Later, More's life and death fit Victorian Romanticism well with Charles Landseer, John Rogers Herbert, Edward Matthew Ward, Lucy Maddox Brown, John Evan Hodgson and William Frederick Yeames milking the legend.

What I did not find was any representation of him in his cell. I learned that no one actually knows which cell he occupied in the Tower, and several sources suggest he was held in more than one. While frustrating for historians, it's wonderful news for artists, for no matter what we paint, no one can call it wrong.

Like a child who has seen a toy in a shop window, I wanted to do this painting and hoped that Stephano would be agreeable.

Content that I had what I needed, I went back to the hotel believing that I had earned my *riposo*.

CR

I went to the hotel bar at around seven and Sophie joined me shortly after I'd ordered a glass of the house red.

"Have you decided where to have your studio?" she asked, leaping over any small talk.

"I think I'd better settle whether I'm painting the people I want to first," I said. "I need to make sure Carrie is agreeable or if this is just one of her mother's batty ideas."

Chiara handed Sophie a Campari Spritz.

"*All atua*," she said, and we touched glasses.

Chiara put some nuts and olives on the table and disappeared.

"I didn't think Francesca was at all batty," Sophie said. "Why doesn't she smile?"

"I don't know, which in those days was odd as she didn't take anything seriously," I said. "Maybe nerve damage, or a traumatic experience, or – "

"Or?"

"Maybe she has bad teeth."

Sophie nearly choked.

"I think what I need to do is to call around at their apartment late tomorrow afternoon when someone might be home and talk to Carrie, Francesca or Stephano."

Sophie raised her eyebrows.

"May I come, too?"

Over dinner, I explained what I had discovered about St Thomas More, the portraits of him and how nothing was known of his incarceration.

"Have you ever performed *Henry VIII*?" I asked. "More's not portrayed badly in that according to what I read today."

"It's not often performed," Sophie replied. "It's not very good. I read it somewhere along the line. It's reckoned to be a compilation of several plays. There was a play, *Thomas More*, or *The Play of Sir Thomas More*, which Shakespeare is thought to have doctored. Chunks of it may have found their way into *Henry VIII*. He collaborated with Fletcher on that one."

Sophie went on to talk about Beaumont and Fletcher, Webster, and a production of *The White Devil* she'd been in as one of her first major roles.

Over dessert, she told me more about her line learning that afternoon.

"I've selected about six sections I'd like to try with you tomorrow morning, if you have time for me," she said.

"Sophie! I always have time for you," I protested.

"Possibly not much more. Carrie Winters just walked in."

Chapter XII

Embarrassed to find us still eating, Carrie was persuaded to sit down and, with some coaxing, accepted a *gelato* and an *espresso*. She was dressed as a student with practical shoes, corduroy trousers, a bulky jumper, and woollen jacket.

"Now, stop apologising and enjoy your ice cream," Sophie said, and being a student, she did.

"I've come to talk to you about my mother's mad idea," she said, when she'd eaten about half the *gelato*.

"It's nothing I would ever dream of doing," she continued, "but I do like the idea of having a pair of portraits of Mum and me by the same artist."

"It's a novel idea," Sophie said. "And, I have to tell you that getting my portrait done was something of a whim, too."

"I am glad you like the idea, Carrie. There are matters of practicality," I said. "I have no studio here, no easel, no oil paints. I can't think you have a lot of time, either."

Carrie nodded and smiled.

"I've thought about all that," she said, brightly. "There is a *loggia* at our apartment. It's open in the warmer months, but windows are slotted in in the winter. It's not on the main heating, so we don't use it much, but it faces almost due West, so it warms up during the day . There is a portable heater, so we won't freeze!"

She returned to her ice cream.

"When would you be available to sit?" Sophie asked.

Carrie looked up looking a little puzzled.

"My agent takes care of the minutiae," I said, and got a kick under the table.

"I have a lot of independent study and am usually at home by four. Would that work?" she asked. "How many sittings would we need?"

I thought.

Normally, after a sitting, there would be work to be done before the next one. I didn't need the sitter to be present to work on background details, clothing, and so forth that could all be done from photographs. Not having my own studio would mean that I'd have to remain at the Polidori's to do these things.

I explained this to Carrie.

"If you could pose for an hour and if I could stay for another hour, I could be ready for the next sitting," I said.

"That will be fine," she agreed. "Mum and Laura are in and out all day. Laura works mornings, but sometimes from home. She likes to be in when Alegra gets back from school. Stephano is usually there by six or six-thirty."

My work didn't usually involve this many domestic details, but in this case, it was necessary.

"I think Nigel will be able to cope with that," Sophie said, her voice rich with irony. "It will mean missing his usual *riposo*, though."

Poor Carrie was missing the fun of this exchange, but Sophie wasn't going to let me off easily.

"My mother has a friend who's a designer," Carrie said, trying to get back into the conversation. "She may be able to lend us one of those collapsible easels, if that would do."

Sophie nodded.

"That should be fine," she said.

I sat back to see what would happen. Carrie caught on and realised we were playing a game of some sort and didn't let it upset her.

"Have you considered what pose you would like?" Sophie asked.

Having been through the process herself, she knew it well.

"What setting or background? Objects you'd like to be included? How you'd like your hair and makeup?" she continued.

Carrie looked embarrassed and bewildered, then suddenly brightened.

"If you'd advise me on all these things, that would be amazing!" she bubbled. "In years to come, I can point to the portrait and say that Dame Ligeia Gordon herself helped me with my dress, hair and makeup."

Game. Set. Match.

Sophie finished her coffee and made a tactical withdrawal leaving Carrie and me to discuss arrangements. I didn't need to impose on the Polidoris until I had a good idea of how I was going to paint her, but we'd have to find a semi-public place to develop the preliminary sketches.

Carrie was keen to begin, and I didn't have that much time left in Rome.

ᐧᑫ

When I spoke to Sophie in the morning, she proposed that Carrie come to the hotel at four and that I work on the sketches in her room – with Sophie present as chaperone. I telephoned Carrie to put this idea to her and she thought this was hysterical. Sophie took the phone from me and explained it was for our mutual protection.

I didn't mind. It was more cramped than my studio but would work well enough.

I spent the rest of the morning shopping. Canvas, paint, brushes, linseed oil, turps, and a few glass containers. I had a large canvas shopping bag, but walking down a windy street with a metre square canvas was an interesting experience for an old man.

Carrie had decided that she wanted a simple head and shoulders portrait. I made a variety of very basic drawings and she chose one where she looked up slightly and straight at the viewer. If I could make the eyes follow viewers around the room, that would be effective.

"What sort of background do you want?" I asked. "With such a simple pose, you probably want more than a soft-focus backdrop like you'd get in a photographic studio."

"Wait until you see the view from the window," she said. "Could you come at three tomorrow? Both of you? Sir Nigel, you could get set up and take some pictures of the view in daylight, while Sophie and I could choose some clothes and look at my hair and makeup."

This was the first time that this possibility had been mentioned but in Carrie's mind, it was a *fait accomplis*.

I drew some squares and asked her where she wanted to be and where the window would look interesting. She looked at the options I'd lightly pencilled in and didn't react to any of them.

"Don't worry about the reality of things," I said. "I can move buildings, change the light, make the window a different shape. . ."

"A regular super-hero," Sophie said, acidly.

"Don't worry, we'll decide these things on-site," I said. "In the meantime, let me draw some features. I'll do your eyes, mouth, ears, nose and hands – even though you might not want them."

I set to work, and Sophie chatted to her, subtly extracting information about her mother, Stephano and Laura, and Alegra.

Nothing scandalous emerged, but it confirmed my feeling that, in spite of all the potential for complications, they got on well. I was curious to know about Francesca and her elderly count, but Sophie would leave that to me. She also knew that I wanted to leave the matter of drawing Stephano until I saw him again.

We finished shortly before six having arranged to be at Carrie's house at three the following day.

"How did you get here?" I asked.

"I walked."

"I'll get you a taxi home," I said, and called the front desk.

"Don't be silly," she said "It's perfectly safe."

"It's not for your safety," Sophie said, as I went to my room to fetch the paint and canvas.

"Still object to the taxi?"

When she had gone, I was aware that I owed Sophie a lot. She had played along brilliantly in the past few days.

"We haven't seen much of Rome recently," I said, preempting the attack I anticipated. "Let's go to the Piazza Navona and get a drink then find some dinner."

&

"I'll give you this," Sophie said, as we settled at our table with a view of the Bernini fountains. "She's remarkably unspoiled."

I drank my Primitivo pensively.

"Are you not happy with the proposed *modus operandi*?"

"No, it's not that, that is completely sensible and can work," I replied. "It's the pose. What we were talking about was a yearbook picture. She needs something more thoughtful, more dramatic. Maybe the room will suggest something."

∽

The room didn't suggest. It screamed.

The *loggia* was now enclosed but had two large horizontal windows facing the city. It was hard to photograph as the sun was streaming in, low in the sky. The sight of the room and the view brought a picture into view. I just hoped it was the picture she wanted.

My things were there along with the aluminium tubular easel. I mounted the canvas and mixed a quantity of burnt umber, linseed and turpentine and began painting in the ground.

Sophie, meanwhile, was upstairs with Carrie looking at clothes and doing things with hair and makeup.

Carrie looked self-conscious when she came in. She still wore the comfortable jeans that she had answered the door wearing, but had on a cashmere navy jumper with a simple V-neck. She wore just enough makeup to highlight her features. Sophie had done well.

"I hope this is good enough," she said, giving a simple twirl and laughing.

She switched on the fan heater before sitting on a stool that had presumably come from the kitchen. She faced me in exactly the pose we had discussed.

"Would you hate it if we tried something different?" I asked.

She looked a little nervous but smiled and said, "Of course not."

"Could you stand by the window."

As she moved to it, I saw there would be a problem. The bottom of the window was too high and Carrie too short for my vision to be realised.

"Is there something you could stand on?" Sophie asked.

She nodded and left the room.

"As soon as you asked her to move to the window, I knew what you were thinking," Sophie whispered.

Carrie returned with one of those metal stools with two steps that fold out that have been around since the fifties and can still be found around the world.

"If you put the lowest step towards the window and stand at it," I said. "Good, now stand on it and turn towards me, but keep looking out the window. . . Good. . . A little more towards me. Good. Are you comfortable? Not afraid of falling."

She giggled.

"No."

"Now, can you put your hand against the window at about shoulder height. . . Sophie, what do you think?"

She came back and stood next to me.

"The windowsill is now too low, but I can paint it higher," I said to her.

"It's good," Sophie said. "We can see both your eyes Carrie, so it works well, but rather than have your hand flat, like a mental patient trying to get out, try a soft fist."

Carrie broke the pose and turned towards us.

"Soft fist?"

"You don't want to look like you want to break the window and jump," Sophie said, and Carrie laughed.

"Now, back into the pose," I said, raising my *telefonino* to take a picture. "That's very good."

Just as I took the picture, Sophie walked into it.

"It needs something," she said, and reached into her handbag and drew out the scarf she'd bought for the filming.

"Put this on," and she wrapped it around Carrie's neck so that it fell down her back and out of the picture.

"*Perfetto!*" we both said.

It took me about five minutes to block in the shapes to the extent that I knew how things would fit.

At five o'clock, Carrie asked to be excused to do some work. She seemed happy with the new idea and delighted with the scarf.

"Would it be possible for you to take a few pictures in the morning?" I asked Carrie. "The light will be right. If you could stand at the window and take a shot left, centre and right, I can print them and stick them together and Monday we can choose what buildings you wish to include."

Sophie sat patiently while I continued to work, laying down some colour and adjusting the shapes.

Although engrossed, I said, "You can talk if you want. The scarf was inspired. I might even call the picture *The Silk Scarf*."

"I loved watching the way that came together. I'll see you for dinner," she said, standing. "You'll want to talk to Stephano and maybe even Francesca – but leave here at six."

Francesca arrived almost as soon as Sophie had left. I showed her the canvas and explained the pose.

"I have no imagination, as you know," she said. "If Carrie is happy, then so am I."

I could hear Laura, Alegra and Stephano coming up the stairs and into the apartment. Stephano and Laura were laughing. Alegra was monosyllabic.

All of them came into the loggia. Laura kissed my cheeks and Stephano gripped my arm. Alegra remained in the doorway, watching but saying nothing.

"If we might have a word," Stephano said.

"I would like to speak to you, too, Stephano," I said.

"Fine, but me first."

He took a deep breath and glanced towards Alegra who straightened slightly.

"Our daughter has something to say."

Alegra's face changed from being sulky to being afraid and embarrassed. She stepped forward and held out her hand which I took.

"I am very sorry about the other night. Sometimes I say and do stupid things. I am sure I offended Dame Ligeia and you."

She stopped.

"And. . ." said her mother.

"Please forgive a stupid girl."

I squeezed her hand.

"I forgive you," I said, "and I will convey your apologies to Dame Ligeia."

She dropped my hand and turned to leave.

"Alegra," her father said, gently, and she stopped. Then he looked at his wife who nodded and left, shutting the door.

"I know your time in Rome is limited," Stephano began, "but since you will be here at the house for a few days, could you spend half an hour with Alegra to help her with her mathematics?"

I looked at Alegra who now looked sulky again.

"Do you want to be helped?" I asked her.

Stephano was about to say something, but I raised my hand very slightly and he stopped.

After a moment of silence, she shrugged.

"I don't want to, but I need to," she said.

"I will do it if you don't waste my time," I said, and hoped it didn't sound mean.

"*Grazie*," she said softly, and slipped out of the room.

"Let me get you a drink, Sir Nigel, and we can discuss the arrangement and agree your fee."

"Rather than a fee, I'd like to propose an exchange."

Chapter XIII

Sophie and I had a leisurely breakfast at the hotel Sunday morning. I filled her in on Stephano's request and how he agreed to pose for some drawings to be used as Sir Thomas More in exchange for me trying to teach Alegra algebra and geometry. I also conveyed Alegra's apology.

"It's easy to be angry with her," she said, "but we have no idea what she's been through. No one knew the reason why I was so withdrawn until I was eighteen.

"Still," she giggled, "I don't envy you trying to keep her attention."

"It's only half an hour. While I'm there, I can either work on my own, or Carrie can come and pose for a while."

We looked at the newspapers in comfortable silence making only the odd comment about the state of the world.

"I'm going to Sant'Ignazio for Mass at eleven-thirty," I said. "I think you'd enjoy seeing the church."

I didn't often ask Sophie to come to Mass with me. I seldom saw her until the afternoon on Sundays, especially when she'd had a full week of performances. However, when I asked her, she usually came.

While the Mass lasted over an hour and was in Italian, I could follow it though not understand the homily. The rest I understood, and the music was wonderful.

Sophie was simply lost in the fabulous ceiling. So much so, that she made no attempt to leave at the end of Mass and we sat listening to the organ playing for ten minutes after the church was virtually empty.

When we were finally gathering our things, the priest I had nearly bumped into on Thursday approached.

"Good afternoon, Father," I said.

"Good afternoon," he said to me, then looked at Sophie. "Miss Gordon, a pleasure to meet you. I'm Gerrard Reynolds."

"Father," Sophie replied.

"You are intrigued with the ceiling? It's quite something, isn't it," Father Reynolds said. "If you walk up the aisle, you will see two circles on the floor. The first is the best vantage point for viewing the main ceiling; the second, for viewing the dome."

Sophie walked up the aisle to the first spot.

"And you must be Sir Nigel Thomas," he said.

"Is my association with Miss Gordon that notorious?" I asked, and Father Reynolds laughed.

"No, but your attendance at Farm Street in London is," he said.

"One never escapes the Jesuits," I said.

"Being a Catholic in England is rare enough," he said. "Are you on holiday?"

"I suppose you might call it a period of reflection," I said. "Sophie – Miss Gordon – suggested I should reinvent myself as a religious painter. So, I'm doing that while she is learning a new part for a play."

We watched as Sophie moved on to the second marker and looked up at the painted dome.

"Is that why you were in the church this week?" he asked.

"One of the reasons," I said.

"And how is being a religious artist?"

"So far, it's been looking at Caravaggios and wondering what I think I'm doing. However, I am making my first serious attempt this afternoon."

"*Buona fortuna*," he said. "I hope to see you back here."

He walked back up the aisle, said a word to Sophie and disappeared to the right of the altar.

"Let me guess," Sophie said when she returned, "he knew you."

"We saw each other when I was here earlier this week," I said, but Sophie didn't look fully convinced. "And he'd heard of me at Farm Street."

"I still think they embed people with chips."

Our late start and big breakfasts meant that we weren't particularly hungry. For fun, we split a pizza and a litre of wine.

"Are you going to rest before heading to the Villa Polidori?" Sophie asked. "Perhaps you should. You're going to be pretty busy for a few hours."

Perhaps I should have. However, I spent the time deciding how I would find out what Alegra knew, what she needed to know and set a course to get there. That's what I agreed with Stephano in return for him spending half an hour to pose for my picture of Sir Thomas More.

I walked to the Polidori's carrying two A3 sketch books, one nearly new, one filled. Laura met me at the door.

"You seem to have become part of our family," she said, with a smile and kissing my cheeks.

She paused at the top of the stairs before opening the door to the flat.

"Anything you can do for Alegra would be wonderful. She's a nice girl, really. We just can't reach her now."

Tempting though it was, I was not about to assume the role of psychologist, psychiatrist, sociologist or confidante, and kept my mouth shut.

Stephano met me when I entered, and we went into the kitchen. There was a large central island with stools around it.

"I thought you might work here," he said. "You can sit either side of the corner. But, please, do what you want."

Alegra entered. She was in a sweatshirt with a faded screen-printed image and jeans. Her hair was tied back in a tangled ponytail. She sat next to me.

"This is only going to take half an hour, and I'm not going to hurt you," I said. "Can you manage that?"

She nodded.

"Do you know your times tables?"

She glared at me.

"I mean, really know them."

"Of course."

I opened my pad which had many of the architectural sketches I'd been doing and tore out a sheet, folded it and ripped it in half.

She gasped.

"Those are beautiful! Don't destroy them!"

I put an A4 section in front of me and wrote the numbers one to ten with my fountain pen.

"What can you divide into one?"

She looked at the page.

"One," she finally said.

"Anything else?"

"No."

"So, what do we call it?"

"*Prima*?"

"Yes."

I wrote down "prime."

"And into two?"

I did this with her up to five then asked her to take over. She remained astonished that I was writing over my drawings and was reluctant to do so.

She completed the numbers to ten, recognising seven as prime and getting the factors correct.

Next, I tore a corner off the paper and wrote a number on it she could not see.

I then played one of the "think of a number" games. In this case it was: think of a number from one to ten. Double it. Add four. Divide by two. Take away the number you thought of.

I gave her the paper and received my first smile.

I then wrote it down in an algebraic form, talking her through it.

"I'll give you another," I said. "When you've done it, I want you to write it algebraically."

And she did.

While she was working on it, I took the next sheet of paper and drew a nine-by-nine grid, stopping when she became distracted by the partial Caravaggio faces I had drawn on it.

She didn't get the equation right the first time but found her error when she talked me through it, and I gave her the paper to unfold showing the answer she had reached.

I then filled in some numbers in the grid, and for the next ten minutes, I explained sudoku to her.

"These are in all the magazines," she said. "I never look at them because they're numbers."

"Do one or two of these every day. It will tidy your mind and make thinking easier."

We stopped at exactly four-thirty. We hadn't done much, but at least I saw a shadow of promise.

"May I keep these?" she asked, picking up the pages.

"Of course," I said. "If you can, try writing the equations for other numbers."

I think she was actually smiling when she left the room for Stephano came in with a surprised look.

"I'm still alive," I said, and he laughed.

We went into the sitting room where he poured a glass of red, and I told him how I'd like him to sit.

"I'll probably paint this one back in London," I said.

I took a number of pictures as the angle I wanted was of one standing at the door – perhaps looking through the grill – looking down at More sitting.

Stephano was very patient as I moved around, asked him to change his position and look up, down, left and right.

"You may talk if you like," I said. "It doesn't bother me."

He gave me a look I later tried to capture.

"There are too few occasions these days where a man can just sit and be still."

At five o'clock, my next client came in.

The concentration, the shift in thinking, and Carrie's bubbly personality made me wonder if I could sustain this in the coming week.

Carrie returned to her pose quickly and needed only the slightest adjustments. I asked her to be quiet while I drew her profile, fixed her jaw line, and painted her hair in some – but far from final – detail. Once that was done, I told her she could talk.

She started talking about her day, one of her classes, how she thought the men on her course were geeks and the rest of the girls thought she was weird.

"My real friends are the ones I swim with or at the football club," she said. "In this final year, there is going to be less and less free time; there's so much work to do and then prepare for the exams. I have – excuse me – "

Preparations for dinner had begun in the kitchen and Laura and the cook were discussing something culinary. Carrie walked to the door and shut it quietly, then returned to her pose.

"Is it cold near the window?" I asked. "I can turn the fan heater towards it."

I did so.

"That *is* better. Thank you," she said.

"Do you play tennis?" I asked.

"Not very well. I had some lessons and liked it well enough, but never had the opportunity to get good at it.

"I did sabre fencing for a while, though," she added.

"I bet your mother loved that!"

Carrie laughed but said nothing.

"As you can imagine, I asked Mum about being painted by you," she said, her voice becoming more serious. "She didn't say much, but I gather it wasn't as pleasant as this."

"We've only just begun."

She laughed.

"I don't want you to tell tales, but Mum said you had been very patient, but she didn't say why. Anything to tell me?"

"Let me say this," I said, after considering the question. "I think your mother was surprised that being painted took longer than having her picture taken. She felt she had other – more interesting – things to do, and I was getting in the way of them."

Carrie laughed easily.

Her face was now taking shape nicely. She had asked me not to make her look "dumpy," so I cut the picture at her waist and adjusted the height of the windowsill to give the illusion that she was taller than she was.

"She did get her life together when I was born," Carrie said. "I don't know what she did or how, but I remember being very happy. When she met Giorgio and we moved to Predore, she grew more and more settled and happy.

"I know what people think and say, but she and Giorgio *were* very happy," she continued. "He was good to her, and though they argued, they never fought. Both seemed to enjoy their debates."

I painted in silence for a few minutes.

"She doesn't smile much, or is that just around me?"

Carrie didn't immediately reply.

"It's not one of those things I like to think about," she said. "I think it's because she hasn't found a role since Giorgio died. She has the house in Predore and this apartment. Stephano lives here because his work is split between here and Milan. He thinks the school here is better for Alegra, and he and Laura have many friends in Rome.

"It's great for me to live here and I try to stay out of their way. When I finish university, I hope to move back to Predore. Most of the things I can do, I can do remotely, but Mum needs to find something to give her purpose again. She's too young to play the role of the dowager countess."

I worked a bit more.

"It's time to decide what you want in the landscape," I said. "Do you want it the way it is, or do you want me to move it around and edit it?"

She looked at me as though this was collaborating in deception.

"Don't worry," I said. "I tell people that even Canaletto did it. Victorian landscapes and cityscapes are pretty ruthlessly modified, and I am sure the same is true of those in Paris. I haven't had the chance to print out the pictures you sent me, but the thing to remember right now is that what you are seeing is not what I am seeing from over here."

She moved from the window and came to look at the picture.

She laughed in surprise.

"You're making me look very elegant," she said, still nervously giggling.

"No, Carrie, I'm painting what everyone sees, not how you see yourself."

"Perhaps that's what Mum needs to do," she said, quietly.

Chapter XIV

On Monday morning, I was able to persuade Sophie to have breakfast with me at Bar 43. She couldn't appreciate the fact that having breakfast in a bar was normal. She may have been afraid of a paparazzi shot appearing in a London newspaper.

When we arrived, more people said good morning to me than before as we settled down at a table.

Sophie either skips breakfast or has a full English. In this case, a full Roman.

I had given her the bones of my afternoon with the Polidoris at dinner, but filled in a few more details this morning, notably about Carrie's comments about Francesca.

"Do you think she'd take me shopping?" Sophie asked, halfway through her second *bomboloni*.

Since this was a prospect I didn't want to contemplate, I simply shrugged.

"I'll call her when we get back to the hotel," she said. "Are you free this morning to help me with the script?"

Having nothing fixed until my math lesson at four, I agreed, but did wonder why Sophie wanted to rehearse with me;. it was something she'd never done in London.

Probably best not to question it.

We spent the time between breakfast and lunch working through the scenes that she thought would give trouble. I read the lines as directed – sometimes a dozen times – but offered no suggestions on how they might best be done. I didn't tell her how to play; she didn't tell me how to paint. Everything else was fair game.

After our big breakfast, another modest lunch at the *tavola calda* was in order.

"Can we find someplace nice for dinner tonight?" Sophie asked, about half-way through her stuffed aubergine.

I laughed.

"And where would you like to go for breakfast tomorrow?"

She put her fork down.

"This is what being in Italy does for me. I can't stop thinking about food," she said. "I think it's the smells that are so tempting. I want to go into every *trattoria* to find out what has such wonderful smells."

"I understand perfectly," I said. "We'll find somewhere nice but think about what you'd like to eat."

I was drinking only water as within the next half hour, I'd have to start walking to the Polidoris'. After yesterday's glimmer with Alegra, I was dreading a new shutdown.

As it happened, Alegra was all right. I made her go back upstairs to get the papers from the previous lesson.

She was reluctant to do so, and when she returned, I saw why.

She had traced, coloured in, or copied my sketches and was embarrassed for defacing mine and of the quality of her doodles.

I said nothing and set out a few progressively difficult algebra problems and a few geometry ones. I tore out a new sheet for her to work on, which gave me the chance to look more closely at what she had drawn.

As I suspected – and perhaps her father, too – Alegra knew what to do, but was unmotivated and didn't care about getting the right answer unless someone was right next to her.

I helped her on the final two algebra problems, but she only needed a few nudges.

She moved on seriously to the geometry, but I stopped her.

"What are these?" I asked, turning her previous day's paper over.

It was clear what they were: they were sketches for skirts, dresses and tops. They weren't good, but there was a flair here and there. Even in the city with the greatest art in the world (sorry, Paris), they no longer bothered to teach their children to draw.

"They're not very good," she said.

"No, they're not. But were you more interested in the drawing or the garments?"

Alegra's attitude was still guarded but the solid sullenness was showing signs of softening.

"I like fashion," she admitted.

"And what a wonderful place in the world you live for it," I replied, and she looked up.

"You know, it's all geometry," I said.

She sat up.

"Look."

Under her sketch of a shirt, I drew a series of cylinders at various angles and of various sizes. Then, with a few strokes, connected them, drew the suggestion of a waist and bust and, finally, added the cuffs and collar her drawing had suggested.

"Now, when you go to make it, you know how to calculate how much material you need using the formulae from your geometry. Do it right, and you can under-cut all your competitors, or use better materials for the same price."

Her face was one of amazement.

"Did you do fashion design, too?" she asked.

"Alas, no. I might have been more famous – and richer if I had," I said. "It's all mathematical: measurements and proportions. I have to draw clothing every day as part of my work – hair and makeup, too – but I don't have to create the style, just copy it – but with the clothes, they are in three dimensions made from essentially a two-dimensional idea, like yours," I indicated her sketch. "It might help your drawing if you thought about the body inside the clothes. Now, can you do the next problem?"

She gave a shrug and slight moan, but it was more a parody of her earlier disposition.

☙

I didn't see Stephano that day, but Carrie came in at exactly four-thirty.

She told me about a cosmology lecture she'd been to while I was refreshing paints and deciding where to pick up.

While a good likeness and striking picture was taking shape, this would be the third sitting and I'd spent less than four hours on the portrait. In my studio, I'd normally do an hour or two from life and several more hours that day. On average about four hours per day. So, by the number of hours painted over three days, I was way behind where I should be and all of a sudden, I didn't know if I could finish before flying back to London.

I worked with Carrie for an hour and a half. For some of the time, she was grilling me about various bits of mathematics, while we'd be silent for other periods. Painting a convincing hand against a window while preserving the illusion of the shape of its plane was tricky. Get it wrong, and it would look like the glass pane ran through the subject's face.

In these cases, use of a photographic print was a huge help as it meant that all I had to do was copy one two-dimensional image to another.

"Here is the full panorama of the city stitched together," I said, taking the sheets I had printed from my pocket. They were taped together to give the entire scene.

Carrie looked at them.

"It's nothing more than a whim, but I'd love to have St Peter's dome more a feature than St Ambrose and St Charles," she said. "Is that disrespectful or irreverent? I love that church but, from here, it always seems in the way."

I laughed.

"If Canaletto can redesign Venice, I can redesign Rome."

"Oooooh!" exclaimed Carrie. "You're beginning to sound like Nero!"

❦

Sophie had found a restaurant near Piazza Farnese, a short walk from the hotel.

"Chiara recommended it," she said, as we walked. "The cousin of a friend runs it or works there. She said to be sure to have a fish course."

We looked in shop windows, commented on what we saw, and I made a mental note to return to an art supplies shop I hadn't seen before. I tried to act casually as we passed it, but Sophie was aware enough to give my arm a tug to speed my pace.

"Come back in the morning to see it," she said.

We found the restaurant without any trouble and the moment we entered, a middle-aged woman who would have been a casting director's dream for an Italian mother came forward.

"*La signora Sophie e Dottor Thomas!*" she exclaimed, taking Sophie's hand and then mine in both of hers.

I glanced at Sophie, but she was focused on the *padrona di casa*.

"*Mille grazie, signora,*" she replied, smiling, but trying to lower the volume as heads were turning.

We were escorted to a table, had napkins unfolded on our laps and handed menus.

The fare, while familiar, ran a wider gamut than more basic restaurants. It was all here: chicken, veal, pork, lamb, beef and several species of fish. There were dishes – meat-based and vegetarian – that could be combined with pastas of all varieties.

While we weren't fussed over, each course felt like an occasion, and we relaxed and enjoyed the special treatment we received. I am sure they had no idea who we were, but knowing Chiara and her father was enough for them.

This was not food to be rushed, so we reduced our normal pace and paid more attention to it than to our conversation.

The restaurant filled up as the evening progressed and noise levels rose. The first impression was that this was a fairly smart establishment, but the look was created with a small number of features: a few pieces of good antique furniture, mirrors, panels of regency striped wall covering, well set tables, low lighting and candles. Not only did it make the room look elegant, but the diners, too.

Sophie became aware of the stage-set effects about the same time I did.

"Well done, Chiara!" she said. "We shall have to ask her to make more recommendations."

We played one of our games, speculating on the different people and couples we saw. It was something we often did and frequently wondered what people made of us.

"The time is going very quickly," Sophie said. "All we seem to have done is work. Me on my script and you on your drawing and painting."

"And I haven't done a single religious picture yet," I said.

Sophie smiled.

"But you have, haven't you? It's all there in your head. All you have to do is get it on canvas. Do you have enough sketches and pictures of Stephano?"

I nodded.

"Yes, he's fine. Thomas More will be in his cell soon," I said. "I had an idea for it that I want to try," I began, and Sophie gave me her encouraging look while tucking into her roast lamb.

"Having someone just sitting in a bare cell can be pretty uninteresting. The shape of the Bell Tower cell – where he almost certainly wasn't kept, but common opinion has him – has an interesting, vaulted ceiling which will give the gothic look to things with some menacing shadows, but it also has a cruciform arrow loop."

I paused to eat some of the pork I had chosen.

"Let me guess!" Sophie interrupted, excitedly.

"Am I that predictable?"

"Of course you are, darling. We all are to our friends."

I sighed and put my fork down and took a drink.

"More is gazing at the floor where there is a cross in sunlight!" she blurted. "Am I right?"

I raised my glass to her.

"The trick will be to position him so it looks natural, and the viewer can see his face."

I was secretly delighted that Sophie had read my mind as well as the signals. It also gave me reassurance that I was on the right track in my thinking about the picture.

"And the one of Carrie?" I asked. "Do you approve of that one?"

"How's that coming along? I love the idea of a bright young lady looking out on the world but not yet a part of it. The hand on the window is brilliant – like a very young child. If you can make it say, 'Just you wait, I'm coming!' that would capture her."

"I knew you were clever when you were fourteen," I said, feeling gratified that at least one person understood what I was trying to do with my portraits.

She didn't reply and I was afraid I'd struck an old bruise. We resumed eating and making speculations about our neighbouring diners.

"She's trying to impress him," Sophie said, glancing to a couple in their late twenties two tables to my right.

"Do you think so? I think she's goading him to impress her."

"How can you say that?"

"Look at her jewellery and accessories. Her shoes, hair and makeup. She's the affluent alpha. He's her reclamation job."

She considered it.

"Maybe they're trying to rescue each other," Sophie said. "Like us."

We talked around this for two decades, but this was the most blatant she'd been.

"I never tried to rescue you," I said. "Though you did make some important changes in my life."

"Yes, I know," she said, dismissively. "I invaded your sanctuary. Boo hoo."

I laughed. There was nothing else for it.

I looked back at the couple.

"I still think she's dominant," I said. "I see no flaws in her character, no hidden past. Poor bloke: she's going to turn his life around whether he wants it or not."

"Thrust him into middle-class morality," she quipped, and giggled.

The couple glanced towards us, Sophie was laughing hard, and I removed the wine bottle from her reach.

Over dessert and coffee, Sophie asked if we might visit St Peter's in the morning.

"Can we get an early bus or taxi? It would be good to get there before the crowds."

"I think – "

We were interrupted by a raised, but still controlled and polite voice.

"*Penso che tu sia meravigliosa, ma mi piace anche quello che sono. Se non è abbastanza, beh, è un problema tuo!*"

Roughly, "I like what I am. If you don't, that's tough."

The young man we'd been watching stood, threw a few hundred euros on the table and left with the girl only feet after him.

There were several shouts of "bravo" from various men. I kept my mouth shut. As I noted, in Italy, everything is an opera.

Everyone watched the door, but neither of them returned.

"I think this is my treat," said Sophie.

Chapter XV

Wrapped up warmly, we took the bus to a stop at the bottom of Via della Conciliazione and walked up to St Peter's Square. The Bernini fountains were still filling up and we watched for a while anticipating the top bowl to spill over, but the speed at which the crowds were already arriving (it was still before eight), we approached the entrance security gates.

Pope St John Paul II liked to give free access to those visiting the basilica and had the chairs cleared when there wasn't a major event. This made the space look massively bigger and let tourists wander more freely. The combination of cost and security risks led to the corralling of crowds to follow a route around the perimeter of the building. It was possible to dip into chapels and sit quietly, rub your feet, drink your bottled water, or pray, but the shuffling crowd continued to move, looking at depictions of events and stories that it neither knew nor understood.

Two thousand years of faith, courage, sacrifice and creativity rolling over minds more used to watching video clips about cleaning a ceramic hob. Well, maybe something might sink in.

As this is neither a guidebook nor a travelogue, I'll say no more than we spent the most time looking at the *Pieta*

– which though a wonderfully moving piece of sculpture, in reality, merely one of a dozen or more of equal merit in the basilica; the high altar and the dome. We were able to sit for these latter two.

When we finished the circuit an hour later, Sophie asked if we could go round again. We paused at some different places and after rounding the high altar and contemplating the window of the Holy Spirit, I maneuvered her to the statue of St Andrew situated in the angle of one of the piers supporting the dome. After making suitable comments about the Scots, I indicated the small staircase nearly in front of us.

"Really?" Sophie asked.

This unobtrusive – and surprisingly little used – stairway is one of many leading to the grottos where there are dozens of small chapels and the tombs of popes.

"The grotto is open the same times as the rest of the basilica," I said. "Visiting priests often come in to say Mass in one of the national chapels or at one dedicated to a patron or favourite saint."

As we moved into the main area, Sophie's eyes widened.

"This is enormous! Are all the popes here?" she asked reading the names, "Benedict VI, Innocent IX, ah! Here's one I recognise: John Paul I."

"There might be someone else you'll recognise here," I said, leading her across the chamber to a marble tomb with a bronze crown on it.

"James III?" she asked.

I smiled.

"The British get everywhere," I said. "James II's son, Henry Benedict, who was a cardinal, and Charles Edward, better known as Bonnie Prince Charlie."

Sophie was stunned.

"Bonnie Prince Charlie?! There?!"

"The last of the Stuarts."

"I guess they took their Catholicism seriously," she said.

"I wouldn't like to say. He abused his mistress who ran away with their illegitimate daughter who, finding herself without money and unable to marry, became mistress of the Archbishop of Bordeaux," I explained.

"Poor girl!"

"She did reconcile with her father, and he named her Duchess of Albany but she died a few years later in her mid-thirties."

"She's not here?"

"No one is sure where she is. The church where she was buried – in Bologna, I think – was destroyed by the French."

She gazed at the inscription, then looked around.

"I don't suppose anyone here led a quiet life."

We continued down the wall passing Innocent XIII, Urban VI and Pius III before coming to a granite tomb.

"That looks really old!" Sophie said.

"It's been recycled," I said.

"Don't be disrespectful," she chided.

"I'm not. It was an early pagan tomb from between two and three hundred, but it now holds the remains of Hadrian IV, the only English pope."

She moved forwards to look more carefully.

"There was a play, wasn't there?"

"*Hadrian VII*. Based on an earlier novel. The writer used the name Hadrian because of this fellow, Nicholas Breakspear."

"Like the beer?"

"Same family."

We moved more quickly along the wall back towards the altar above.

"Two things to see," I said, "Actually, one thing, two sides."

We were near the stairs we'd come down, and we looked through the grate to the Pallium Niche, behind which was where St Peter was thought to be buried.

"We saw that from upstairs," she said, and I nodded.

"Now come around here to another chapel. This is an earlier one and the stone band marks the place, too."

We looked for a while, but there were now crowds at this end of the grottoes.

"And, during World War II, a whole new level beneath was discovered and excavated under the noses of the Nazis. The whole basilica is built on a Roman cemetery."

Sophie nodded with enthusiasm.

"I know that one, too! To make the foundations, half the hillside was pushed over the cemetery, wasn't it? But is St Peter really right there?"

"I think so, but you may decide for yourself."

We walked the length of the space again, picking out one or two other names, including Pope St John Paul II, Pope St Paul VI and Queen Cristina of Sweden.

I thought Sophie must be bored with all the papal history and monuments, but we spend considerable time looking at various artifacts and carvings excavated on the site over the years.

When we emerged into the air, we were surprised to find it was nearly eleven thirty.

"What shall it be?" she asked, brightly. "Coffee or a drink?"

"Ladies' choice."

ဆ

The lady chose coffee.

"We can drink with lunch," she said, and I thought it made sense.

I felt her patience with things Catholic and the tombs of popes she'd never heard of and whose authority she rejected was exceptional, so I talked about her forthcoming play.

"It's hard to believe that this time next week I'll be in a draughty rehearsal hall drinking bad coffee and eating a grim sandwich," she said.

"Do you have pre-show dreams? Or performance nightmares?" I asked. "I've painted several headmasters and headmistresses (head teachers don't tend to get painted) and they told me that in mid-August all teachers start having back-to-school dreams where they do something horrible or can't find their books, classrooms, or schools."

"You've known this for years and never told me!" Sophie exclaimed.

Her vehemence was approaching anger, and the café went quiet. I was taken aback, and she later told me that I'd lost all my colour.

"It's *normal*?" she shouted again.

It took a moment for me to nod and squeak out, "Yes."

She fell back in her chair with a loud laugh.

The waiter approached.

"Too much coffee," I exclaimed discreetly, and asked for a carafe of water.

"I'd never dare tell you what I dream before an exhibition," I said, and Sophie laughed harder.

The water came, Sophie calmed down and the rest of the patrons considered us uncouth British (or worse, Americans or Germans) and went back to their espressos.

Sophie leaned forward.

"You know, I can't rely on anything in my life being normal," she said. "I question everything I do or think."

"Teachers really have back-to-school dreams?"

"I think every working person has dreams about not being able to do his work or telling off his boss," I said.

"I can't tell you what a relief that is."

"You really didn't know that?" I asked.

She shook her head.

"No one has put it in a play and dreams are private, so I don't talk to people about them."

I suppose we all wonder from time to time what it must be like in someone else's brain. Sophie had told me more than enough when we first met (or re-met) to prevent me from asking questions. [3]

Sophie drank some coffee and nibbled on her biscotti.

"You don't know what a relief that is," she sighed.

"I think we all have certain types of dreams that recur," I said. "I suspect many are of a sort that we wouldn't want many people to know. Most of mine make very little sense."

"Do you think it's a way that God talks to people?"

___
[3] Ibid.

"I never thought so," I replied. "I think most of it is a clearing of the cache of the brain; dumping all the things that are not necessary for your life. I also think it's a time when the subconscious mind works out problems – though that may not manifest as dreams. There's also a good amount of wish fulfillment."

Sophie gave me a naughty smile.

"Probably best not to go there."

☙

We wandered down the streets off the main roads, looking in shop windows and reading menus in the various restaurants. By the time we reached Piazza Cavour, we were hungry. While busy with businessmen having lunch, we were able to find a friendly place for pizza (Sophie) and pasta (me).

While I had to be able to do algebra and hold a paintbrush later in the afternoon, Sophie did not and ordered a litre of wine.

I returned to the topic that had previously been derailed.

"November is not an ideal time to launch a new play – unless it's a panto," she said. "It should have been much earlier, but the renovations to the theatre ran behind. If we don't get a decent run, a lot of people could lose a lot of money.

"Because I am old and established, I know I'll get paid for at least two weeks even if we close after opening night," she explained. "Should it be a success, my contract is for ten months with an option to renew."

"Are you word-perfect yet?"

"Pretty nearly."

I took that as a yes, because I knew from experience that she knew everyone else's words, too.

"Will it be a hit?"

She thought for so long that I began to think she hadn't heard me. She stared out the window, picked a mushroom off her pizza with a fork and drank some wine.

"It could be," she said, at length. "It needs to be played right and I'm not sure the director is experienced enough. I don't think the writer has a full understanding of what he's written, either.

"In November, the audiences will be British," she continued. "That means they will have a greater sense of irony than the summer, more foreign, audiences. The playwright is young and earnest and those lines if delivered with the earnestness that's in the script will come across as being ironic which, in turn, will make the play funnier and better."

She looked at me.

"Did that make any sense?"

"Who else is in the cast?"

She gave me a list of names. Some I knew, others I did not.

"That's what could make this work," she said. "There are enough members of the cast who will know how this should play. They are the more experienced actors. Together, we should be able to move the play in our preferred direction."

Revealing such things was not something Sophie generally did, which I took as an indication of her reservations. She wasn't asking for advice but trying to work something out that had been percolating for some time.

We declined dessert and coffee and decided to walk back to the hotel. Although we'd been on our feet much of the day, even Sophie thought a small penance was in order after the meal.

We didn't rush and poked about some shops, squares and picturesque alleys so by the time we reached the hotel, it was nearly time to head back to the Polidoris'.

For that journey, I would indulge in a taxi.

I rang the apartment bell at exactly four o'clock and Carrie answered the door.

"You have two hours with me, today," she said, when we reached the top of the stairs and entered the apartment.

"Oh?"

"I'm afraid so," she replied. "Alegra couldn't add two and two at the moment. She's up in her room, stoned out of her mind."

Chapter XVI

I have had people show up to be painted drunk, drugged and both. Not painting them would have been the preferred option, so not teaching algebra to someone incapable was fine with me.

"Mum's up there with her to make sure she doesn't do anything else stupid," Carrie said, matter of factly.

"Does this happen often?"

"Her current boyfriend's brother's a dealer."

"It's a bit unfair on your mother," I said, thinking that Francesca seemed to have pretty good reasons not to smile.

We walked into the loggia, and I took out my paints and set up.

Carrie stood by the window but didn't take the pose.

"Let me know when you're ready," she said. "I suppose I'd better fill in some blanks for you."

"You don't need to tell me anything," I said.

Carrie turned to face me and gave me a very grown-up look.

"I don't think you're someone who just paints the superficial," she said. "Believe it or not, I learned more about some things by looking at your portrait of my mother than she ever told me.

"No, I'm telling you because it's important that you have a little more insight in how we all function together."

She stopped, perhaps feeling a little embarrassed, then turned to the window.

I had decided how to move St Peter's Basilica and the grand church of Saints Ambrose and Charles but would do that while Carrie was having a break.

"I'm ready now, Carrie."

She adjusted her pose and posture and put her hand on the glass. I later saw that this clever girl had marked both the floor and the window to ensure she did it properly.

After a few minutes of adjusting some things I wasn't happy with, I asked:

"Any further with the cosmology?" I asked, and she laughed.

"It frightens me," she said. "I laugh because it's the only way I can cope.

"It's scary enough as it is, but when you bring in quantum theory, the whole thing gets rather closer to 'Music of the Spheres' which I find unsettling to say the least. Did you find that?" she asked.

"What I ultimately found – and have discovered no reason to change my mind since – is that those who have belief and faith (and they're not the same) in an all-powerful God, have no problem with cosmology," I said, trying not to sound preachy or dogmatic. "It's not that the theory or mathematics is any easier, but that realising the possibility – and probability – of *creatio ex nihilo sui subiecti* – and it's important to remember the second bit – is an acceptable option. Not only does it offer peace of mine, but it also reveals many new doors to be opened."

"So only believers can do cosmology?" she challenged, but not aggressively.

I laughed, which seemed to disconcert her.

"It is certainly not easier for them, but I think only a believer can fully appreciated what creating something from nothing means.

"Please look back at your focus point," I said, gently, lest the painting stop.

"You remember the simple diagram of the mediaeval universe with the big heaven, the big area of Chaos, the universe hanging by a golden chain from Heaven and the Void surrounding it all?"

She nodded.

"With hell in Chaos. Yes."

"Well, understanding the Void makes understanding *creatio ex nihilo* easier," I said. "However, the Void is as ineffable as Heaven. Who can grasp the absence of space itself? But that's what *nothing* means.

"It's easy for us to understand a potter as a creator of pieces of pottery from a lump of clay but suppose there were no clay. What would the potter be making his pots from?"

"Nothing."

"Exactly. In that case, there are two possibilities, either there is, in fact, nothing there, and what we are seeing is an illusion or something made from the essence of the potter/creator himself.

"And the illusion – "

"And the illusion," Carrie interrupted, "could either be generated by the potter or by us in our own minds."

"Either way, in the absence of blue smoke and mirrors, it's the emperor's new clothes," I said.

"So, the universe is created from the essence of God himself?"

"And the Devil can only create illusions. He can neither create nor break *anything*."

We were quiet for a while.

"So do you create illusions?" Carrie suddenly asked.

"I make a slightly more accurate representation of the shadows in Plato's cave."

I don't know if she found that satisfactory, but she was quiet for a few more minutes.

"You can relax and take a break now, Carrie," I said.

She sat in the chair and leaned back, closing her eyes. I worked on. I needed to find a time when I could paint her face in daylight. The colours and shadows were close, and I did have several photographs, but understanding her more now meant that I could see more of what her face was saying.

"Would you like a glass of wine?" she asked. "I'm getting some water for myself, but there's a bottle of Franciacorta open."

She went into the kitchen. When she returned and handed me the glass, I nodded to the painting.

"Do you recognise yourself yet?"

She said nothing but looked closely at it. I asked if she'd be available in daylight to finalise her face and she asked if nine o'clock Thursday morning was all right. She could give me an hour and a half if I agreed to talk to her about Markov Chains.

"I'm beginning to understand the pose," she said. "It's curious how different the image of oneself is compared to that of how others see you."

I thought she'd elaborate, but she returned to the chair and relaxed.

"Mum's only here because it's so lonely in Predore," she began. "It's beautiful, and the house is comfortable – the views are amazing! Stephano is back and forth to Milan but because of schools, they are living here. Laura works in the Italian equivalent of a large teaching hospital. Although she's not a doctor, she teaches image analysis and various tricks for getting the best scans and information from them. When Stephano's away, she's good company for Mum, though I don't think they'd choose each other as friends.

"I mean, they get along well but don't have that much in common. Mum and I feel very foreign sometimes."

"And you? Are you comfortable with this, or would you have preferred to get away from family for university?"

Carrie considered this.

"I did at one point, but growing up with Giorgio, I learned the importance of family – and I think Mum did, too," she said. "You really wouldn't believe how devoted to him she was. To the outside world, it looked like a gold-digging young lady with a past going after a vulnerable much older man, or an old roué chasing a bright young lady, but it wasn't like that at all."

She stood and took the pose by the window again.

"I can understand that well," I said. "In partial answer to Alegra's question the other night, I never recovered emotionally from the death of my wife nearly forty years ago. Sophie never recovered from something else and sharing that – which we discovered when I painted her when she was in her forties – became the basis of our companionship."

Carrie said nothing for a while but was very still and I took advantage of that to fix her eyes.

"That's very sad," she said.

ରଓ

I'd made good progress in two hours with Carrie and was disappointed when she asked if we could skip the next day. It would be cutting things fine to get the picture finalised, but it was virtually done now. If it hung in Predore for the rest of time, it wouldn't matter, but other artists and good critics would recognise it as unfinished.

I told Carrie that she could stop posing and was finishing up when Francesca came in.

"How is she?" Carrie asked, with concern.

"Finally asleep."

Francesca looked weary but satisfied.

"May I look?" she asked, moving next to me.

"Of course, it's yours."

I backed away to give her room. She moved to where I stood to paint and looked back and forth from the painting to the real window and wall in the background.

"That's very clever," she said. "You've changed the proportions of the window to make Carrie look taller – but when you look at her in the picture and in real life – they're the same."

She shifted her gaze from the portrait to her daughter and back as she spoke.

"Are you objectifying me again, Mother?" Carrie demanded. To me, she added, "She's always doing that. Especially when she wants to introduce me to some man."

"You're lucky I'm trying – you're not," Francesca retorted.

"Can't I just graduate first?" Carrie said.

"Yes. 'Just let me graduate,' then it will be 'Just let me do the next two years.' Then, 'Wait until I've finished my doctorate,' or 'finish an article,' or 'have been made – Astronomer Royal!'"

"Oh!" exclaimed Carrie. "I think I'd like that. That sounds *worth* waiting for."

Francesca rolled her eyes and, with both hands, made a grand Italian gesture of exasperation. It was all good humoured, if pointed, banter but Francesca's refusal to smile gave it an edge.

The exchange was interrupted when we heard the front door closing and Laura Polidori coming up the stairs.

Francesca left the room. Shortly after, we heard a cry of fear, and then steps running up to the top floor.

"Laura is a nice person, really," Carrie said. "She's quite shy with strangers. You may have sensed that when you were here for dinner."

I was nearly finished cleaning my brushes and putting the paints away.

Carrie lowered her voice.

"Laura was jealous of Mother when she arrived in Predore. They are virtually the same age. Stephano was very sweet," she said. "He hadn't seen his father so happy in years and accepted Mum. I think he was glad that he no longer had to keep an eye on his father. He treated both of us very well which Laura didn't always like, but he regarded us as family."

She reflected for a minute.

"It would be easier if Mum didn't get so lonely in Predore. Stephano would miss her – even Alegra – but Laura would be relieved."

I put my coat on quickly. These were just people I painted. I didn't want to get tangled in family matters. I took a last look at the portrait.

"We've made good progress. One more session should finish it," I said. "Nine o'clock Thursday."

"And, to talk about Markov Chains."

$\wp$

I'd barely had time to clean up from the day when Sophie tapped on my door at seven.

"I'm starving and I want to talk to you," she said through the door.

"I'll meet you in the lobby."

I couldn't judge Sophie's mood when I met her, and we walked to the Trattoria della Pigna. She held onto my arm but seemed irritated by something.

Fabrizia greeted us and showed us to a table.

"Has your visit to Rome been a success?"

I replied yes, but Sophie drowned me out saying, "Good question."

Fabrizia said nothing but a moment later, Tonio placed a carafe of *rossa della casa* on the table.

"*Complimenti*."

We stared at the carafe.

"Oh, dear," Sophie said, softly.

I poured two glasses.

Sophie took a good drink, then picked up a piece of bread.

"Did something happen in my absence?" I asked, as soon as she had put the bread in her mouth.

Timing is everything.

Her eyes widened in outrage that I'd use that tactic. Then, she feigned calm, swallowed the bread and took a leisurely drink.

"While you were chatting up the Polidoris – "

She was cut off by the arrival of Tonio to take our order. Rather than admit we hadn't even opened the menu, I told Tonio to bring us things that we might like but might not know. He began to ask whether we wanted beef, pork, lamb or veal, but Sophie had warmed to the idea.

"*Lasciamo la parola allo chef, Tonio.*"

"*Grazie, Signora.*"

When he had left, Sophie returned to trying to look cross.

"You probably thought I had my fill of churches this morning, but I was so amazed by the ceiling and fake dome at St Ignatius that I went back late this afternoon."

"Ah, there's hope for you yet."

Sophie dropped the pretence and burst out laughing.

"Probably not after today," she said, still giggling. "I walked all round the church, poked into the side altars and read the various inscriptions where I could. Then I sat near one of the floor markers and gazed upwards. Even I can see it's an extraordinary piece of work."

Tonio arrived and placed dishes of *zuppa imperiale* before us with a fresh breadbasket. The portion was carefully rationed, otherwise it could have been a sustaining and delicious meal on its own.

"*Buon appetito*," I said.

We tasted the soup and smiled at each other, then Sophie resumed.

"While I was sitting there communing with the saints on the ceiling, Father Reynolds came by, sat next to me and asked if I were staying for Mass. *Don't snurkle*! I told him I wasn't Catholic. 'But you come to Mass with your husband,' he said."

Now, I was doing more than snurkling.

"He knows we're not married," I said.

"I told him we were living in sin."

"Sophie!" I exclaimed.

"Father Reynolds didn't flinch. He nodded and said, 'That's somewhere in Oxfordshire, isn't it?'"

Sophie was clearly amused at the time and said that she had corrected her earlier statement and explained our curious friendship. We must have been giving these same explanations at exactly the same time. And some say God doesn't have a sense of humour.

We finished our soup, and Sophie's expression darkened.

"Father Reynolds and I continued a quiet chat. He explained how episodes of the life of St Ignatius were on the ceiling along with his reception into heaven."

"His apotheosis."

"That's the word!" she said. "He then went on to say that he had heard about you from the Jesuits in Farm Street and understood you had been involved in several art intrigues."

It was my turn to say, "Oh, dear."

"He asked if you – he said I could come, too – could come to the English College after lunch, around two-thirty tomorrow and that he might have something you could 'help the Church with.'"

That final phrase meant that this was not an invitation but a command.

Chapter XVII

Our soup dishes were cleared, and the next course of beautifully grilled fish was placed before us on a bed of tiny broccoli florets, and glistening with butter and herbs. Tonio was followed by Fabrizia who delivered glasses of white wine.

"It's a good thing we just have to go around the corner," I said "A bad combination, being unable to move and liberally dosed."

The fish was magnificent. We seemed to have half a fillet each which was perfect for a fish course. Along with the expected herbs, there was the tang of lime which lifted the flavour to a more complex level. The wine (a Grave, perhaps?) was the perfect complement.

"And about what does the Church need my help?" I asked, trying to indicate that I was as displeased about this as she was.

Sophie didn't acknowledge the question but focused on her fish and wine, pausing only to glance around the room, presumably to see if we'd be treated to another floorshow.

When she'd finished and taken another drink, she said:

"Don't pretend you're not intrigued, flattered, and other things you'll probably have to confess," she said.

Her tone was teasing now, but I knew she wanted me to get on with religious painting while this time in Rome seemed to be a simple extension of my life in London.

Our plates were cleared and we were given a few minutes before our main course.

"And how was Alegra today? Eager to talk about multiplication?"

I told her how I had found things. Sophie was horrified.

"Was Francesca able to cope?"

"She seemed to have things under control. Carrie said that she really did turn her life around when she married, though doesn't seem to have enough to do," I said.

I told her what Carrie had said about her loneliness in Predore.

"She's caught in that place where you don't have to work and can't get motivated to do much of anything," Sophie said. "I've seen a lot of that."

Fabrizia arrived with our main courses.

"I am giving one of you a choice," she said, holding two tempting plates. "I have a *scallopine al limone* and an *ossa bucco*."

"May I have the *veal scallopine*?" Sophie asked me.

"As if I could say no."

Side dishes began appearing, from sauté potatoes and mushrooms with sun dried tomatoes, to green beans with fried onion flakes and garlic and side salads.

"Enough?" I asked Sophie.

"How's the painting going?" she asked, after trying all the dishes.

"Carrie couldn't do a session tomorrow, so I'll finish it at nine o'clock Thursday morning. Francesca seemed to like it, but Carrie hasn't said anything."

"I expect she was badgered into having it done."

"Perhaps, but she's a wonderful model. Quiet and still when she needs to be and chatty otherwise."

I told her about the marks she'd put on the floor and window so she could duplicate the pose.

"She's definitely not stupid," Sophie agreed. "So how are you going to spend the morning tomorrow?"

"I have to mug up on Markov Chains," I said.

"Oh!" she said, her voice rising. "Someone into bondage there?"

And then she got the giggles. It was at moments like this that I felt most profoundly sorry for Sophie. She should be sharing this unguarded side with a husband and children, not just a friend, however close. On the other hand, maybe it was just too much wine.

It took a while, but we managed to finish these dishes to the satisfaction of the chef. We were able to prevent

Fabrizia from putting large desserts before us and finished with espresso and limoncello.

"What do you want to do tomorrow morning?" she asked.

"Our days are getting short, so we should go see something. The beginning of the Apian Way, or the Baths of Caracalla?"

"Thank you for not suggesting we go to some obscure church," she replied. "I'd like a lie in and then go shopping. Down the Via dei Condotte."

"You won't miss out on churches completely. You'll probably get a tour of the Venerable English College," I said.

Sophie didn't look thrilled at the prospect.

"Father Reynolds will want to talk 'Church business' with you. Do I have to go?" she asked, semi-seriously.

"He invited you and told you to bring me," I said.

She drank some coffee.

"What would you like to do tomorrow morning, then?"

"A lie in does sound good," I admitted. "I'd like to work on my Thomas More drawings. It's starting to come together."

"You'll have to do it back in London now, won't you? It rather defeated the purpose of coming to Rome," Sophie said.

"Should I have not painted Carrie?"

Sophie thought about this.

"I think you were right," she said. "Painting mother and daughter twenty-two years apart is special. Think what it will mean to them in the future."

Then she smiled to herself.

"What?"

"If Carrie were pregnant now, you could paint her daughter when she is twenty-two. You'd only be ninety-seven."

೮ა

Going to bed on a full stomach wasn't a good idea and it certainly didn't make for a promising lie in. When we rather noisily left Trattoria della Pigna, we walked to the Piazza Navona. Though mild, it was dark and threatening to rain. We walked around the square, pausing at the far end to walk up to a fountain.

"When do they come to collect all the coins from the fountains?" Sophie asked.

"I expect there's a complicated timetable that changes to prevent others from collecting money. The Trevi Fountain gets the most – about four thousand euros a day. I don't think the others get too much."

"Where does the money go?"

"This is Italy. Don't ask."

The church of St Agnes loomed over us against a very black sky. While not crowded, there were enough people about to make it feel safe. I had read a detective novel where some hapless European man had been mugged or murdered in Philadelphia. The detective noted that it never occurred to most Europeans that walking around at night was dangerous. Even with many recent stories to suggest the contrary, this is still broadly true.

We passed several couples dreamily making the circuit and Sophie mused at their nationalities, backgrounds and compatibility as companions in life. The diversity in modern Europe is ubiquitous, but I still find it disconcerting to hear Asians speaking German or Italian.

When we reached where we'd begun, Sophie asked if I'd like to go round again or wander off somewhere else. We were not far from the hotel and this was familiar and a long enough walk to remain interesting, so we continued as if in the ruts of chariots.

"This trip was a remarkably good idea, Sophie. Thank you," I said.

"We don't seem to have done much more than eat," she said, giving my arm a squeeze.

"You've made a film appearance, I've done a portrait and have another ready to do. I've done a lot of research and seen some wonderful things," I said. "By the way, Carrie said to ask you if you really want her to keep the scarf."

"Yes, of course."

"I'll take a good picture of the painting on Thursday. Does Carrie know the scarf is in the film?"

"*I* didn't tell her."

"We must make sure she sees it, but I don't know how often she goes to the cinema," I said. "According to Francesca, all she does is study."

"Girls don't tell their mothers everything."

That was certainly true in Sophie's case.

"And are you really intrigued by painting something new and different?"

"I've been thinking of some other possible subjects," I replied. "Thomas More is a good choice. He's someone that a lot of people feel they know – they can picture him from all the paintings of him, so he's a good one to start with. I've been thinking about others whose stories feel familiar – no matter how wrong it is – but whose looks don't readily come to mind."

"Dare I ask?"

"I was thinking of a fictional scene with St Robert Bellarmine and Cardinal Orsini with Galileo."

Sophie thought.

"Interesting. Could be controversial, too," she mused.

"I thought the three of them might be playing a game. Chess would have been the logical one, but that's for two. Then I thought they might be looking at a partially constructed scientific instrument and pile of different sized coloured spheres with some brass rods and trying to assemble the first orrery."

Sophie laughed.

"You might even get the Science Museum to buy that one! Other possibilities?"

"Oh, there are lots that could be fun. Julian of Norwich – not a saint yet, but she could be, another might be St Simon Stock who lived for a while in a tree trunk."

"I like the idea of English subjects – though the one with Galileo sounds intriguing, and controversy never worried you."

I had thought it might be amusing. The question of controversy hadn't crossed my mind. I'm not sure I've done any paintings that were controversial. On the odd occasions that I've deviated from my normal jobbing form, the art writers and other artists have noticed the change. Surprise maybe, but controversial?

My triple portrait of Sophie was a departure for me, but it had been done at her request, so was her vision. The other portrait that entered new territory was the one of Fletcher Bailey, already mentioned.

Sophie's comment made me now see that simply starting to paint in a new genre might not be straight-forward. That had never occurred to me, but it did make me want to get on with *Sir Thomas More in his Cell*.

We finished our second lap, and Sophie walked to an empty bench near the *Fontana del Moro*. I sat next to her, but not too close. She surprised me and moved closer to me and took my hand.

"How do you cope with the loneliness?" she asked.

I believe the modern expression is that I was gob-smacked. Never in all the time I'd known her had she asked this – or anything like it. She had sealed herself in her own protective carapace when she was fourteen and, seemingly, had let nothing penetrate it.

She gave my hand a squeeze as a prompt, then drew it away.

"I keep looking forward, planning, thinking," I said, eventually. "I keep busy. I have friends in London – as do you."

"That might be part of it – missing the familiar routine and people," she said, "but you're the one who keeps me entertained and grounded."

"Your personal court jester."

"No, it's not like that at all!" she exclaimed. "Oh, please tell me you don't think I'm that shallow."

"I don't," I said, truthfully, "but what are you trying to say?"

She shook her head and was silent.

"Tell me something I don't know," she said, once she'd collected herself.

"These three fountains have the same source of water as the Trevi Fountain, an ancient Roman aqueduct that's running underneath us."

She gave one of her clear laughs of amusement.

"You see – you've given me something new to think about! It's hard to wallow in pity when you're around. You used to tease me more when I was younger."

"You mean when you were forty-five?"

She laughed again.

"Don't start being an actress who frets about her age," I said. "I'll do my best to keep you amused, but," I added, trying to sound serious, "I'm too old to take on a sixty-something teenager."

Sophie gave a gentle giggle.

"You'd be so easy to hate," she said.

"Would you like to go back to the hotel, or do you want to risk another *digestif*?"

We went to a café opposite St Agnes's near the main fountain. Sophie asked me to order something for her. I didn't relish the role of oracle, but she was not resilient enough at the moment for me to tell her.

I ordered a *mirto* and a *genepí* and she could decide which she preferred, or disliked least.

We watched the people and the fountain in silence while we waited. I thought about the day and realised how full it had been, from the breakfast in the bar and the trip through St Peter's, then my painting session and Sophie's visit to Sant'Ignazio. It was no wonder Sophie was out of sorts. I suspected she was fretting about what Father Reynolds wanted me to do, too.

Our drinks came. I passed the *genepí* to Sophie.

"I think this will suit you well," I said.

She held it up to consider its colour, yellow with a tinge of green, then tentatively tried it.

"It should make you sleep very well tonight," I said.

"It's bittersweet. What is it?"

"Wormwood."

"Like in absinthe?"

"You can tell me about your experiences with absinthe tomorrow," I said. "This is very pure, unadulterated apart from the sugar, and supposedly an excellent herbal remedy."

"What are you having?"

"*Mirto*. Also herbal. Made from myrtle."

"How do you know these things?" she asked.

"You're not the only one with secrets," I said.

She laughed hard.

"By that, I expect you mean the Jesuits."

"Shh!"

We drank quietly and were just finishing when I felt the temperature drop.

"It's going to rain soon," I said.

"Oh, I was hoping I could have another two or three of those," Sophie joked. "It was good."

There was a low rumble of thunder.

"Come on."

It was still well before midnight, so the hotel doors were open. We said good night to the night clerk (Giancarlo, I think) and took the lift to our rooms.

Before going to her room, Sophie turned to me.

"Tell me one thing," she began. "Did I really jump into the fountain last week?"

Chapter XVIII

I could have told her. There was no way she'd remember in the morning, but I just said goodnight and went to my room. Sophie's question about loneliness inevitably led me to consider my own position – again. I understood what she – we – felt, but always supposed the rest of the world felt the same. I knew there was a limit to how long I could live on my own in Albany, but it was my wish – like everyone else's – that when the end comes, it comes quickly. So quickly that I wouldn't have to worry about it.

By the time I climbed into bed, the rain had started. There was no more thunder, and the sound of the rain soon put me to sleep.

It was still raining in the morning when I woke up at around nine-thirty. The sound of wet tyres on the streets was a universal one and, dozing for a few minutes, I realised that I could be anywhere.

I took a book down to the lobby with me and ordered coffee. My murder mystery was resolving and the blind – and presumed mad – old aunt who had been pitifully sewing bits on the curtains hanging in her nephew's house turned out to be a long message in braille accusing his wife of embezzlement and murder. So engrossing was this – and welcome antidote to high art and religion – that I did not see Sophie enter. She was in the process of sitting down when she spoke.

"Did I behave last night?" she asked, softly. "I can't have been too bad, my shoes were dry."

"Of course, you were fine," I said, surprised that she considered her behaviour inappropriate.

Of all the well-known stage and film actresses, she was among those who had the least scandal associated with her. I had experienced – first hand – how the low-end media tried to make stories from nothing. Over the years, I had been photographed in restaurants and in the street with Sophie. Apart from speculations about who I was, and some gentle ribbing from friends at the Royal Academy and my club, the invasions had been minor. It helped that I never escorted Sophie to any premiers or awards ceremonies. Although we had said nothing about it, we accepted that some paparazzo would spot us here and pictures would appear in due course. As long as we weren't pursued in the streets, we'd have to accept it. If asked, Sophie could always say that she'd been in Rome to meet with Gaetano Minetti.

A coffee arrived for Sophie.

"Are you feeling fragile this morning?" I asked.

She looked embarrassed, which she seldom did.

"I remember every mouthful of that wonderful meal, but once we left the restaurant, things get foggy," she said.

"Did we walk all over the city? I have a memory of walking but little idea of where. How much did I have to drink?"

"Not that much," I said. "You had half a litre of red wine, a good-sized glass of white and a limoncello. Later, you had a *genepí*."

"Whatever that is," she said, trying to remember. "I didn't do anything to offend your sense of propriety?"

"You never do."

She relaxed and laughed.

"You didn't always think that."

"You have nothing to worry about," I said, and she seemed mollified. "Are you still planning on shopping this morning? It's filthy weather."

She looked at her watch.

"I'd like to. I won't melt," she said. "What are you going to do?"

"I thought, I'd go back to the library and see if anyone has painted the saints I mentioned yesterday. Picking up some of the symbols and conventions could be useful."

Sophie nodded.

"How long will it take us to get to the English College?"

"Fifteen or twenty minutes," I said. "We can take a taxi if it's raining or you don't want to walk."

"Do you want breakfast?"

"No. I'd rather get to the shops," she said. "Let's meet here at one and go for lunch."

☙

The fact that there wasn't a lot of time worked in my favour as the lists and variations of symbols associated with saints was seemingly endless. The catalogue had every sort of object, animal, flower, fruit, and religious object imaginable. There was quite an assortment of weapons: swords, spears, axes, halberds and maces, not to mention hammers and tongs. I also found about sixty variations of the cross.

St Simon Stock is visually associated with the brown scapular of the Carmelites – a long cloth with a hole in the middle to go over the head and hang down the length of a cassock, front and back. He is often shown holding a long lily with several blossoms at the top. There are a number of paintings showing the Blessed Virgin handing him the scapular and others that are more like simple icons.

Julian of Norwich was rather different. Not (yet) a saint, she lived as an anchoress in Norwich. Her cell had two windows, one into the church, and one onto the street through which she could speak to and counsel people. During the time of the covid lockdowns, she was seen as a source of spiritual help, having lived through the Black Plague. Somewhere along the line, the notion that Julian had a cat crept in, so there are a number of modern paintings and icons with cats. I'm not convinced, but that may be because I just don't like cats.

I considered it a successful morning as I collected what I needed to move forward, and judging by the bags

Sophie was carrying when she entered the lobby, her morning had been successful, too.

Sophie suggested we go back to the *tavola calda*. I think she liked seeing and eating "ordinary" food in a daily setting. We got the odd stare as obvious foreigners, but having been there before, we knew how things worked.

"Is the Via dei Condotti empty now?" I asked Sophie, when we sat down.

"Pretty much," she said. "I only brought back what I'm going to wear in the next two days. The rest is being shipped home."

This was one of our set-piece exchanges. Sophie's flat simply didn't have enough room for Hollywood actress wardrobes. She, like many other sensible public figures, had mastered the art of altering outfits so they looked different depending on their interchangeability. For smart dresses, Sophie, of course, knew many costume designers and seamstresses who could remake a dress so that not even the fan magazine fashion writers would recognise it as something she'd worn before.

We compared our mornings and decided that we were both satisfied with them. Sophie displayed a rare feeling of contentment as we reached the end of the meal. It was raining steadily now and there was a comfortable fug in the restaurant, replete with the smells of good food.

"It would be nice to just curl up with a good book this afternoon," she said.

"Why don't you? If it would make you happy."

"No," she said, "I'd better see that you don't get into too much trouble. If I leave you alone with Father Reynolds and his other Jesuit henchmen, your 'service to the Church' would end up being painting a portrait of the pope!"

She said it loudly enough that I could almost see it as tabloid headlines.

She looked at her watch.

"Come on, we mustn't keep the good Father waiting."

⊳

I didn't know the Venerable English College well. I'd been to Mass there a few times over the years, but those who worked or studied there usually met me in cafés or restaurants.

We took a taxi and found our way into an area that served as "Reception." A novice, nominally "on duty" went to find Father Reynolds.

We had a cursory look at our surroundings.

"I feel like I've entered a men's locker room," Sophie said.

"Oh, yes? What was that like?"

Judging from her eyes, she was about to give me a seriously sharp reply, but the novice returned with Father Reynolds.

"With classes in session, I can't give you a full tour," Father Reynolds said, after greeting us. "But I will show you our small domestic chapel."

We walked through a series of passages and entered a long narrow chapel with black and red tiles. There were a few pews facing the altar at the back, but along the length of the room, there were pews facing each other, collegiate style.

"Why is it called the Venerable English College?" Sophie asked.

"Forty-four students were martyred between 1581 and 1679. Forty of them have been canonised or beatified," Father Reynolds explained.

"Why not the other four?" she asked.

"They were guilty of talking in class," he replied, without hesitation. "There have been several students and former students martyred since, too. Be sure to see the frescos in the main chapel, too.

"What I brought you here to see, Miss Gordon, is our ceiling. Father Andrea Pozzo who did the ceiling you like so much at Sant'Ignazio designed much of the college and he either worked on or influenced our ceiling here."

We moved down the aisle to view the *trompe l'oeil* painting of the Assumption.

"It's not as grand as St Ignatius, but it's uplifting," Father Reynolds said.

From there, we moved to the refectory which was a similar room to the chapel. It also had a large ceiling painting, this one of St George slaying the dragon. A number of large round tables with table cloths filled the room.

Father Reynolds pulled out a chair at one of them for Sophie and we sat down. He checked his watch.

"We will be joined by a few others in a couple of minutes," he said. "Miss Gordon, you are welcome to comment at any stage of our discussion. I did not invite you here to be left out."

We'd only been seated for a few minutes when two more priests approached the table. We rose to greet them. Father Reynolds introduced a Benedictine, Father Malcolm Muldrew and a French priest, Father Bernard Mézard.

When we sat down again, Father Reynolds began.

"As you know, I teach ethics and theology here, and that is my only role. However, Father Muldrew is – how can I express this best? – a what used to be called a 'fixer,' but 'facilitator' is probably more acceptable today."

Father Muldrew showed no displeasure in either term.

"It was in a chance conversation about meeting you both that led Father Muldrew to have a word with Father Mézard about a situation he wandered into last week.

Father Mézard was far more ascetic looking than the other two priests, but he did not appear to be irritated by the conversation. Indeed, a charming smile and gentleness revealed themselves when he spoke.

"I am a property manager for the Holy See," he said. "I'm in charge of what we call extraterritorial residential property. I have two lay assistants, and there is an equivalent team that looks after commercial property."

"Extraterritorial?" Sophie asked.

He smiled at her.

"Property owned or leased by the Vatican, but not within the city itself," he explained. "However, the definition of that is not clear, either. There are a number of properties that are technically in Rome but have Vatican City addresses. So, some of the property we manage is, arguably, within Vatican City."

He said this in an amusing way and we laughed.

"More complicated still are buildings in Rome that are owned by the Vatican and have Roman addresses," he continued. "So, if a country owns land in another state and that land has the address of the owner-state, what country is it in?"

"You have two hours and your answer is worth forty points," Father Reynolds said.

When our amusement died down, Father Muldrew asked me.

"Have you heard of Monsignor Basso?"

Purely by chance, I had.

"The one who allegedly tried to sell fake antiquities?"

"Indeed," said Father Muldrew. "He died in January 2023 and left a collection of statues, ancient pottery and paintings of dubious origin and authenticity."

"Yes," I said. "Remembering more. Several of the art newsletters mentioned it. I don't remember reading anything further."

"No, you wouldn't have," Father Muldrew said. "The Vatican is usually pretty good about keeping quiet about things it wants to keep secret."

"But not always," Father Mézard said. "And that's why you're here."

"In 2019, an elderly cardinal, Giuseppe Cardinal Mauro, was moved from one of the extraterritorial apartments I manage into a hospice. The apartment was cleared of perishables and personal items like basic clothing and toiletries, and the apartment was locked.

"The cardinal died in June 2020, but because we were locked down, we were unable to clear the apartment – and we knew that it wasn't urgent.

"Other properties have taken priority and it wasn't until about a month ago we revisited the cardinal's residence."

He paused and looked to Father Muldrew.

"What Father Mézard and his assistant found caused him to contact me," Father Muldrew said. "I visited the apartment and thought it was best not to repeat the considerable publicity that Cardinal Basso attracted.

"Your appearance and your imaginative work on the fringes of the art world – not to mention your reputation as a leading British portrait painter," he added hastily, "seemed a propitious coincidence."

I didn't know how to respond.

"What is it that you would like Nigel to do?" Sophie eventually asked.

The three of them looked at each other. The fixer then spoke.

"We would like to invite you to view what we have found and help us to make sense of it."

"Surely the Vatican museums have better resources – "

"That's part of the point, Sir Nigel," Father Muldrew said. "Given the leaks about Monsignor Basso – and subsequent departures from the Museum's service – we'd like to keep this quiet until we understand things better."

I nodded.

"So, what do you propose?" I asked.

"We'd like to show you the apartment and its contents, evaluate what's there and see what conclusions you draw," Father Muldrew said.

"Why do I get the sense there's something you're not telling me?" I asked.

"You'll see."

Chapter XIX

When we left the college, we walked in silence for a while. I was uncertain as to what Sophie thought about me getting involved in this vague project. The rain had stopped, at least temporarily. Having sat for more than an hour, we were glad of the movement and fresh air and walked back to the hotel.

"Something tells me this is going to take longer than two days," she said.

I couldn't read anything from her voice: it had been a simple statement.

"No, I don't think so," I said. "We visit the apartment, I look at whatever it is, I tell them I haven't the expertise and we go for drinks."

Sophie gave a sigh.

"I still don't understand you," she said, holding back her exasperation. "You are sensitive to all sorts of nuances, shadings, hidden meanings, deceptions, and lies, but you fail to recognise that three priests took the time to talk to you about this."

She stopped on the pavement and turned to face me.

"This wasn't, 'Hey, Nige, let me show you this dead cardinal's apartment and his odd stuff.' They were unfolding the first bits of what they all see as a serious problem," she said, firmly. "*They want you.*"

"We'll see," I said, and we walked on.

I was surprised that Sophie was delighted with the intrigue. With our days in Rome drawing to a close, I was surprised that she jumped at the chance to accompany me to the late cardinal's apartment. We arranged to meet Father Reynolds at our hotel in the early afternoon the next day, and we would proceed by taxi.

Before that, I had my final sitting with Carrie. I picked up a bottle of champagne for her as per my "Varnishing Day" custom, but it would be too early to open it. I was looking forward to completing the portrait in the morning and was satisfied with the result.

"You didn't get one for me?" Sophie asked, as I was paying.

We regarded each other with our usual indulgence.

"I'll buy you a bottle if this business with the cardinal goes beyond tomorrow," I said.

"Deal!"

The skies opened almost as soon as we reached the hotel, and we made the instant decision to eat there rather than venture out again. I had to be at the Polidoris' by nine, so that suited me well.

Over dinner, it was clear that Sophie had been flattered to have been included in this afternoon's discussion and was genuinely looking forward to visiting the apartment.

"It's not a crime scene," I said.

"No, but their reluctance to say much was very revealing."

Our conversation moved on and we enjoyed our meals. I think we both relaxed from our good behaviour with the clergy, helped by the bottle of Primitivo that accompanied our Tuscan chicken.

"Are the maths lessons over, then?" Sophie asked.

"I suspect they are with Alegra, but Carrie wants to pick my brain one last time."

"How did she end up so normal? Girls usually grow up like their mothers," she said.

"That is their tragedy."

Sophie gave me a warning look.

"It appears that the old count was a very good influence on both of them," I said. "I never knew much about Francesca's background, so I don't know what accounted for it. All I knew was what was in the papers and what was standing before me."

I told her what Carrie had said about Francesca's loneliness.

"She needs a role," Sophie said.

"I'm not sure what she can do."

"I didn't say she needed a job, I said she needed a role. There's a difference. From what you've said, she doesn't need money."

"I only know what Carrie has said," I replied. "I'm not certain how much children ever know about their parents' finances."

Sophie considered this.

"If she owns that apartment at the top of Spanish Steps, I doubt that she's poor."

"Who knows?" I said. "I don't know about Italian inheritance taxes, if the property is mortgaged, or if the ownership is shared or otherwise encumbered."

"Well, if she ever wants to sell it, let me know," Sophie said, with a smile. "I could find a bunch of friends who'd go in on it and run a very nice boutique hotel or B&B. It could work well – whoever was resting could come run it for a few months."

I laughed at the idea that out of work actors would have the money to come to Rome or the patience to put up with cranky tourists. It was an idea suitable for a farce.

We moved to the bar with its more comfortable chairs and ambience for coffee and *digestifs*. We could see through the glass front doors that it was still raining and the lights from the traffic and the shiny wet streets made it feel cosy to be inside and wrapped around warming drinks.

"What are your plans for the morning?" I asked Sophie, who was perusing a map of Rome.

"I've never been to the Baths of Caracalla," she said. "I've seen them from buses and taxis to the airport, but never properly."

I must have looked surprised by her choice.

"Apart from the Pantheon, we haven't been to any ancient sites since we first got here," she said. "I'd even like to go back to the Forum before we go home, if there's time."

"I'd like that, too," I said.

Sophie thought for a moment.

"Perhaps I should have suggested you paint the ruins here rather than religious subjects," she said.

I wasn't sure whether she was teasing.

"A bit too capital 'R' Romantic for me, don't you think?"

"I don't know. Just another untapped vein in your creativity."

Now I knew she was teasing.

"Actually, painting orgies or toga parties could be good fun," I said. "Marketable, too. Maybe Carrie and Alegra would pose. . ."

Sophie held up her hand.

"All right! Enough! Stop! I don't want images in my head that I can't get rid of!"

She was laughing and it was tempting not to wind her up further.

If anything was a hallmark of our curious affection for each other it was that we both knew when to stop. I felt that Sophie got closer to my bruising points than I did hers, but, of course, I had no way of knowing. In any event, she stopped and we chortled for a few moments longer at the prospects.

"Did you ever think what you would have done had you not painted portraits?" she asked.

"Do you mean if I'd never painted at all, or if I had decided to paint something else?"

"Hmm," she said. "I was thinking of painting other things, but I suppose I'd like to know what else you'd considered doing."

Sometimes you make enormous decisions without thinking about it. While the Jesuits had pointed me towards the Royal Navy – however indirectly – I had begun to paint portraits first as therapy and then as a career, but it had all been serendipitous.

My first portrait – ironically from death, not from life – was of my late wife, Vera. On a whim, I'd entered it for the Summer Exhibition and all else followed from that. I received a commission for a portrait and then another and so it went.

Had I actually *thought* about becoming a painter, what might I have painted?

I looked up to find Sophie staring at me, waiting for a reply.

"The painting I did of you asleep at Versailles remains one of my favourites," I said.

"Mine, too," she agreed. "If you haven't left it to me in your will, I'll never forgive you."

It was the first small-scale picture I'd done of Sophie on our first – slightly less than successful – trip to Paris. She had fallen asleep in the sun in the grounds of the palace and I'd sketched her and then painted it in a looser, more abstract style than I usually used.

When Sophie had woken up, she knew I'd been drawing her and dreaded that her knickers were showing where her short skirt had ridden up.

"I liked that style," I said.

There's an American artist I found not long after painting Sophie who works in a similar style. The "secret little painting" done for Fletcher Bailey, referred to above, is the only other one I painted in that style.

"So did I," Sophie said. "You could have done eight of those a week and made a fortune."

"I never wanted a fortune," I said.

"What did you want?"

"What does anyone want?" I countered. "To be safe, secure. To find a comfortable niche where I could work and another where I could live."

"Was that all?"

That was a good question. Was it?

I took a deep breath.

"What I wanted was to be able to live a reasonably contented – if not happy – life without Vera."

Sophie nodded and gave a small smile.

"Well, you've almost done it," she said. "It's a huge pity – for you and for someone else – that you could never let yourself fall in love again."

"It's not a question of *letting*."

She went very quiet, then said, almost inaudibly:

"No, it's not."

Had I pushed too far?

"Not to go all religious again, but there's a prayer by Cardinal Newman that I say fairly often," I said. "It has the lines in it, 'God has created me to do Him some definite service. He has committed some work to me which He has not committed to another. I have my mission. I may never know it in this life, but I shall be told it in the next.'

"I find the first part very comforting, but the second part terrifying," I said. "Can you imagine meeting your maker – your *maker* – and discovering that you had not used the special talent He had given you?"

Sophie had put her coffee down and was staring at me intently.

"Do you know how often I think that?" she asked, in a whisper. "When my innocence was taken, so were all my dreams. I told you this once – I could no longer be myself, so I found a career where I could be other people.

"Is that running from destiny, or making the most of it?"

It was seldom that Sophie and I talked about our pasts in this way. Curiously, when we did, it was always away from home. It was in conversations like this that I realised how little we really understood each other. We could predict each other's movements and finish each other's sentences; we could sense when we were upset, discontent, or otherwise out of sorts, but as to understanding each other's motivations and *weltanschauung,* that was a different story.

We shared secrets, but we still had ones we didn't. We knew what was concealed, but not the details. Sophie knew that I still missed Cambridge, but had no idea how much I had loved and missed teaching. I knew that Sophie believed she had murdered her uncle, but had never dared to ask how.

I mean, one doesn't. It wouldn't be polite.

"All right," Sophie said, bringing me back to the conversation, "you never considered painting anything but portraits, but suppose you hadn't been a painter? Before the exhibition, you'd been recovering and contemplating your future in Cornwall."

"Devonshire."

"What else had you been considering?"

I had gone to Devon, stayed in a small guest house and walked for miles each day. Eventually, I began to draw again. It had been something of a passion at school, and I found I could think better if my mind were engaged on something else. Rather like saying a rosary where you're reciting the prayers but contemplating the mysteries. For much of the time, I was doing mathematics in my head; dreaming up new theories, asking endless "what if" questions, and coming to appreciate how little I knew.

"I think you know the answer to that one, Sophie," I said.

"Yes," she said. "The priesthood. But why didn't you?"

"The question every would be priest – and priest – wrestles with," I said, "and very few can answer."

"What's that?"

"Am I good enough?"

The case is that no seminarian ever feels good enough, but rather feels the call to act is stronger than he can resist. While I felt the twitch upon the thread, the line was not tugged and the hook not set, so my life with paint began – and in a very curious fashion, has led me to Rome.

Chapter XX

Thursday

Though the rain had continued for much of the night, the morning was bright, clear and mild. Sophie and I were brighter, too, even with our early start. Our uncharacteristic sharing of our intimations of mortality had passed.

Father Reynolds would be coming at one-thirty so we opted for a large breakfast, anticipating that we'd have little, if any, lunch.

"Another Varnishing Day," Sophie said. "That's quite a lot of champagne you've got through in your career."

"Always ready for more," I said. "I won't get to drink this one, but the morning should be fun."

"Is there much left to do on the picture?"

"A few highlights," I said. "Maybe an adjustment to a few shadows, but basically nothing."

"Have you signed it?"

I smiled.

"Yes, I have. There is a rather tangled signature in the folds of your scarf," I said. "Oh, Carrie asked me again if you're sure you don't want it back."

"No, it's hers," Sophie said. "It will be mine forever in Gaetano's film – if the scene doesn't get cut."

I laughed.

"You know, that's the easiest film I ever made," she continued. "There was no waiting around, no arguments, and Gaetano knew just what he wanted to shoot – even though he had no clear vision of which version he wanted to use, he knew exactly how to set it out."

We finished our coffee.

"Are you looking forward to getting back to London?" I asked.

"It's home," she said. "I'm happiest when I'm working – as are you."

I went up to my room to collect the things I wanted to take with me and hoped the electronic mini-bar didn't charge me for my own bottle of champagne.

"Enjoy the baths, Sophie," I said. "Don't drown."

She laughed.

"And no getting sentimental with college girls."

∞

The freshness and beauty of the morning, surrounded with the noise and bustle of Rome caused something of the inevitable cultural shock. How did I come to be here? What was I doing portrait painting in Rome?

As I climbed the Spanish Steps and turned towards the Polidoris' apartment, I was chuckling at the idea of visiting a dead Cardinal's apartment with Vatican officials. Well, Sophie couldn't accuse me of staying in my comfort zone.

I paused to look at the view from the piazza and was probably smiling when I rang the bell at the Polidoris'.

In a moment, I heard footsteps on the stairs and several locks and bolts being opened. Carrie dramatically threw the door open and threw her arms around me. Sophie's admonition flashed through my mind but I soon realised that something was not right: Carrie was sobbing.

I moved her inside and closed the door and held her as far as I could in the narrow staircase. While wearing the dress I was painting her in, her hair and makeup had not been done.

"Are you all right? What's happened?"

She caught her breath.

"Yes, I'm all right, physically, at least," she managed to say as she composed herself.

"Your mother?"

She shook her head and started up the stairs. When we stepped into the sitting room, she looked at me again.

"They've arrested Stephano."

"They *what – ?*"

I steered her to the kitchen and topped up the glass of *minerale* that was on the island. While she drank, I put the bottle of champagne in the refrigerator and sat on a stool across from her and waited.

Only then did I realise how quiet the apartment was.

I looked at Carrie.

"I'm sorry," she said, sadly. "You told me how your final sessions were always particular fun."

"Tell me what happened."

She took another drink.

"Yesterday Alegra was much better and was going to go to school. I don't know if she went or not, but she met up with her dealer boyfriend and after lunch, they came back here. Mum was out, Laura and Stephano were at work, I was in the library studying.

"Stephano came home unexpectedly and found Alegra in the sitting room, barely able to move. While looking after her, he heard noises upstairs and went up and found her boyfriend, Enzo, putting stuff in a pillowcase."

Surprisingly, as she told the story, Carrie became more calm. The pace of her speech slowed and she even gave a flicker of a smile.

"You know Stephano was in the army? Well, with one move, he grabbed Enzo and threw him down the stairs. When he reached the bottom, Stephano followed him down and threw him down the steps to the street, too."

My eyes must have opened.

"Don't worry," Carrie said. "He didn't kill him. Just a broken shoulder, wrist and leg."

I grimaced.

"Stephano called an ambulance and the police," she continued. "While waiting for the police, he went to

Alegra to make sure she was all right. All this time, Enzo was moaning at the bottom of the stairs."

She paused, topped up her water and had another drink.

"This is Italy. Stephano is well-known and well-respected," she began. "Being a count helps a little, but not a lot of people know it. Anyway, in Italy, defending one's family and home – by virtually any means – is accepted as justified. However, Enzo's father is something in the mayor's office, so they took Stephano into custody.

"Alegra spent the night in hospital and poor Laura was torn between being with her and being at the police station with Stephano."

"I'm here partly to watch the house in case any of Enzo's friends try to retaliate – though I doubt any of them could make it up the steps – and just to be here if anyone comes home."

I felt as any stranger might intruding on a family crisis.

"We can do this tomorrow, if you like," I said, rather feebly.

"No!" she exclaimed, as though the idea horrified her. "I need something to do, and it would be lovely to have the picture finished."

"Are you sure?"

"Yes. Very sure," she said. "You get set up and I'll make us some coffee."

Seeing the picture after two days made me realise that there was a section of the dress that wasn't quite working, but it would be easy enough to adjust and complete. The face, room, view and window were all to my satisfaction. A slight adjustment to the shadowing on her hand would be the final touch.

When she arrived with the coffee, she took the pose without being told.

"May I tweak the skirt of your dress?" I asked.

She laughed.

"It's surprising how many men don't bother to ask."

I tugged on the hem.

"Don't be cheeky," I said, feigning displeasure. "By the way, Sophie said she was sure about the scarf and wishes you many happy years wearing it."

"She's lovely," Carrie said. "Tell her thank you."

I returned to the easel and painted for a few minutes. We both drank coffee as I worked, until after about forty minutes, I stepped back.

"I think that's it, Miss Winters," I said. "Just one last thing."

She came over to watch as I painted $\frac{\omega}{\pi}$ in the corner of the window, as though it were etched into it.

"That's deep!" she laughed.

"Now, you have avoided telling me about Markov Chains," she said, disapprovingly. "I'll make you another coffee and you can give me your tutorial."

◌

Carrie kissed my cheeks when I left and I wished her and her family well. I didn't like leaving not knowing the outcome of their family crises, but I'd done my job, and my sittings often concluded before the end of good stories.

I related all this to Sophie over a simple lunch at the hotel. She was shocked to hear about Stephano's troubles but felt certain he'd be released once various feathers and egos had been smoothed.

"What's going to happen to the painting?" she asked.

"It will go to Predore to join the other one," I said. "They call the house a castle, you know. It's not, but it's built on the ruins of an ancient fortified villa.

"If Carrie does well in her exams and then does her master's, she'll be able to work online from there and keep Francesca company," I said.

"That lady needs to find something to do," Sophie said. "She's been in mourning long enough."

She finished her pasta.

"Are you going to keep in touch and see how things turn out?" she asked.

"I don't think so," I said.

Sophie looked shocked.

"It's not a good idea," I said. "Look what happens when I do."

She was about to shout something at me when Father Reynolds walked in.

Sophie and I both hastily looked at our watches.

"I'm early," he said, casually, then greeted us.

We invited him to sit and help us finish our carafe of wine.

We dropped the subject of the Polidoris and talked generally before gathering our things and meeting Father Reynolds outside.

"Is there anything more we should know before going?" I asked.

"Only that this should be considered confidential," he replied. "Not secret, but the fewer people who know at this stage the better."

"And by that, you mean the Vatican curators," I said.

Father Reynolds' look said it all. He was not going to put it into words. I nodded.

Sophie took my hand and squeezed it. Something she almost never did except around very good friends.

The taxi ordered by the hotel pulled up. Father Reynolds sat up front and Sophie and I were in the back, where she took my hand again.

"I'll let Father Muldrew explain," Father Reynolds said, turning to us.

Again, it surprised me that Sophie continued to hold my hand. The duration of this – albeit slight – physical contact was approaching a record for her, so I knew that she was anxious. I also knew that, apart from asking objective questions, she would keep quiet until we were alone again, at which time it would all reveal itself.

"Undici Via Plauto per favore," he said, and we drove off.

Part Three

Chapter XXI

To say that nothing in Rome is straight forward was demonstrated by the taxi ride from the hotel to the cardinal's former residence. I recognised the bridge across the Tiber and a glimpse up the Via della Conciliazione as we crossed it. After that, there were more twists and turns than I bothered to count until we entered a street so narrow that the taxi had to stop in an intersection so that we could open the doors.

The entrance to number eleven was as anonymous as any of the others that I could see. There was an arched relief and a solid, plain wooden door. There were buttons and entry codes, and on the building itself, the standard European white square with the house number.

Father Reynolds checked his watch.

"Father Muldrew and Father Mézard should be here by now," he said.

He pushed a button and the door buzzed and was released. The entry hall was small with locked mail boxes, a staircase that went up the sides of the walls and a small lift that went up between the stairs.

As it was only big enough for two, Father Reynolds went up with Sophie. I buzzed the lift down and followed them up. They had waited on the landing. A glance around showed that there were three apartments on the floor: two at the front and one to the rear.

Father Reynolds tapped on the door that simply said "A" and Father Mézard answered and let us in.

"OMG!" Sophie exclaimed, in a vernacular that I wasn't aware she was familiar with.

"This is exactly like your set!"

The indulgent clergy said nothing as Sophie faced me. I couldn't deny it: the room had one old and warn oriental rug, two almost-comfortable armchairs, a sofa and at the far end a table with four chairs. (I had six.) There were no ornaments, nothing beyond functional lighting, and much empty space.

The walls, however, held a number of paintings of various sizes, as well as faded areas where more paintings had hung.

The only piece of furniture in the room that was not in mine was an *escritoire*. Mine was in a separate, small study.

"I know exactly what the bedroom looks like," Sophie said.

There was a brief silence.

"I'm not sure the good fathers need to know what you know about my bedroom."

I had no idea how Sophie would react to this, but she simply burst out laughing. She turned to them:

"Not that I have to explain myself," Sophie said, only minimally flushed, "but though this Protestant might be guilty of many things, one is not any impropriety with Sir Nigel. All I can say is that this apartment is incredibly similar to his. If I may predict, the bedroom is virtually bare: a single bed, a chest of drawers, a small rug near the bed, and on the walls maybe one picture and a crucifix."

It was now time to see how these priests would react. For a moment, it seemed that they wouldn't react at all.

"To facilitate our work, perhaps you should inspect the bedroom now," Father Mézard said, without expression.

He moved to the end of the main room and opened a door. I let Sophie go on her own; I'd see it soon enough.

She disappeared for a moment, then reappeared. When she did, Father Mézard was the first to speak.

"It seems that the lady is not only talented and lovely but very perceptive, too."

Sophie just gave me her smug look.

I had been looking at the paintings. Their sizes and conditions varied greatly. Several appeared to have been restored. While Father Mézard confirmed Sophie's assumptions about the cardinal's bedroom, I moved from picture to picture. I am unable to give values, but I recognise good art, and, as a painter, like to think that I can see something of the artist's mind at work in the way works are executed. There are the little hints of the objects chosen to be included. While most of these relate to the sitter or subject in figurative painting from live subjects, they can be more revealing in historical paintings.

Often they instantly identify a subject and the educated viewer fills in what is not explicitly shown. For example, a noblewoman dressed in colourful robes standing near a riverbank carrying a baby can suggest several stories, but the inclusion of a crude wooden basket floating away from the bank pins the story absolutely.

This composition was unusual as it is the discovery, with the child still in the basket, that is usually portrayed, not the embracing of the child and the affirmation of its future.

"Have you seen anything you recognise, Sir Nigel?" Father Muldrew asked, moving beside me.

Sophie and Father Reynolds had finished looking around and were sitting at the table by the window. Father Mézard stood a few feet behind me, presumably to ensure I didn't suddenly start spraying graffiti on the walls.

"It's an interesting collection," I began, "and, I think, some of these are quite good, while others – "

I stopped as I had moved on to a small painting, about sixteen by twenty, and stared at it.

I looked back at Father Muldrew.

"I think, Sir Nigel, you are beginning to understand the need for confidentiality."

I looked back at the painting. It was a well-painted interior scene of a room in a Central European home. A mother, father and three children were at a simple wooden table with a white table cloth partially covering it. On the table were a bottle of wine, a loaf of bread, two small, worn, once-gilded cups and a pair of candles in simple brass candlesticks. The mother held a lit taper as the rest of the family regarded her with reverence.

I looked at the other paintings and my initial impressions were taking firmer shape.

"That's not all," Father Muldrew said, and went to the *escritoire*.

It wasn't a particularly elaborate one but it did have a generous, drop-down writing area with pull-out supports. There were slots for letters and a number of small drawers under two bookshelves. It was well made, possibly late nineteenth century, but to me it looked like a factory piece.

Unsurprisingly, it had several secret compartments which Father Muldrew revealed.

"It's almost like a Chinese puzzle box," I said, as he removed two hidden drawers, one from each corner.

He handed one of them to me.

In it was a tangle of chains, gold, silver and base metal. Attached to these were stars of David of various metals and designs. Several of them looked to be gold. There were other simple pieces of jewellery, bangles, pendants, and simple brooches in the drawer and half a dozen mezuzahs, mostly of brass.

Sophie and Father Reynolds heard our voices drop and came to see what we'd found.

My immediate reaction was that these pieces had a long and unhappy history. Their link with the paintings was obvious, but none of them had said anything about it yet.

I passed the drawer to Sophie who understood what they were, but appeared not to have made the link with the paintings yet. As she looked at the jewellery, Father Muldrew handed me the second drawer.

It contained only a small book.

It was battered and its covers were barely hanging on. I opened it and turned it around a few times to orientate it properly.

Unsurprisingly, it was in Hebrew.

"It's a *siddur*," Father Muldrew said. "A Jewish prayer book with a collection of Old Testament texts and additional prayers and blessings."

While I knew more Jews than most English people, I had only the basic Christian's understanding of the practices and customs of Judaism.

I turned the page.

"Joseph Schlesing, Wein 1929."

I turned back to the inside cover. A name was written in a spiky Germanic hand. It was written in badly feathered ink making reading it nearly impossible. After flipping through the thin pages, I put the book back in the drawer.

Father Muldrew put the drawers back and shut the desk.

The four of us went to the table and sat around it. Father Mézard was making his routine checks of the windows and plumbing, ensuring the integrity of the property.

"We can go for coffee – or something more – in a few minutes," Father Muldrew said, "but we should only discuss what we've seen here in this room."

Sophie and I nodded.

"Would you care to speculate on what you have seen, Sir Nigel?" he asked.

Why did I get put on the spot?

"I think the following may be objectively deduced: we are looking at some of the personal effects of Jewish refugees who came to Rome, possibly before the German occupation. The artwork indicates that they are from Central Europe: Poland, Austria, Hungary, Yugoslavia – of course, they also could have come from Italian, or Roman Jews.

"The subjects of the paintings are either everyday scenes – landscapes, cityscapes, or Old Testament scenes. I'm sure the Vatican collection has many similar pieces, but I suspect it doesn't have many of the candle lighting to begin shabbat."

Fathers Reynolds and Mézard looked satisfied, and Sophie looked proudly impressed, however, Father Muldrew wanted more.

"I did ask for speculation, Sir Nigel," he said. "Is there anything you'd like to venture?"

"I'm afraid the Jesuits taught me to seek evidence," I began, glancing at Father Reynolds whose eyes twinkled but head moved slightly, indicating that this was not the path to follow just now.

"Yet, I think I can help define things better with some key questions – again, which I do not presume you have not thought of yourself, Father."

"Just go on," Father Muldrew said, but his tone was more indulgent.

"First, it would help to know more about Cardinal Mauro. When did he come to Rome? Did he, perhaps, work with Jewish refugees? Did he have a personal interest in art? He does not appear to have anything he collected himself.

"Secondly, are there any records here that he might have kept about these pieces and the jewellery? Are his papers still here? Did he have another office? What did he do? What were his different jobs? Do these pictures relate to his time as a cardinal or before?

"Thirdly, several of the pictures appear to have been cleaned or had restoration work since the War. Who did this? Why? Who paid?"

I paused.

"My last question is the big one – why did Cardinal Mauro have these paintings? – and I can't begin to answer that."

It had been a long time since I'd delivered a monologue like that and wasn't certain how it was received. The fact that no one was saying anything – not even Sophie – led me to believe that either they didn't like what I said, or I got it all wrong.

After what seemed a very long time, Father Reynolds took pity and asked:

"Do you have any ideas who the artists might be?"

I shook my head.

"My knowledge of Central European artists is poor," I said. "I haven't looked at the back of the paintings, and something might show up after cleaning or black light examination."

"Like a signature?" Father Muldrew asked.

"Or a date, place, or something that would give a hint of its origin," I said. "There might be a detail in a picture that has some lettering on it or a few numbers. . . "

Father Muldrew looked at Father Reynolds who simply opened his hands to indicate that we were done.

"Thank you, Sir Nigel," Father Muldrew said. "Let's find ourselves some refreshments, but though we can talk of pictures in general terms, let us say nothing of the War, the Jews or his late eminence.

We left the building as we had come with multiple trips down in the lift.

"That lift wobbles even more than the one to your studio," Sophie said, as we waited for the others.

We moved out into the street and Father Muldrew took the lead. I didn't know such things existed but tucked between the Vatican museums and the Sistine Chapel was an anonymous doorway which he opened and we followed. It was a typical corridor in an old building: worn floors, dim lighting, peeling paint, but as we walked further down, there was the distinctive smell of coffee.

He opened a wooden door and inside was a fully equipped modern coffee shop. The only difference between this one and those found around the world was that nearly everyone in it was wearing black.

I glanced at Sophie who was uneasily looking around to find a female face, then spotted a gaggle of nuns and some ordinary women in mufti.

While voices were low, there were enough people speaking to make it sound like a normal, civilian, café.

"One of Vatican City's many secrets," Father Muldrew said, smiling for the first time.

We ordered espressos and found a table.

"I hope that was worth your time," I said, when the coffees were delivered.

Father Muldrew glanced at Father Reynolds before speaking.

"Very much so, Sir Nigel," he said. "Father Reynolds was fairly certain that this little puzzle would appeal to you and you seemed to engage well with it."

I smiled, glad to be of use, but Sophie appeared anxious.

"It would be interesting to see it solved," I said.

"I'm glad you agree," Father Muldrew replied. "It seems to follow on from your other investigations at the fringes of the art world."

I heard the words but didn't take in the meaning until I looked at Sophie. Her expression told me there was more going on here than I'd appreciated.

I put my cup down.

"I'm sorry?"

Father Reynolds replied:

"Father Muldrew was being tactful. Since I know you – at least via your friends at Farm Street – I will be more direct.

"Father Muldrew would like you to *solve* the little mystery you saw this morning."

"But I'm flying back to London on Saturday."

Father Muldrew picked it up:

"The Holy See would like you to investigate these objects and how they came to be in the cardinal's possession."

I chuckled at the idea.

"Even if I could do it, I couldn't do it alone," I protested, but knew their minds were made up.

"The Vatican owns the whole building where the flat is," Father Mézard said. "As it happens, there is an apartment on the same floor that is empty. It would be yours until your work was finished."

I stared at Sophie, unable to think of a reason not to stay. I had no immediate pending commissions or other important engagements.

"Don't look at me for an excuse," Sophie said. "I'm going to be in rehearsals and then performances. I'll survive."

I was about to speak when the penny dropped.

"They got to you!" I exclaimed, looking at Sophie, then turned to the priests. "Rather, Father Reynolds got to you! This has Jesuitical fingerprints all over it."

Chapter XXII

We walked back to the hotel in near silence, and I reflected that since lunch, I'd been coerced into a potentially very messy business, acquired an apartment, and received an invitation to meals at the Venerable English College. Father Mézard told me I could also use Vatican City's secret café since I would be part of the staff of the Holy See. "Semi-officially, of course." Of course. To be "official," people would need to know what I was doing.

I did make a resolution on the way back and that was to do whatever Sophie wanted the next day.

On arrival at the hotel, Chiara gave me an envelope. I confess that the words, "What now?" crossed my mind. I slipped it into my pocket in the hope that Sophie hadn't seen it.

Opening it in my room, I found it was from Francesca.

> *I am so sorry that you walked into domestic turmoil this morning. The good news is that Stephano has been released without charge. The little runt has been given a restraining order, and the mayor's minion is mollified, if not totally happy. Alegra is safe, so order is re-established.*

Carrie is delighted with the portrait and so am I. I hope you found her a more cooperative and appreciative sitter than I was.

Enclosed is a cheque for the balance for the portrait plus a little more for embarrassment, inconvenience, and giving Carrie a level of conversation that I cannot! In no way is this to be considered hush-money.

[Ha!]

Stephano says that you are extending your stay in Rome. I hope you can visit again.

Love,

F.

PS Will you collect your painting clobber or shall I bring it to you?

Though proud that the portrait was well-received, and heartened to know that Stephano had been returned to his family, the comment about him having heard that I would be remaining in Rome set alarm bells ringing.

I had no phone numbers for any of the priests but called the English College and left a message for Father Reynolds to call me at ten o'clock or afterwards.

Before going down to meet Sophie, I tore a deposit slip from my cheque book, filled it in, and put it in the envelope with the note from Francesca to give to Sophie.

She could drop it into Drummonds when she got back to London.

"Chiara recommended two places we haven't been to," Sophie said when I met her downstairs. "We can look at the menus and decide how hungry we are."

We didn't get beyond the first recommendation. While visually uninspiring, the smells drifting out to the street were compelling. Sophie thought to mention Chiara when we entered, and we were shown to a table in a better than average position. Once we'd ordered and clinked our first glass of wine, I handed Francesca's note to Sophie.

"Fan mail?"

"Almost."

When she re-read it, I knew that she'd caught the line that concerned me.

"How did Stephano – "

I put my finger to my lips.

"Good news about him being released," Sophie said. "And about the portrait. I'm sorry I didn't see it."

I took out my phone and showed her the pictures I'd taken.

"Oh, Nigel! It's beautiful!" she exclaimed.

"Hard to miss with an attractive lady, that view and a beautiful scarf."

"I can put a word to most of your paintings," she said.

"Oh?"

"Yes, but none has been 'beautiful,'" she said. "Did you ever name it?"

"I told Carrie I call it *A Matter of Time* and wrote it on the receipt for Francesca," I said. "Carrie seemed to like it."

"What did you call the one of her mother?" Sophie asked.

I laughed.

"I called it *Finished at Last*, but when she showed it at some club in London, she'd called it *Une Jeunne Fille á la Mode*."

Sophie made a face that made me laugh.

"So, what label did you give Marissa's?" I asked.

Sophie considered this.

"Stately," she said. "Did you ever give that portrait a name?"

"Oh, I gave it lots of names," I laughed. "*Hellfire, Mad Woman of the Manor, The Red Menace*."

"Seriously!" Sophie scolded. "The Summer Exhibition catalogue called it *Portrait of a Young Lady*. Not very imaginative, darling."

"No, I suppose it wasn't," I admitted. "If I had to name it now, I think I'd call it *Lindum Gothic, or Lindum Lady*."

"Better."

Like many artists, the name of a painting is unimportant. The trouble is that if you don't name them, someone else does and it's usually wrong.

"And *The Yellow Frock*?" I asked.

"Radiant."

"And yours?"

"'Dramatic,' of course!" she laughed.

Our appetizers appeared, and after sampling and making positive comments, Sophie returned to the portrait.

"This picture is full of beauty in the present and potential beauty in the future. I don't think other pictures of yours have that.

"Does it reference the portrait of Francesca?"

"Not really," I said. "It lost its spontaneity because her appearances were so erratic. I worry about her idea of displaying them together as they might not gel. Francesca was *agitato* where as Carrie's is *cantabile*."

"Do you have it on your phone?"

The exaggerated portrait format of the phone meant that my square pictures could only be seen in full in near postage stamp sizes. The result is that I don't keep many on my phone.

"I'll have to download it. I'll email it to you."

"See that you do."

We focused on our food for a few moments.

"Now, enough of my ancient history," I said. "Tell me how you got on at the Baths of Caracalla."

"Well, at least my feet were dry when I got back to the hotel."

଼

Although not late, it had been a very demanding day, so Sophie and I said goodnight when we got back to our rooms. The only thing I did before getting ready for bed was to email Francesca to tell her I'd collect my things Saturday. I also said that I was pleased that Stephano had been released and the portrait had met with favour.

Almost simultaneously with my pressing "send," the telephone rang. I had forgotten that I'd asked Father Reynolds to call. He seemed more concerned whether I'd changed my mind about staying than the fact that Stephano knew that I was. He made little other comment than he'd talk to Father Muldrew in the morning and thanked me for my diligence.

This left me more bewildered than ever, but I was too tired to worry about it. Keeping up with Sophie on tomorrow would take some stamina, and I wanted her to have a good last day.

෨

Friday

I was up at seven and went down to the lobby to wait. I read several newspapers and made notes about how I should set about my study of the cardinal's effects and look into his history. As an outsider, I didn't expect this to be easy. I would need some tools, too: lenses, lights, polish for the silver and brass, and some experts on Eastern Jewish art and artefacts. Eventually, I need the pictures to be unframed and possibly cleaned to look for signs of identity.

While I'd have access to libraries, there would also be a time when I'd need the benefit of someone with languages. I expected Father Muldrew would facilitate.

Sophie appeared shortly before ten and announced that she was hungry, and we set off for Bar 43. She was more stylishly dressed than usual and slightly more made up, though she was never excessive.

"I'm sorry if I kept you waiting, but I was tired," she said. "It takes a long time for me to slow down and really relax. I reached that point last Saturday which made that day so enjoyable. By the way, I know what you said about painting ruins, but you ought to have a go at the baths. The geometry would fascinate you, if not the history and atmosphere."

We ordered our breakfast and exchanged greetings with those we'd seen before.

"I thought you wanted me to do religious subjects. I've done my research and made a list," I teased.

"You just need a break from portraits," she said. "I don't care if you paint famous people's Pomeranians."

I drank my cappuccino.

"You must have loved it when I painted Carrie."

"Actually, that didn't bother me," she said. "It was rather special, but if I haven't seen *Thomas More in his Cell* before you come back to London, I shall be very cross with you."

After breakfast – which Sophie was in no rush to finish, and even ordered more coffee – we went out into the clear morning sun.

"London's not going to be like this," she said. "Never mind. Today. I want to look in every shop on the Via dei Condotti."

"Look or buy?"

"Probably just look, but I wouldn't mind replacing that scarf I gave Carrie. And, should a pair of shoes present itself. . ."

It took nearly three hours to complete the expedition, and I had to do it in the same pair of shoes, while Sophie tried on about nine. She did manage to find a suitable replacement scarf which I bought for her in thanks for her tolerance of my diversions during the week. She reciprocated and bought me lunch in a small, basic pasta place where we ate dishes of spaghetti, garlic bread and drank a carafe of surprisingly good wine.

Satiated with shopping, Sophie suggested we walk in the Borghese Gardens before returning to the hotel to put our feet up.

What I noticed most while walking the paths, remarking on the vistas and the carefully selected and tended trees, was how distinctively Italian it was. The handsome cypresses and pines were unlike the deciduous parks in London and the studied randomness of the French.

From time to time, Sophie would take my arm or hand but never for long. For most of the time, she walked beside me, just out of reach. Whether that was to discourage me or her, I didn't know. It was probably just out of habit.

We sat on a bench facing the sun. It wouldn't be long before it sank below the surrounding buildings, but for a few moments, we had its light and warmth.

"Do you want to get a taxi back?" I asked.

"Yes, but let's not," she said. "I don't want to get back to dreary London and think I passed up a last chance to walk in Rome."

We took our time and arrived at about five.

"That *was* a lovely day," she said, when the lift deposited us on our floor. "I'll see you downstairs at seven."

Back in my room, I checked my email. No one appeared to be missing me in London, though they might next week when I failed to show up.

While I was intending to put my feet up for an hour, I expected Sophie was still working on her play. She wanted to know her lines on day one of rehearsals. One of the things she said to me not long after we met was, "We do the same thing: we make the difficult look easy. The only difference is you do it in private while I do it in public."

৪৩

Later, downstairs, I reflected that it would be odd not to have her in Rome. I had a whole new experience ahead of me, and I wasn't fully comfortable with it. Sophie's goal of pushing me out of my comfort zone had succeeded, perhaps even better than she had hoped.

When she joined me, she still looked modestly elegant. I was surprised to see her wearing her new scarf. My face must have shown that as she gave me one of her red carpet smiles. She looked relaxed, younger and more confident than she had when we arrived, but that could have been from lack of sleep on the train.

We strolled to the restaurant which was not yet busy. The evening felt balmy to us, but others had remarked that it was turning colder. That was another reason I was pleased to be remaining but refrained from telling Sophie.

"Do you feel ready for the rehearsals?" I asked, after we'd ordered and toasted.

"Like all things, it depends," she said. "The director may have a completely different view of the play and my character than I do."

"He can't have read it more than you."

She gave a shrug.

"The play isn't bad, but with the right direction and pace, it could be very funny and powerful," she said. "We'll see."

Our first course arrived, and we stopped talking, except to note our satisfaction.

Just before our main course arrived, Sophie asked if I intended to see more of Francesca Polidori once she'd left Rome.

"I don't see why," I replied. "I'll go there tomorrow to pick up my things and take them to Via Plauto.

"I might ask Stephano to come by for a sitting if I have time to begin *Thomas More*."

"What do you think he knows about Cardinal Mauro's pictures?"

I had to think about that. Was her question just an extension of her occasional jealousy, or was she buying into a Vatican conspiracy theory?

"That, Sophie, is something I'm not going to worry about," I said. "I told Father Reynolds what Francesca had written. It's now over to him. I'm just helping out."

We said nothing more until we finished that course.

"Have I stopped you from working?" Sophie asked. "I suppose I was naïve to think you'd have a bunch of paintings done."

"But I *have,* Sophie! It's just that they're still all up here," I said, pointing to my head.

She smiled.

"Really?"

"Yes, really."

We had dessert, coffee and limoncello before we finally left. It was busy now and people were waiting to be seated.

We walked around Piazza Navona and the Pantheon before heading back to the hotel.

"Promise me you'll be careful," Sophie said. "They are spending a lot of money to keep you here. No doubt, there's more than they've let on."

"I don't think there's anything to worry about."

Sophie said nothing, but gave me one of her, "I warned you," looks.

Chapter XXIII

Saturday

I offered to go to the airport with Sophie even though she had a very early flight. She told me to stay in bed as her taxi was coming at five-thirty, but I did meet her in the lobby to say goodbye. Miraculously, she had the same amount of luggage as when she arrived.

Goodbyes were one of the emotional things she could not handle and so it consisted only of a brief arm around my waist as I carried her suitcase to the driver. She smiled and waved from the back of the black Mercedes, and I returned to my room.

While climbing back into bed was tempting, I had my own departure to prepare for. My plan was to have breakfast, and if no one from the Vatican had contacted me by ten, take a taxi to the Polidoris' and collect my things. I would then call Father Reynolds when I returned to the hotel.

As it was, in the middle of breakfast, Father Mézard arrived. I persuaded him to have a cappuccino while I finished. I explained what I had been planning.

"That will work well," he said.

I hadn't paid a lot of attention to him when we visited the cardinal's apartment. He had seemed efficient and businesslike, but today he struck me as a remarkable ascetic. He was tall, very thin with a long face that took inscrutability to a new level.

This contrasted with a gentle manner and voice, but he was not given to smiling. I could see him in my Galileo painting.

When we finished, he said that I could check out now and that after the visit to the Polidoris', he would install me in Via Plauto. He did offer to help me down with my things, but I was of the generation that would never dream of asking a priest to help with physical personal service. I just had the suitcase and my computer case stuffed with papers.

I said goodbye to Chiara, Angelo and a few others who had generously come from the kitchen and other nether regions to say goodbye.

I walked outside to be met by a young man in his early thirties holding the door open to a dark green Fiat Tipo. He put my suitcase in the boot, and Father Mézard and I climbed into the back seat.

When we were in the car, Father Mézard introduced me.

"This is Richard," he said. "He will join us and Father Muldrew at the apartment."

Richard turned to me and smiled and then we set off.

Since it was Saturday, I wasn't sure who would be home at the Polidoris'. My impression was that Francesca would be there, but in the event, Laura opened the door.

She greeted me warmly and kissed both cheeks.

"Francesca has gone to Predore," she explained as we went up the stairs, but Carrie is here and will help you."

Carrie greeted me just as warmly and apologised for the absence of her mother. She looked much more like a student with a sweatshirt, old jeans and worn loafers. Her hair was carelessly pulled back and she wore no makeup. Still, her personality radiated and although looking considerably different, it was unmistakably the same young lady.

My things were arranged as I had left them in the loggia, and the two of us took the lot down in one trip.

Carrie gave me a quick embrace before I got in the car.

"Would it be possible to have another tutorial before you leave?" she asked.

"You have my email," I said, cautious about arranging assignations in Vatican-owned apartments.

Father Mézard and Richard were silent as we made our way to Via Plauto.

Arriving outside the building, we blocked traffic as we unloaded and horns blasted until we moved into the building and Richard could drive away.

It was cramped in the lift with my luggage, easel, paints, carry-on bag and Father Mézard, but we managed to move everything into the hallway. Hearing the noise, the apartment door opened and Father Muldrew stepped out to help move my things in.

Neither priest made any attempt to show me where things were, but I moved from the large bright sitting room which also had a dining table and looked into the first bedroom and then the second. There was a kitchen with a large opening to the main room and one bathroom that appeared to date from the 1950s.

The apartment took up the whole back of the building and had windows on three sides. The furnishings were Cistercian, but there was one comfortable looking arm chair, and the old sofa – reminiscent of a Chesterfield – was so worn that it was hard to believe that it would not be comfortable.

I put my easel and paints in the second bedroom. Its two windows would make it better for painting than the other rooms.

Though without the warmth and comfort of the hotel, this would serve me well enough. After all, I did not expect to be here long.

While I was inspecting the apartment, Father Mézard sat perfectly still at the dining table and stared out the window.

I began looking around again, thinking of what I would need to conduct my "investigation" when the door opened and Father Muldrew and Richard entered. After short pleasantries, Father Muldrew took a seat at the table with Father Mézard and Richard and I joined him.

Without a word, Richard drew a notebook from his pocket and waited.

"If you are going to do this for us, then we need to be clear on the working parameters," Father Muldrew began. "As discussed, you will live here and have access to the cardinal's apartment, the refectory at the English College, the café, and the Vatican museum and libraries, should you need them.

"A housekeeper will take care of your laundry, cleaning and such meals as you wish her to prepare," he said.

"Today is Saturday. By Wednesday – say, lunchtime – I would like to see a detailed outline of your plan of action. What you need, who you would like access to – whatever it takes to accomplish this as quietly as possible," he continued.

"What I would like is – "

He gently raised his hand.

"Tell Richard what you want and he will arrange it. He will be your liaison."

"I'm perfectly capable – "

"We know you are, Sir Nigel," Father Muldrew replied. "This, however – and should be – considered a clandestine operation. It will not do to attract attention or do anything that will raise suspicion."

Here, he paused and gave me a smile.

"Your cover story – "

I laughed and so did he.

"Your cover story is that you are in Rome to work on your new interest in religious painting, and, perhaps, paint the odd cardinal or college rector," he said, still smiling. "That should provide the necessary excuses for your library and museum research.

"If you require anything – including spending money – ask Richard. He's very enterprising – but he also has his own work to do. He will explain.

"You may contact Father Reynolds about visiting and dining at the English College, and Father Mézard if the plumbing doesn't work, but do not contact me. Richard will do it for you."

Richard had been making notes, then looked up.

"Do you have immediate needs, Sir Nigel?"

"Good coffee and a means for brewing it, and internet access."

Richard merely nodded.

"I think you two will get along fine," Father Muldrew said. "We'll leave you to it.

All three stood up.

"Before you go, can you tell me how Stephano Polidori knew I was staying in Rome."

Father Muldrew paused.

"Ah."

I waited.

"In Rome – especially in the Vatican," he said, slowly, "it's a good general rule not to insist on answers to some questions."

I sighed.

"I assume from that answer that he can be trusted."

"Absolutely."

The two priests left first and descended in the lift.

Richard smiled reassuringly at me.

"I've got to drive them back and get rid of the car, but I'll be back soon with a router and we can go to lunch."

ო

I glanced at my watch. Sophie would nearly be back to Albany and headed for a long hot bath. I proceeded to unpack my things and set up my easel in the second bedroom. I'd only come for two weeks and would need my laundry done. Such practicalities that one doesn't think of at home become major concerns when travelling. House-keepers are never heard of these days, but Rome and the Vatican were in different centuries to the rest of the world, so I shouldn't be surprised.

I pictured an elderly lady of no discernible shape who was either totally silent, or voluble only in incompre-hensible Italian who would go through the motions of providing a basic level service with food that could be used for ballast.

No wonderful *arancini* or black spaghetti lovingly prepared by Adelina. Detective fiction managed to create such wonderful images and impossible expectations.

I had to admit that whoever had prepared the flat did an excellent job – it was spotless. The bathroom and kitchen had been scrubbed, drawers were empty and clean, linens and blankets were carefully piled, and there were plenty of coat hangers.

A glance in the kitchen showed it to have the essential pots, frying pans, cutlery, knives, tin-opener and corkscrew. I even found a Melitta funnel and an unopened box of filters, but, alas, there was no coffee.

Apart from remedying that, I made a list of other things I needed. I'd need to find a stationers for a notebook, ink, and a ruler. If I were to present the image of a painter, I'd need canvases, more paint, and at least two lamps to paint by and maybe a third for reading, plus whatever was needed to look at the cardinal's pictures properly.

I began to understand what Sophie meant about a serious investment being made in me. I would have to live up to some demanding expectations. Presumably much on my list could be sourced from Vatican attics and basements.

This would be no holiday.

I sat in the old armchair – which was as comfort-able as it looked - and began to think about how I should organise my life over the next few weeks. I told myself it would all come together because it had to. I had no intention of returning to London without the job done, at least as much as I could do alone.

I deferred beginning on the work to-do list on the cardinal's effects until Monday and focus on my own needs in what was left of the weekend. I could also see that the proximity of St Peter's would take me there for Mass.

Richard arrived in about an hour and a half and I was hungry. He was carrying a floor lamp from somewhere, anticipating one of my requirements. He also deposited a canvas carrier bag with it in the sitting room.

"How many more would you like?" he asked, as I let him in.

"We can discuss it over lunch," I said, putting the lamp in the room I was already thinking of as my studio.

We walked down Borgo Vittorio and crossed over to a bright trattoria that still was serving at tables outside which was good to see, though we opted to go inside.

"You will find this place useful," Richard said. "Apart from being less than five minutes from your apartment, it's almost never closed."

After ordering lasagne, salad and bread, I asked Richard to tell me about himself.

"You are clearly not just an odd jobs man," I began. "So is looking after me some sort of punishment?"

He laughed.

"It would never have occurred to anyone to fill you in," he said. "I'm a student at the Venerable English College. I had my deaconate ordination – in Saint Peter's – last December."

"My congratulations," I said, seriously. "And your ordination?"

"Ah."

"Doubts? In the soup?"

Richard gave a charming smile.

"Nothing colourful or serious," he said. "My theological studies have been augmented – or diverted – depending how you look at it. I'm an astronomer."

I nodded, and other wheels began to spin.

"At present, I am working at the Vatican Observatory as well as at my normal studies," he explained. "I really want to have a parish, but at present, Mother Church wants me to continue astronomical training with post-doctoral study and practical work."

"You are working with Brother Guy?"

He nodded and smiled.

"A lovely man with a lively mind, but with characteristic Jesuitical meticulousness that I can't always live up to."

Our meals arrived and their smell was so inviting that conversation ceased for a while.

When we spoke again, I ventured a question that my sixth sense already knew the answer to.

"Where are your academic studies?"

"La Sapienza."

I knew that I would have to be quiet about Carrie if I wanted this talented novice to continue to his ordination.

"If you are at the English College, I gather you are not training to be a Jesuit."

"No," he replied, quietly. "I never considered myself clever enough for them. Also, I don't want to miss out on parish work."

"It's often the biggest sacrifice," I said.

Richard ate some more lasagne.

"I've read your biography," he said, almost guiltily.

"Then you know you have an ally."

He laughed, and I took the opportunity to divert the conversation.

"How did you get into astronomy?"

He thought, drank some water and began.

"You can tell from my accent that I'm not English," he said.

"Canadian."

"Yes, very good. Cow Moose Bay, Nova Scotia."

I laughed.

"Let me guess, not much light pollution there."

"Not a lot. I had a childhood watching the sea and the sky. I suppose I could have been a marine biologist, but my father's tales of the great myths of the constellations fired my imagination," he said. "He helped me restore an old telescope and it spiralled from there."

"And the priesthood?"

His smile became more wry.

"When you look at the universe, you look at God's second revelation," he said, simply.

We discussed this mediaeval idea which had intrigued me as much as the other one I've mentioned in these adventures: that all things exist simultaneously in the mind of God.

"The links between mediaeval theology and philosophy and quantum physics never cease to astound me," he said.

We finished our meal with a delightful *gelato* and returned to the apartment.

On the way back, I promised I'd make a timetable for his assistance and not to waste his time.

"I'm sure you consider this penance for some-thing," I said.

"Not yet."

Chapter XXIV

Saturday

The canvas bag that Richard brought held a broadband router which he set up while I fiddled with the light. It didn't take him long before I was ready to log in and reconnect with the world. I tell myself I could live without it, but as a communications, accounting and research tool, it is invaluable.

"I hope you will come to the college for lunch tomorrow at twelve-thirty," Richard said, before leaving.

I said I looked forward to it and asked if he knew a local supermarket so I could get some food for the weekend.

"Your pass for the café will work at the Vatican supermarket," he said. "Also at the department store in the old railway station, the pharmacy and the post office. Just wave it around and you'll be able to get into most places. It will even get you into St Martha's, but, believe me, this is far more comfortable even with its basic furnishings."

St Martha's is the residence for the cardinals when they come for conclaves and other events. No longer do they have to be sealed into the Sistine Chapel, sleep on cots in cells divided by curtains and use chamber pots.

Pope Francis still occupies the room he had there when he came for the conclave that elected him.

It wasn't long before Richard called me in and asked me to log into my email. Once a handful of messages had downloaded, he dictated his email address to me to send him a message as a test and to give him mine.

"I'll send you some useful links to the libraries," he said. "Needless to say, only a small percentage has been digitised, but the catalogues are pretty much complete."

When he left – with a reminder to come to lunch at the college Sunday – I checked my email.

Most were art-related newsletters, auction announce-ments, gallery private views, the odd bill, and an email from Sophie.

Dearest Nigel,

Thank you for making my Roman holiday memorable. I hope you found it as refreshing and inspiring as I did.

I'll remember Paris and the wonderful trains forever, but hope to forget the flight home. We hit turbulence over the alps making it difficult to keep the champagne in my glass, and circled Heathrow for nearly an hour. As you will imagine, my first destination was a long, hot bath.

I am sure you are excited about your new work just as I am looking forward to starting rehearsals on the play. It's what we do. It's what we are.

I hope you get to see Stephano and Laura again. I liked them.

Good luck with the project and let me know as much as you can about how things are going.

I'm sure you will be looked after.

Love,

Sophie

Attached was a selfie she'd taken of us in the forum. Typical of Sophie, it looked like we were still practising social distancing.

☙

Sitting in the bare apartment, I felt something I had not experienced in a long time: that feeling of strangeness, of newness, of not knowing how things worked, or what to do next. It wasn't a comfortable feeling.

It was still relatively early, so I went online to see if I could find an art supply shop that was in the area where I might buy a canvas or two. I found one improbably close on the Via dei Penitenzieri across Via della Conciliazione. The listing merely gave the address and *"forniture d'arte,"* which sounded like it could be code for dirty pictures.

It took only ten minutes to reach the narrow street, and I found the shop between an undertakers and a wine bar. The dusty window display assured me that it was what I was looking for.

After a very old-fashioned entrance with worn, dark wood counters and shelves, the shop surprisingly opened in to a large, bright, modern area. I was reminded of the contrast between the eighteenth century ground floor of Blackwell's in Oxford and the large modern basement.

The door had set a bell clanging and it wasn't long before someone appeared and asked what I was looking for.

I had not expected to find metre square canvases in stock, but he had two which I bought. The helpful chap, whom I took to be the proprietor, secured the canvases with a cord that enabled me to carry them. With luck, I wouldn't take flight into St Peter's Square if a gust caught me on the way back.

Friends who are writers tell me that they feel uneasy if they don't have access to adequate supplies of ink and paper. I feel the same about canvases. There has to be at least one in reserve for an unexpected commission, opportunity or attack of serendipity.

The lift at 11 Via Plauto was barely wide enough to accommodate me with the canvases, but all three of us returned to the apartment undamaged. I was, however, suddenly tired. The fresh air, and the general runaround of the day was making itself felt. Before I surrendered to an hour's kip, I mounted one of the canvases on the easel and covered it with a thin layer of burnt umber. Inspired by that, I found my sketches for the Thomas More picture and began blocking it in.

Being able to paint in my own time, not in scheduled sittings of an hour or two, was a luxury I had missed. With my sketches, it was like having a model who kept still, didn't prattle, fidget, take breaks to check his messages, drink my sherry, or ask for another coffee. As a result, before I knew it, it was really time for bed, and I had something that was beginning to look like my first religious painting.

༄

Sunday

Early the next morning, I walked to St Peter's for the seven o'clock Mass in St Joseph's chapel. The square was empty and quiet. The fountains were still and drained. They'd begin to fill shortly, but now the silence was striking. There were probably seventy or eighty at Mass, but no great numbers of tourists. It lasted about forty-five minutes and when I re-entered St Peter's Square, the top bowls of the fountains were spilling over.

I made a detour to pick up a few pastries and a loaf of bread while looking for a bar that might do breakfast. Perhaps the Vatican café was open. I'd look tomorrow when I began the real work.

I spent most of the day on the painting but had a break for lunch at the English College, where I was made to feel at home. Daily meals at academic institutions are mere interruptions to the students' work. They are not social events, though Sunday lunches usually make the effort. More likely, it's a brief stop to take on fuel. Many would adopt the old jerkwater approach and eat at their desks, but here at the Venerable English College, their home dioceses pick up the tab for meals in the refectory whereas snacks at the desk come from the students' own, shallow pockets.

I was invited to sit with the Rector, his parents, and a visiting sister of one of the novices, and Father Reynolds. The novice's sister - his own sister, not a nun, who – while attractive – could do with time in a Carmelite convent as she talked nonstop throughout the meal. So much so, that it was something of a challenge to catch the moments when she actually ate something, but her plate was one of the first ones bare. On reflection, perhaps this was a reaction to time served in a Carmelite convent school.

The meal itself was very good. On Sundays, meals were served by all members of the college in rotation. Sundays were family style dining and we enjoyed roast pork.

This was a college. A place of work and prayer, not my club in Mount Street, so I should not have been surprised that within two hours of my arrival, I was crossing Via della Conciliazione on my way home.

I made more coffee and took a close look at my painting of More. There were many problems, but I was concerned with the one of balance. More was seated to the right of the picture and the arrow slit very slightly off centre to the right. Its cruciform image, projected onto the floor crossed the centre line, but something else was needed to the left to balance the picture. There was another small window, and the hint of the stairway, but something with more mass was needed. A bed? A table?

I had already simplified the Bell Tower cell. The actual one has an improbable number of arches which, were they all included, would have been a distraction from the focal point, More and the highlight of the cruciform arrow slit on the stone floor.

Readers might get the impression that I paint very quickly. That's not wholly true. I get the ideas down quickly; making them presentable takes considerable time and patience. The inspiration and artistry are finished, now it's just hard graft.

I think that's why abstracts and less finished art is popular now: few have the patience – or talent – needed to deliver the standard, so another form of "art" has been created to accommodate the lazy and talentless.

There are, however, many painters who know their craft and produce magnificent pieces: landscapes, architectural paintings, portraits, murals, still lifes, flower paintings, seascapes and all manner of other works that will endure.

Regardless of what else I do tomorrow, I have to get more lights.

❧

The walk back from the Venerable English College served to wake me up, so I wasn't tempted by a *riposo*.

Although eager to get back to work, I told myself that I wouldn't be in Rome forever and that exploring my new neighbourhood would be a good way to spend part of the afternoon.

The Piazza del Risorgimento was very near Via Plauto and I spent nearly an hour walking around it, looking into shops, and enjoying an espresso watching the people, busses and trams. The mass of the wall surrounding Vatican City was a solid reminder that it was a separate country, entitle to defend its borders. It was a marked contrast to the welcoming arms of the Bernini colonnade around St Peter's Square and the benevolent, but consuming nature of the basilica itself.

As in all of Italy, two thousand years of history could be found in almost every glance. Time compacted into the quotidian.

Did other people's minds work like this? I'm not sure anyone knows for sure.

A look at the posted tram timetable showed that the line served La Sapienza so it was possibly used by Richard, or could be if he were dropping by my apartment.

Thinking of La Sapienza made me think of Carrie. Was there a reason that the two students – both scientists – I had met in Rome both attended the same university? Was this some pattern, or was I the only common denominator?

I finished my second espresso and fourth biscotti and decided it was time to check my emails, drop Sophie a line and do some work. I was looking forward to starting on my main project but also determined that it would be a Monday to Friday job.

The apartment looked bare and the basic lighting didn't help, but at least it was warm. I switched on the computer, deleted the junk, wrote a brief note to Sophie wishing her success in the next day's rehearsal, and browsed my normal exhibition and gallery sites. I didn't appear to be missing anything.

I moved the LED floor lamp into my painting room. While not ideal, it was a big improvement on the overhead bulb.

I was at the point where I would soon have to decide if I wanted realistic detail or a more suggestive, impressionistic one. I decided the More was worth the effort, but needed a live model to get the subtle flesh tones right. This is where artists can rely on their own skin, but my only mirror was screwed to the bathroom wall. There was plenty else I could be getting on with. The colour of the cell walls, its textures and the masonry joints could be taken from photographs on the internet.

It was then that it occurred to me that there might be pictures of Stephano online. He was, after all, a successful engineer in the construction industry as well as a count who might turn up at various social events.

I started to do the search when I realised the source of my restlessness: I was missing London, my set, Sophie. The realisation itself didn't cure the feeling, but it made me feel less uneasy about it. I chided myself for feeling sorry for myself – especially in this city which was never boring.

Although not my usual practice, I poured a glass of wine, found some good music on the web, plugged in my headphones and began making lists for tomorrow.

Lists of things to do, things that I'd need, things that would need research, things that I needed to know were in my assignment, and even a few things I wanted for myself.

Chapter XXV

Monday

I'm not one to attend daily Mass often, but not feeling up to the task I'd been given took me back to St Peter's at seven in the morning. I'd always been taught not to ask for physical things or particular outcomes in prayer, but to ask for abstract virtues and capabilities like patience, wisdom, humility and, in my case today, presence of mind.

It was another clear morning (I must check when Summer Time ends here) and I was just a little less intimidated by St Peter's Square and the silent fountains standing like alien guards.

Today, I was in the Clementine Chapel in the crypt, directly under the high altar. It was an "extraordinary" Mass, said in Latin. There was one in Italian at the same time in the Chapel of the Choir, but my Latin is better than my Italian. The extraordinary form means that the readings and prayers are on an annual cycle rather than on the three-year rotation that's been in place since Vatican II. I'm not a theological pedant or reactionary and figure that any version of the Mass said here must be valid and licit.

As it was a short daily Mass, the top bowl of the Bernini fountain had not filled by the time I came out into the air again.

No doubt, talk about the Catholic faith will make many feel uncomfortable, but one cannot be in Rome or write about it without acknowledging its presence here and in the world.

There's a scene in *Brideshead Revisited* – nicely played in the 1981 television version – where Charles Ryder asked Cordelia Flyte:

> *"Does your family always talk about religion all the time?"*
>
> *"Not all the time. It's a subject that just comes up naturally, doesn't it?"*
>
> *"Does it? It never has with me before."*

I remembered the conversation I'd had with Alex Josephson before leaving London and how he'd said that Jews and Christians had some of the most tremendous stories in the history of the world but that as artists we had failed to retell them.

It had taken two weeks, but I did feel I had made a small start, and I wondered what Alex might think of my present task. Standing here, yards from the spot where St Peter was executed and where so much history had taken place, it was difficult not to feel the imperative of that mission. I had let this new task intervene – and who knew where it would lead and how long it would take?

Now, the practicality of getting breakfast intervened.

I had not found a bar for breakfast on Saturday and began to explore the streets behind Via della Conciliazione. Clearly, God was smiling that morning as I almost instantly found Bar Latteria Giuliani on Borgo Pio, about two minutes from 11 Via Plauto. This establishment had been around for more than a hundred years and offered the selection of pastries and other dishes similar to Bar 43's, so I felt immediately at home.

It was later than I'd planned when I returned to the apartment and began working for real.

◌੪

I will not bore readers with a blow by blow description of the method I followed beyond saying that cataloguing and photographing everything was how I began. It took nearly two days to measure things and move various tools from my apartment into the late cardinal's.

One by one, the paintings were taken down, measured, given a light dusting (I didn't want to remove clues that might be there, pollen, for example), and basic descriptions written. I also made a note of anything that might indicate age or origin. I'd do an inch by inch examination using a new pair of magnifiers with LEDs that I found at a curious shop that had small tools for engineers, electricians, plumbers, and other artisans.

Tuesday was much like Monday. I had breakfast at Giuliani's again, a small lunch in a cafeteria and cooked myself dinner. I finished the basic work on the paintings in the early afternoon and moved to the jewellery, sorting the pieces by gold, silver or other. I had not begun to do the cardinal's effects which, I felt, had to be checked to see if there was anything that related to the Jewish artefacts.

On Tuesday afternoon, I began to make notes of my proposed method, based on a two week schedule.

I knew I would need help with translations and would also need contact with someone who knew about Eastern Euro-pean Jewish art. A call to Alex Josephson would yield both, but for now I would have to follow Vatican Rules.

I was anticipating difficulties at the scheduled meeting Wednesday. It would be at my apartment, and I brought in some pastries while we chatted. In the event, it was only Father Muldrew who came. He was easier to read than Father Mézard, but his serious nature made me cautious. One encouraging sign was that he seemed to enjoy the *cornetti*.

I explained my thinking, perceived needs, and proposed schedule. From time to time, he asked for more details, but for the most part, he just listened.

When I finished, I expected a grilling or some suggestions about my method, but it was time allocation he queried.

"You've given yourself a generous amount of time for your own activities," he observed, and indicated my painting time on the schedule.

"If you had expected an eight-hour day, you would have chosen someone younger," I replied, hoping it sounded casual.

"Quality, not quantity, eh?" he said, laughing for the first time.

"Modesty forbids," I said, and he laughed again. "So are you doing anything with your painting time?"

I led him to the other room and showed him Sir Thomas. He moved the lamp to see better.

"Can we move it to the window?" he asked.

As if on cue, the sun broke through the overcast sky and flooded into the room. He stared at the nearly finished picture, then glanced towards the window.

"I'll take that as a sign," he said, his eyes laughing. "We'd both better get back to work. Do all you can before we call in the experts, then we can give them each precise instructions."

"So they don't see the big picture?"

He gave a slight nod, then added, "And have Richard get you some decent lights."

I laughed.

"Thank you."

"Now," he said, standing by the door, "is there anything more you need from me?"

"Yes, Father. I would like a detailed account of everything Cardinal Mauro worked on, who he worked with and when. Say from the time he became a seminarian to 1950, for a start."

Father Muldrew raised his eyebrows, but nodded.

"Let's meet for dinner next week," he said, and left.

After tidying up, I went to the cardinal's rooms and continued cataloguing. I was nearly done and was finishing the jewellery. Some of the pieces had maker's marks and other inscriptions and stamps that might help to identify them, but for now, I simply noted that they had marks. I would need a *loupe* to see them, then probably someone who could translate them.

I wanted to study the paintings – unframed – with magnifiers and under decent lights, but began going through his eminence's books looking for loose papers, notes or anything that might give a clue about his collection. There were several hundred books and, in a bottom drawer, stacks of simple notebooks of about thirty pages each. From what I could tell, based on the dates and headings, these were homilies and other talks he'd given over the years.

I'd completed looking through one drawer when I realised it was nearly two o'clock and I hadn't had any lunch. I judged this to be a good opportunity to see what might be available at the Vatican Café and walked to the anonymous doorway and went in.

I went down the long corridor and opened another nondescript door to enter the café. I had to show my card before being admitted to the serving areas.

It was still busy, but there were now plenty of seats. The short cafeteria line had about half a dozen dishes – pasta, stew and salads, with a selection of fruit and yoghurts. My card was swiped at the end of the line and I found a seat.

What this room was before its current use was anyone's guess. It had high ceilings and almost no decoration apart from a simple moulding running around the perimeter. Signs of a large doorway, now bricked up, suggested that it might have been a garage or stable.

I slowed my speed of eating by making the odd entry in my notebook. Not unexpectedly, I saw no one I knew in the café. It was pure vanity to think that I might.

I was keen to find out what the old cardinal had been up to during the war, and I also had an idea of how to short-cut a lot of research on the paintings.

After lunch, I was going to walk around St Peter's Square, but the crowds and barriers prevented that, so I returned to the Piazza di Risorgimento and walked around it before going back to the apartment.

Stepping out of the lift, I was alarmed to see my door ajar. Could I have forgotten to lock it? Approaching it carefully, I glanced at the door jamb and lock. They were undamaged. While I hardly considered this my home, the sense of violation was no less strong, and it was that which gave me the sense of outrage to enter without fear – albeit cautiously.

There was noise in the kitchen and I stepped in further.

"*Buon giorno*," I called, making my voice artificially deep.

A light burst of laughter came from the kitchen, closely followed by an apparition in black, wide eyes and a huge smile.

"*Buon pomeriggio, mi chiedevo quando sareste tornato dal pranzo. Sono Pasqualina, stavo riordinando e preparando la cena. Spero che ti piaccia la parmigiana di pollo con le farfalle. Ho pensato che fosse abbastanza sicuro finché non avessi avuto la possibilità di scoprire cosa ti piaceva davvero. Ho quasi finito qui dentro: dovrai solo scaldare il forno per venti minuti e cuocere la pasta, poi darò una leggera spolverata e mi toglierò di mezzo.*"

As this torrent of Italian washed over me, she came forward with her hand extended, took mine and gave one sharp shake, and turned back into the kitchen, clearly expecting me to follow.

I was pretty much lost after "my name is Pasqualina" but I recognised the chicken parmigiana in the baking dish, and the bag of farfalle on the counter. As for the rest of it – well, I suppose I'll find out.

I managed to thank her, repeat her name to confirm it, and managed the phrase I had recently found most useful:

"Il suo inglese è migliore del mio italiano?" [4]

This released another unrestrained burst of laughter.

"I am sorry, Dottor Thomas, no one told me you didn't speak Italian," she said. "It's good that you try. We'll manage."

She made coffee and we sat at my dining table, and she seemed to calm down. She was much younger than her black clothing suggested. I guessed she was around forty, and her long black hair – by nature or design – revealed no grey. Despite her constant and natural exuberance and smiles, her eyes reflected an experience of hardship, illness or loss.

"You were expecting me?" she asked.

"I knew someone would come, but not when."

"It is okay. Is Monday, Wednesday and Friday all right?" she asked. "I can prepare food for two days, and leave you a chicken, and lamb, beef or pork on weekends. Do you like fish?"

Pasqualina was refreshing – but exhausting – company after the parade of priests I'd been dealing with. In twenty minutes, I learned that she was a widow (no details were given of how or when), she had no children,

---

[4] Is your English better than my Italian?

she was from Latina in the Lazio region, she loved cooking, and also worked at the Venerable English College.

She wanted to know what I wanted her to do. Make the bed, do the laundry, change the sheets? Cook more often? Clean more often? I had the impression that if I had a car, she'd offer to change the oil and adjust the spark-plugs.

Before she left, I realised that there was something else she could do for me, but now was not the time to mention it.

As we sat at the table, the sun broke through and illuminated her face. I instantly knew that I wanted her to model for my Julian of Norwich.

Chapter XXVI

Tuesday

Pasqualina returned to her cooking, cleaning and tidying while I began the next phase of my work. The cataloguing done, I transferred the photographs of the paintings onto my laptop and opened an imaging program.

I made a folder for each painting and immediately copied each one so I had an original reference picture. Using a few basic tricks, I squared the image and gave them a digital cleaning, removing the cast of dirt and old varnish. In several cases, the results were exciting. I was in no way proficient at this and would hand over anything I might discover to an expert.

However, I next uploaded each of the images to a reverse photo-search website in the hopes that something might get a hit, as they say.

My theory was that if any of these were known stolen pieces, the search engine would track the Nazi-looted art sites. I had to fiddle a bit to ensure the pictures were in the right sizes for uploading, which I did one at a time on three different sites.

What came back was frightening in its returns. While none had matched any of the pictures, those sites claiming to be "AI-powered" recognised Biblical, Old Testament or Jewish subjects. The returns on two pictures included the probable identity as nineteenth century pieces, and one identified a painting as Polish, suggesting it was in the style of Gierymski. While this partially confirmed my suspicions, I was also relieved that these paintings did not appear to be actively sought.

As for Gierymski, this was not a name I was familiar with, so the next half hour was spent looking for information on him. The first problem was there were two Gierymskis, brothers, Aleksander and Maxymilian. Aleksander looked the more likely as he was known for paintings of Jewish life while his brother was known for his watercolours. There was another satisfying bit of information: Aleksander had died in Rome.

Although I had only one simple, tenuous lead, and writing up an index card, I was pleased enough to finish that work for the day and head into my "studio" to work for an hour or so before dinner.

Once moving the lights so I could work, I realised that I was very close to finishing St Thomas More. I fetched my laptop and brought up a number of the photos I'd taken of Stephano as well as laying out the sketches I'd done of him.

Pasqualina had left dinner in the oven, so all I had to do was turn it on, set the timer and pull the cork on the bottle of red wine she had brought. Unsurprisingly, it was from Lazio.

I continued my work until the timer went off indicating when I should cook the pasta. I wanted to see the painting in daylight, but felt that it was complete.

I don't find dining alone pleasurable and I was missing Sophie's company. I usually ate too fast, or became absorbed in a magazine article or book and failed to appreciate whatever I was eating. Not eating something I'd cooked myself was a pleasure, however, and this chicken was excellent.

I remained at the table reading and drinking my second glass of wine when there was a knock on my door.

I opened it, and Richard stepped in with a bright greeting. He was carrying boxes which he set down when I invited him to take off his coat.

"Father Muldrew said you had urgent need of more lights," he said. "You said you liked the one I brought, so I bought three more of them."

I cleared my plate and brought in another glass and gave him some wine as we spent the next fifteen minutes assembling them.

Standing together next to each other, they reminded me of the Martians in *War of the Worlds,* and I expected them to glow green when I switched them on.

"I brought two extension cords, too," he said. "These old buildings never have enough outlets."

We took one of the lamps into the studio where the first one was. I set it up so the painting was illuminated from both sides with a warm, if faux, incandescent glow from the LEDs.

Richard stood back when I switched them on and moved them into position.

"St Thomas More?" he ventured. "Wow! You did that since you moved in here?"

I nodded.

We returned to the main room and drank the rest of the wine.

I asked about his work at the observatory and at university. He was modest but it was obviously very advanced. He didn't know about my former connection with mathematics, and it was a pleasure to listen to him enthusiastically explain what he was studying and how he was assisting at the observatory.

About half an hour after the wine was gone, he looked at his watch, apologised and said he had to get back to the VEC, as he called it. I thanked him for the lamps and went to the door with him.

"I've no knowledge about art but I thought St Thomas was very powerful. He rather reminded me of Count Polidori."

੪ఄ

Days quickly fell into a pattern: work, painting,, Sunday Mass and lunch at the English College, and setting tasks for Richard to undertake. Pasqualina was making me more elaborate meals and gave the apartment (and the late cardinal's) a thorough cleaning.

To my relief she worked quietly and didn't chatter if she knew I was working. She asked no questions about what I was doing – either about the cardinal's artifacts, or my painting.

During my time at the English College, I made sketches of Father Muldrew and even persuaded Father Mézard to let me sit in a corner of his busy office and sketch him. I think he was secretly flattered that I wanted to portray him as St Robert Bellarmine, Doctor of the Church, even though Father Mézard was much younger than St Robert, who in 1615 – the year before heliocentricity was declared heretical – would have been seventy-three. Father Muldrew was amused to play Galileo, but was close to his age of fifty-one.

I had yet to broach the possibility of Richard posing as Alessandro Orsini, then a young man of eighteen, but a patron of Galileo. Later, Galileo would dedicate his book on the tides to him. Orsini himself would perform great works of charity during a famine, lead an ascetic life, and be made a cardinal in this twenties.

The figures were already blocked in and the overall composition was taking shape.

Richard had been taking one or two of the pieces of jewellery and religious objects to a succession of jewellers and pawn shops to see if anyone could tell him anything. While choosing the pieces to give Richard to show around, I looked in the battered leather pouch with a zipper that lay in one of the open compartments of the desk. On my first visit, I'd had a quick look inside and it seemed to contain ordinary pens and pencils, and I put it aside.

Now, I looked more closely and emptied the contents onto the desk. There were three thin metal pieces variously decorated but each had a hand with a pointing finger at the end. Two of them were brass and the third looked like it might be silver. At first I thought they might be dip pens, as I had had at one time a nib where the link flowed from the extended finger, but they were solid.

I showed them to Richard on his next visit and he recognised them immediately.

"They're *yads*," he said.

"What's a *yad*?" I asked.

"When reading the Torah in a synagogue, rabbis use the *yad* to keep their place in the text," he explained. "Boys use them when studying and at their bar mitzvah ceremonies, too. I expect girls use them now, too for their bat mitzvahs."

"Would they be used in domestic circumstances? These brass ones are very basic. Even the silver – or silver plate – one is very plain."

Richard thought.

"I expect in ghettos or small villages the synagogues were pretty basic, so brass might be used," he said, considering it. "We had a rabbi speak to us about modern Jewish worship last term. If a family had Torah scrolls at home, they would probably have a *yad* but it would be unlikely for those coming from Eastern Europe."

I thought he was right, but the discovery that one of our possible painters died in Rome opened other possibilities.

Richard's visits to the pawnbrokers and jewellery stores only confirmed my suspicion that these bits of items, no matter how precious they were to their owners, had little monetary value.

So why were they in Cardinal Mauro's drawer?

చ

Thursday the following week

With my new lamps, illuminated magnifying headset, and lots of time, I went over the front and back of all the paintings. Only on one of them did I find the hint of a signature. A full examination with x-rays, UV-lights and other digital magnification and deconstruction could probably turn up a variety of clues that I could not see, but would come later.

I did manage to remove the frames to look under the mouldings at the edge of the canvases, and that was where my one possibility was found. As I scanned the images with the bright light on the headset, I had to remember that I should be looking not only for letters in the Roman alphabet, but in Cyrillic and Hebrew as well.

I was reaching the end of what I could do. I'd been there three weeks and finished one painting and was getting to the end of another, but I sensed the end of my stay in Rome approaching.

While painting in my apartment at the end of a frustrating day, I was comforted by the smell of Pasqualina's latest creation developing in the oven, and thinking that this was a good evening to retreat into a good book and finish my wine in the most leisurely way I could, but like all dreams, reality intervened.

There was a knock on my door simultaneously with the timer going off for my dinner.

"*Mannaggia!*"

I opened the door in less than good humour.

"Hello, Sir Nigel! Mmm! Something smells good!"

It was Carrie.

"I should have called or emailed, but I was in the area and thought I'd take a chance," she continued.

I sensed that she was embarrassed and/or nervous, but was braving it out.

"Come in. Join me for some supper or at least a glass of wine," I said, putting her out of her misery.

She dropped her bluff, gave me her usual smile and mouthed, "Thank you."

Dumping her backpack, presumably filled with books and notes, she moved to the table where I placed another glass.

"May I tempt you to some lemon and garlic shrimp pasta?" I asked, putting the dish on the table.

"*Ah! Linguine ai gamberi al limone e aglio! Grazie!*" she said, with delight.

I fetched bowls and cutlery for her and poured the wine.

"How is your mother?" I asked. "Poor Alegra and her parents?"

"*Sante!*" Carrie said, raising her glass. "Alegra's clinic is this side of the city – which is why I'm in the area. She is also one of the reasons I've come to see you."

I served her some linguine as she began to explain.

"Before you go on, how did you find me?" I asked, passing her the dish.

She laughed again.

"Rome isn't that big," she said. "I bumped into Richard Durand at the university. I've known him for several years. He's older and doing more advanced things than I, but in the library one day, we got in an argument about a book we both wanted.

"We are interested in some of the same things, but have little else in common. I said I hadn't seen him about as much, and he said that in addition to his academic, religious and observatory work, he'd been lumbered with looking after an old English artist doing something secret for the Vatican."

While this could be dangerous, I laughed.

"Sorry. I made up the bit about being lumbered and old," she said, with a smile. "Don't worry, he likes working for you. He said it was a welcome distraction. You can imagine how stunned he was to hear that you'd painted me! As I said, Rome is small."

"You were telling me about Alegra."

She took her time finishing her mouthful.

"It's been a very tough two weeks. She's been on an intensive detox programme with lots of physical exercise – and what she hates most – school work. She looks healthy, but tired and unhappy."

Carrie drank some wine.

"I told Alegra I was going to try to see you," she resumed. "She seemed genuinely embarrassed by her behaviour while you and Miss Gregg were there. I actually think she means it."

We finished the meal and I made coffee.

"Suppose you tell me why you really wanted to see me."

Carrie gave me a Cheshire cat-like smile.

"I'd like your advice about what to study next year."

We talked about mathematics and cosmology until it was nearly ten. I offered to call her a taxi, but she said she was happy to take a bus or walk.

"Before I go, may I see your painting of St Thomas More?"

I must have looked surprised.

"When I told Richard I knew you, he said something under his breath which he repeated for me. He said, 'That makes sense now.' I asked him what made sense, and he said – "

"He said, that was why the painting reminded him of Stephano," I interrupted. "Yes, of course, it's in here."

Chapter XXVII

Thursday

Although I have not said much about Sophie since her departure, we have remained in touch. We emailed and spoke when she had time. Her play was scheduled to open in a week and, while she had expressed few opinions about the merit of the play or the standard of the rehearsals, I knew her well enough to tell that it was not a source of anxiety.

My own work was approaching an interesting stage. I had gone as far as I could with the pictures. Subjects have been identified, dates within a decade had been deduced and evidence provided, and the artists of two of them suggested, with a good possibility for a third.

It is now late Thursday afternoon of my third week on the project and more than a month since coming to Rome. *Galileo Builds an Orrery with St Robert Bellarmine and Alessandro Cardinal Orsini* is finished and work has begun on *Saint Julian of Norwich,* but more on that later.

Father Muldrew and Father Reynolds are coming tomorrow morning. I have the feeling that this is the beginning of the end of my time here.

Things have been happening in the background that I am not aware of. Good Richard has faithfully acquiesced to all of my requests, digging out answers, requesting translations, visiting the pawnshops as well as helping me with practical matters.

As an indicator of the seriousness with which my project was being taken, each of my requests was relayed to Father Muldrew for approval before Richard was given the nod to fulfil it. Once he had the answers, he had to liaise with Father Muldrew again before he could pass them to me.

Needless to say, there were numerous requests that were unfulfilled.

When I became aware of this process, Richard entreated me not to press him.

"What's the phrase the Americans use, 'I can neither confirm nor deny that I secured a reply to that request,'" he said, with admirable wit.

I did not press him, but it made my work more difficult and less satisfying. I had not yet received the long-requested details of Cardinal Mauro's activities during the 1940s. I felt that if I had a single clue, I might be able to follow it myself.

For some time I had also been urging that professional art historians look at the paintings, but I had no idea whether this was being considered. Still, I had not remained entirely on *piste*.

With the help of my laptop, I had found a dozen organisations active in researching, documenting and recovering or seeking restitution for art looted by the Nazis. These are based in Israel, Europe, the United States and Canada, and each has remarkable stories of success. It was tempting to mention the provenance sites in Quebec and Ontario to Richard, but I knew he'd have to pass it on.

What I did do was telephone (using VIOP) the specifically Jewish ones (World Jewish Congress, the Holocaust Art Restitution Project, the European Shoah Legacy Institute and a few others) as well as the Commission for Looted Art in Europe and the American Holocaust Memorial Museum. I couldn't email and give my personal details away. These organisations would have been able to trace an email right back to Via Plauto.

It was difficult to have any sort of credibility as I couldn't say who I was, who I was working for or what, specifically, I was asking for. Honing my tactics and terminology, I settled on asking if they were actively seeking lost Jewish art from Eastern Europe *not* looted by the Nazis. For example, works that may have been sold along the way. That seemed to cover what I was dealing with.

As I expected, the primary interest was in recovering art that was looted or seized specifically for the collection of the Third Reich or the personal collections of its commanders. The – not unreasonable view – was that art that was taken with the refugees and lost, sold or stolen along the way was probably not of sufficient value or historical importance to trace, and probably untraceable anyway.

I was sympathetic to this as their job was already so monumental that it needed some basic parameters to bring it down to a manageable scale. Worthy individual pictures that showed up in sale rooms would be investigated as needed.

By the time I heard from the ninth organisation on my list, they knew who I was – at least they knew the alias I was using. This revealed a very powerful network.

Everyone was courteous, and no one gave anything away. Several stressed that I had a duty to report anything I suspected. One even suggested I'd be complicit if I did not.

There was only one thing I had not finished doing and that was going through all the cardinal's notebooks, books and papers. I had been delaying that until I had some sense of his working biography so I could sort things into the periods of his life with some confidence that they had nothing to do with my project.

After the meeting tomorrow, I hoped I'd be granted enough time to do that before being shipped back to London.

The meeting preparation done, I locked the cardinal's door and went back to my rooms. I'd have to paint before and after supper, so I returned to *Julian of Norwich*.

I'd had little idea how to compose this painting, but I had a vision of a lonely nun in her small cell with a pious face showing faith, patience, wisdom and similar virtues.

While willing, Pasqualina was totally unable to maintain a serious, pious face for more than ninety seconds.

"I'm averagely religious, but I don't understand this!" she exclaimed.

I put my brush down and we went into the kitchen. In the next twenty minutes, over a desperate cup of coffee, I tried to generate the requisite gravitas by ex-plaining Julian's solitary life in a cell as an anchoress.

Pasqualina's response was to ask me what the holy woman was best known for. I explained her few writings and the importance of *Revelations of Divine Love*, only to be met with an impatient wave of the hand.

"Surely there's a prayer, a story or a few sentences she is known for like every other saint," she retaliated. "I don't want an English history lesson!"

Her delivery was humorous, but her intent clear.

I found the notes I had made in my first week in Rome, leafed through the many pages until I came to the lines that stopped me.

I looked at Pasqualina – who had never revealed any of her troubles and whose laughter lit wherever she was.

"Julian is known for repeating words that encapsulalted her faith and fed her spirit, 'all shall be well, and all shall be well, and all manner of things shall be well.'"

Pasqualina looked up at me with a huge smile, and we went back to the studio to begin again.

What I painted was a nun, sitting straight, but comfortably on a chair, showing her full face, but looking down, pupils nearly unseen, but with the trace of a smile on her face that spoke of satisfaction, pleasure, and of a vision beyond her cell and beyond time – and it *amused* her.

In terms of Julian of Norwich, this was the dawning of her revelations; in terms of Pasqualina, it was the moment before she looked up and exploded into laughter. We had something we could both understand.

When the idea clicks, it's only a matter of getting the paint on the canvas. Each painting needs that moment. In the Sir Thomas More painting, it was when the idea of making the highlighted cruciform arrow slit the focus of More's attention, or the moment when Carrie put her hand on the window glass.

I was excited by this idea now and decided to delay supper and do all the painting before eating.

80

Friday

Friday morning's meeting was frustrating. I wanted to write that it was difficult, but in a sense, it wasn't because, as the Americans say, I had no skin in the game. What the Vatican decided to do with its things was nothing to do with me. I'd done some work for them, enjoyed being in Rome, eaten well, had some memorable conversations, and enjoyed an intriguing puzzle. Perhaps it was time I went home and did my Christmas shopping.

The two priests were in excellent spirits when they arrived and happier still when they saw the assortment of pastries I'd brought from Bar Latteria.

"Sir Nigel, you have given this whole business a very valuable push," Father Reynolds said. "We couldn't have asked for more."

This surprised me, for obvious reasons. I'd accomplished next to nothing, but I let them go on.

"Father Mézard has been wanting to renovate these apartments since the cardinal moved out," Father Reynolds said. "Then there was Covid, then the problem of what to do about these pictures and other bits.

"You immediately grasped the solution saying that the Vatican Museum should be dealing with these," he continued.

I sat, waiting for one of them to continue.

"All right, I'll ask," I said, after nearly a minute. "Why isn't the museum dealing with this?"

Father Reynolds looked at Father Muldrew who, after a moment sighed.

"Once the museum takes them and catalogues them, it will be up to them to explain how they acquired them, and, more inconveniently, how Cardinal Mauro acquired them."

"And you don't know the answer to that?"

"No."

This conversation was clearly more uncomfortable for them than it was for me. The pauses between my questions and their answers told me that. I did, however, feel that for the first time I was beginning to see the bigger picture.

"And I have helped how?"

A longer pause.

"As an outsider, you were able to root around, ask questions and send your envoy to ask questions," Father Muldrew began. "This attracted attention.

"The Vatican remains very sensitive about its perceived lack of action during the War and Pope Pius XII's alleged collaboration with the Nazis."

"That all stems from one calumnious play," I said.

"And created a myth that continues today," Father Muldrew said, sadly, adding, "and delaying the canonisation of one of the holiest men ever to be pope."

Although those who had studied the Vatican's role in World War II knew of the network of anti-Nazi spies connected to the Vatican under the personal – and extraordinarily cautious – supervision of Pope Pius XII, knew the truth of the matter, most people did probably accept the other version.

"The Vatican has done very little to set the record straight," I said. "How many know that more than four thousand priests were killed in Dachau? And how many elsewhere?"

More silence. Then Father Reynolds spoke, quoting a well known TV drama:

"You might think that. I couldn't possibly comment."

Father Muldrew looked uncomfortable.

"All right," he said, a note of impatience in his voice. "You have attracted just enough attention so that the people at the museum feel that they must now become involved. The paintings will be collected this afternoon along with the other bits and pieces of Judaica.

"Yes, we have used you," he added, seeing me about to react. "However, as Father Reynolds said, we could not have asked for more."

We sat in silence for some time.

"When do I have to leave?" I asked. "I am sure Father Mézard is anxious to get on with his decorating."

Father Reynolds nodded.

"How would by next Saturday suit you?" he asked. "If you needed to stay longer, we could accommodate you at the VEC."

This was acceptable to me. The Vatican could probably be persuaded to ship my paintings. I would pack them. I had accumulated little to take back with me. The only real thing I had to decide was whether to finish *Julian of Norwich* here or back in London. It would need at least five days before it would be dry enough to ship, I'd need some wax paper and a means of preventing the packaging to press on the surface. Minor damage could be easily fixed, but I didn't want giant smudges to arrive in London. Thomas More would be fine and Galileo safe enough, but Julian would need care.

Packing them would take time and I wanted to supervise, so the sooner it could be started, the better.

I mentioned this and Father Muldrew said he'd arrange for the museum to take care of it and suggested the pictures might even find their way into the diplomatic pouch.

"Apart from my pictures, may I ask one other thing?" I asked.

Father Muldrew nodded cautiously.

"I have not been able to look through all the cardinal's papers and books. I won't be able to paint, so I'll have time."

Father Muldrew glanced at Father Reynolds who answered.

"I see no problem with that. Keep everything in the cardinal's rooms, as you have."

"There is one last thing," Father Muldrew said.

It was my turn to sigh.

"I can guess. You want my notes."

He nodded.

"And photographs," he added.

I tried to look as unhappy as possible.

"Do you want to watch me delete them?"

"On Monday, when the paintings themselves are out of here," he said.

Mannaggia.

Chapter XXVIII

Although I had done what they asked me to do and they had expressed pleasure at what they saw as my success, I was dissatisfied. I was ready to leave Rome. I loved my time here, but today made it bitter-sweet.

Somehow, I'd done four paintings in five weeks. I was excited by my saintly subjects, and I had enjoyed meeting and painting Carrie.

There is a joke that goes, "God moves in mysterious ways, bishops move diagonally." I have always refrained from believing the Church is deceitful, but it can be incredibly opaque and subtle. It has suffered from that with unrelenting critical attacks.

I take some comfort from the Hilaire Belloc quote, which is one of the few things anyone remembers about this remarkable man: "The Catholic Church is an institution I am bound to hold divine – but for unbelievers a proof of its divinity might be found in the fact that no merely human institution conducted with such knavish imbecility would have lasted a fortnight."

Saturday and Sunday were beautiful days and I spent much of them outside, walking, sitting in cafes, and visiting a few places I wanted to see before leaving Rome.

I would have preferred to go to an early Sunday Mass in St Peter's, but I didn't want those at the VEC to think I was sulking, so I went there and enjoyed lunch with the students, Father Reynolds and Father Muldrew.

None of us spoke of the cardinal's pictures.

In fact, both priests told amusing stories which we all enjoyed. Several of the students appeared not to have seen Father Muldrew laugh.

I met Richard after lunch and we walked back to my apartment and had a glass of wine while talking through what needed to be done. He was sympathetic to my feelings.

We were in the cardinal's flat, and I was looking at a large pile of papers and notebooks I'd put on the table.

"Do you really expect to find anything?" he asked, looking at the stack and at the bookshelves.

"No," I admitted, "but I need to look. For my own satisfaction."

We locked the apartment and carried our drinks into my studio where I gave Richard instructions on how my paintings needed to be packed. He made notes that he'd pass to Father Mézard who had the contacts with the museum and removal companies.

He looked at Galileo, leaning against the wall.

"Where's Galileo and the Orrery going?"

"I thought I'd try it in the Royal Academy's Summer Exhibition, after that – well, it depends if anyone wants to buy it."

"I wish my parents could see it," he said. "They'd get a laugh at me in all the period clothing."

"I'll have them photographed professionally before they go into the show. I'll send you a copy," I said.

He stood awkwardly for a moment and looked embarrassed.

"Sir Nigel – look, I'm sorry I had to deceive you with all your requests and the answers," he said. "Believe me, I – "

"You were just following orders – no, Richard, that's unfair. We were both minor but necessary pieces in a much bigger game. Let's just hope it was worth it."

He smiled and shook my hand rather formally.

"Can you be free tomorrow for dinner?" I asked. "I'd like to show you my appreciation for all your help."

When he left, I returned to the cardinal's rooms and began going through the stacks of papers.

❦

I was up early on Monday despite having looked through notebooks and papers until eleven-thirty. Apart from the homilies, there were reflections that appeared to be for events and publications, book reviews, and methodical commentaries on what his eminence had read.

There were calendars, a few pocket agenda, and piles of programmes from ordinations, elevations, installations and consecrations.

My fear was that I had missed something. My lack of fluency in Italian and Latin meant I had to rely on seeing key words. What made me feel a little better was that Cardinal Mauro not only had wonderfully clear handwriting, but he appeared to be extremely well organised.

In spite of this, I learned little of the man's actual duties. There were letters from all the major congregations and dicasteries, so it was impossible to tell which he belonged to.

As it was another bright morning, I went to Bar Latteria Giuliani for breakfast. With no tourists at that hour, the bustle and noise was all from people who lived or worked in the neighbourhood. Secretaries and priests were buying boxes of pastries to take to their offices, while others drank their *cappuccini* and read the sports pages.

I wanted to appear busy and still committed when the good fathers came to collect my files and delete my photos when they came at ten.

I walked around the piazza after finishing breakfast and returned to find the cardinal's flat full of people. There were four porters and a curator from the museum along with Father Reynolds and Father Muldrew. Richard was also there, helping to move furniture so the paintings could be reached.

Father Muldrew was putting the jewellery and other artifacts into a small box and gave it to the curator.

After saying good morning, I went to my apartment to get my notebook and laptop. I set up the latter on the table and booted up and opened to the file directory (Windows Explorer for pedants).

All that remained on the laptop were my own pictures and the research notes I'd made for my own projects.

It didn't take long for the seven paintings to be removed. The curator hadn't said a word, or even acknowledged my presence, and Richard left with them, but not before saying he'd come at seven so we could go to eat.

Once the door had shut, I turned the laptop towards Father Muldrew and held out my notebook and papers.

They both relaxed and sat down.

"This is it?" Father Muldrew asked, taking the notebooks.

"That's it."

He opened it and saw that nearly every page had something on it: the catalogue, the measurements, the condition reports such as I could do, subject descript-tions, and other bits of information and speculation.

He stopped turning pages and read a large section – I couldn't tell what – but he was silent for several minutes before looking up and giving a satisfied smile.

"This is good," he said. "Once I've read it, I'll pass it to the museum. It will save them a lot of time – though they will never admit it."

He then turned to the computer.

"This is the master folder with all the photographs, some notes, information on possible artists. Basically everything."

Father Muldrew took a USB stick from his pocket and transferred the files, then deleted the folder. All four-hundred twenty-two files. Next, he emptied the recycle folder. Then, he went somewhere into the invisible folders and deleted various other files and folders, before turning the screen back to me.

"If anything doesn't work properly, tell Richard. He'll fix it.

"This is down to trust," Father Muldrew continued. "I will presume that you put nothing on a USB stick on your own or uploaded anything to a great holding tank in the sky."

"I have not, Father," I said.

"Good. I think we're finished here. We'll see you before you leave, but I cannot tell you how much we value your work."

And I cannot tell you that I emailed everything to Sophie a week ago.

୧

Richard seemed to be embarrassed when he came to the apartment that evening. We stayed there long enough for me to tell him not to worry. I did what I had to do, just as they did what they had to.

"I can think of it as 'service to the Church' and hope I can get time off in Purgatory for not holding a grudge," I said.

Richard laughed.

"I suppose you've seen some changes in the Church," he said.

"Probably more since the Reformation," I said. "It survived that, it will survive this. Come, let's find a taxi."

We went to Trattoria della Pigna. I had not been there since Sophie left, and Fabrizia greeted me with delight and ran to find her father.

After introducing Richard to them, Tonio showed us to a table but wouldn't give us menus.

"I'll make something special. If Father Richard eats at a seminary, he'll eat anything," he proclaimed. "He will remember this meal and believe in Heaven all his life."

"I'm not a priest – I haven't been – "

"Forget it, Richard. By the time we leave, you'll be a monsignor."

As we were enjoying the bread and wine, Richard asked how I felt about my time in Rome.

"The city? My painting? Or 'The Vatican Project'?"

He laughed.

"You have had an adventurous time," he said. "I didn't mean any particular aspect, but let's start with the painting. I saw Carrie again and told her you'd painted me! I didn't tell her I was incognito as Cardinal Orsini."

I was pleased to see his nervous formality was gone.

"Actually, Orsini may not have been a cardinal at the time of the painting – "

He laughed.

"I know," he said. "When you told me who I'd be painted as, I looked him up. Not bad, becoming a cardinal at the age of twenty-three."

"He lived up to it," I replied.

Our fish course arrived. This would not be a meal to be rushed or to talk through.

When we'd finished the last of the whitebait, I asked about his university work. He told me about some of the complex research he was studying. He gave me an overview of the mathematics in layman's terms. I was interested in what he was doing, so I let him talk. Then, he suddenly broke off.

"I asked Brother Guy again this week, how he coped with the minutiae of the math, physics and chemistry of the cosmos without losing sight of the simple awe and wonder of the night sky."

He drank some wine as our dishes were cleared and before he continued.

"And what was his answer."

"He only had to think for a moment before he replied, 'AMDG'."

"That sums it up pretty well," I said. "For the greater glory of God. It goes right back to our earlier conversation about creation being God's second revelation."

Richard coughed.

Are you all right?

"I'm just amazed that you'd remember anything I said."

"When you are a priest, you must prepare to realise that people will remember everything you say," I replied. "More often than not, it will not be the bit that you think is important, but some little thing that resonates with their lives."

He thought about this while our next course arrived and some fat ravioli was placed before us.

"That's a humbling thought," he said.

As we ate, he returned to the subject of my feelings about being in Rome.

"Do you know that I was here with Ligeia Gordon, aka Sophie Gregg," I asked.

He looked embarrassed again.

"I didn't think it polite to ask," he managed to say.

"I can assure you that Miss Gordon is not my mistress – no matter what you might hear or suspect."

"I never – "

"Careful, it's not good for novices to lie."

He laughed.

I couldn't tell him the real reason, but used an alternative version.

"When you've known a woman since she was fourteen, and I was thirty, there is a distance that is not usually bridged."

He nodded.

"That's not why I raised the matter, either," I said. "I brought it up because painting religious subjects was her idea."

"Is she Catholic?"

"No. I think she's nominally Church of England. Even though I've known her for a long time, there are parts of her life that we don't discuss."

He seemed surprised by this.

"You should try to bring her back to Rome," Richard ventured.

I laughed.

"That was possibly the most difficult part of being here with her. I kept wanting to show her churches, statues and paintings," I said.

"Cramming religion down someone's throat is never a good idea," Richard agreed. "Yet, the religious paintings were her idea. That's very interesting – and intriguing. How did you handle it?"

"In the morning, I'd tell her where I was planning on going and let her choose whether to come. That was before I got tangled with Carrie's family and Father Reynolds."

"I call it God's sense of humour," Richard said.

"That's very interesting, so do I."

Chapter XXIX

Tuesday

God's sense of humour would be severely tested if today was anything to go by. It certainly tested the trust and patience of everyone I spoke to once the day got going.

After the previous nights memorable meal, it was hard to believe that I could even think about eating a *sfogliatella,* but one must eat something with one's *cappuccino* at Bar Latteria. There was nothing on my agenda apart from continuing to go through the cardinal's papers and pack. The latter would take no time, so I had a few days in hand. There was no need to rush on this beautiful Roman morning.

I did something I'd thought of doing since moving to via Plauto: I walked to Piazza del Risorgimento and walked the perimeter of Vatican City. It was about two miles, but on a lovely morning, moving in and out of the shadows and seeing centuries of architecture was a unique experience. Watching other people going about their business while one has nothing pressing always feels like a holiday.

By the time I stepped in the lift at Number 11, I was ready for another coffee before settling down to work, but it was not to be.

Once again, I found the door to Cardinal Mauro's apartment open and went in to investigate.

Inside were Father Muldrew, Father Reynolds and a layman I did not know. They stood, reading divers newspapers and did not look pleased.

"We thought you'd got lost," Father Muldrew said, in a tone that was less than friendly.

Father Reynolds shot him a look which he ignored.

"I wasn't aware I was punching a time-clock," I said as mildly as I could. "What seems to be the trouble, Father?"

He pushed a tabloid newspaper in my face. Big headlines screamed something but I only recognised two words: Vatican and Nazi.

Still trying to lower the temperature, I said that my Italian wasn't good enough to appreciate the full impact of the headline.

"It says that it has just come to light that a cache of valuable paintings and jewellery has been hidden by the Vatican since the War!" he bellowed.

The layman quietly went to the door and closed it. I hoped it wasn't to muffle gunshots.

"I had his eminence the Secretary of State on the telephone at quarter to six this morning," he continued.

"Ah! And so you are cross with me," I said, calmly. "Would you like me to have a word with his eminence on your behalf?"

Father Muldrew looked about to explode, but if being educated by the Jesuits and dealing with clergy all my life taught me anything, it was to be impervious to what my own blessed father called "ecclesiastical fascism."

Father Reynolds recognised that bluster was not going to work and intervened.

"This has worldwide implications," he said, as calmly as he could. "The story has appeared just about everywhere already."

"And the Vatican has said – let me guess – nothing."

Father Muldrew had recovered himself and spoke.

"I should introduce you to Mr Bonardi of the Press Office of the Holy See," he said.

We exchanged greetings, then I asked him.

"What has happened so far? It cannot have escaped anyone's attention that I worked with these paintings and artifacts for three weeks and the day after people come in to remove them, it's all over the press and all hell breaks loose. Sorry, Fathers."

Father Reynolds actually smiled.

"We have not been idle since quarter to six this morning," Father Muldrew said, slowly returning to better humour. "One porter and two juniors on the curatorial staff are already looking for new positions. We did not come here to accuse you."

I sensed that was the closest to an apology I'd get and didn't want him delving into my email history.

"I'm afraid you're the first person Father has encountered this morning who's not in a superior position," Father Reynolds said.

"Shall I make some coffee, and we'll see what can be done," I said, then turned to the press man. "Mr Bonardi, I am sure you are evolving a plan of action."

"Giovanni," he said. "And, yes, coffee sounds a good idea."

While he had been silent, he knew he was in the driver's seat in terms of managing this latest perceived scandal. We went into my rooms and I got the coffee underway.

"What is the response going to be?" I asked.

"That's the problem," Father Muldrew grumbled. "We've got no evidence of anything."

"Did you bring me the cardinal's file?" I cheekily asked. "There are so many letters from different congregations and dicasteries that I can't tell who he worked for or with."

There was the expected silence.

"You'll have it this afternoon," Father Muldrew said. "We need you to keep digging. Take as long as you need."

"Are you planning to say anything?" I asked Bonardi.

"I've got a draft holding statement but it hasn't been approved and. . ."

He paused and look at Father Muldrew who nodded.

"We need your permission, too."

I put the coffee pot down.

"Mine?"

Bonardi opened the small document folder he had with him and drew out two pages.

"The first bit explains the circumstances of the discovery of the paintings – more or less – then says that an independent art consultant had been appointed to look into things and make a report."

I gaped at them.

My brain raced. This looked lose-lose to me. I couldn't see that even with a *Deus ex machina* that this could be good for me.

"Whose brilliant idea was that?" I demanded.

"Mine," said Father Muldrew.

"I – "

"May I?" he said, more gently than I expected, and I nodded. "You already know this situation better than anyone. It would take two weeks for anyone else to learn as much as you do now. Access to the pictures will be difficult now as no one wants leaks from the museum.

"The report doesn't have to be long or detailed."

"But you will want some account of where they came from, how they were acquired and why Cardinal Mauro had them," I said.

"Yes," Father Muldrew and Bonardi said together.

I shook my head.

"I've been trying to find that out for two weeks and I'm no nearer now than I was when I began," I said. "I have one tenuous lead on one of the artists, but nothing is certain."

I stalled by pouring the coffee. We were seated at my table. No doubt their minds were running as fast as mine.

"There will be some conditions," I eventually said.

"What do you need?"

"Access to the Vatican's relevant art historians and anyone they think I should talk to."

"Agreed," Father Muldrew said.

"Translations already done and access to translators."

"Agreed."

"No one gets thrown under the bus unless they deserve it. Specifically, I don't want to explain to St Peter my part in defaming a dead cardinal."

"Agreed."

"This article – and those around the world – will compel those organisations that recover Nazi plundered art to be on the Vatican's doorstep tomorrow morning. I would like you three to agree today with the museum curators what access you will give them to the pictures.

"I won't set the terms, that's your area, not mine," I continued. "I would recommend that you let them see everything but take nothing – but whatever you decide, I will accept."

I paused for some coffee.

"This makes good sense," Bonardi said, before Father Muldrew could protest. "If we can get some of those organisations to state that they've been given access and that no hugely valuable Old Masters are involved, nor jewellery and artifacts of any great value, then we might get some perspective on the affair."

Father Muldrew pondered this.

"It's a big ask," he said. "Ultimately, it's not my decision."

"But it could be," I said. "Presumably your instructions were something like 'just sort it out!'"

"Actually it was, *'Fac!'*"

"Are you certain that's what he said?" Father Reynolds asked, with equanimity.

Bonardi exploded with a laugh which he tried to cover with a coughing fit. Father Muldrew glowered, but then looked resigned.

"Then, the decision is yours," I said.

"Oh, don't *you* go all Jesuitical on me! I get it all day from him!" he exclaimed, looking at Father Reynolds.

The tension was broken and we had a plan.

Of sorts.

◌

The three of them left shortly after that. I had what I thought I needed, and Father Reynolds told me I could continue to use Richard as a runner. Giovanni Bonardi and

I exchanged emails and telephone numbers and told each other to call about anything any time.

There was little I could do until the requisite files arrived and I had the name of an art historian to work with. I picked up a notebook and my pens and set out for the Vatican café for lunch.

It was busy, but by the time I'd placed my order and collected a drink, it was easy enough to find a space. I began evaluating what I might be able to do – even with the resources I'd been promised. At this point, I was most eagerly looking forward to receiving the answers to the questions I'd already requested. That and something about the elusive Cardinal Mauro.

My lunch was the Italian equivalent of a charcuterie board with a modest glass of Cesanese. I paid it inadequate attention and was nearly finished before realising how good it was.

Trying to get back in the moment, I looked around the room and listened to the congenial babble in several languages, including an animated discussion near me in Latin. I was trying to count the different tongues when I saw a man move from the counter after placing an order and taking a place with an elderly priest wearing the simple black suit and collar.

It was Stephano Polidori, and as I looked more closely at the exposed piece of the priest's white collar, I saw the flash of red. This at least gave me a clue as to how

Stephano had known about me remaining in Rome before it was general knowledge.

I had no reason to suspect anything other than coincidence, but then again, this was Rome.

കൗ

Things now began happening quickly and most of it was out of my control.

There was an email from Sophie, marked urgent and in red type,

> *Darling, Presumably this is somehow linked to what you're doing. Do be careful. Better still, get out of there as soon as you can.*
>
> *The play's going well and the cast has really hit its stride. Four days to opening night. I wish you could be there!*
>
> *Love,*
> *Sophie*

This was a predictable reaction. It was a bit frustrating as she gave no details about what she had read, and I realised that needed to be my first priority: to read what was actually written.

Most of the UK newspapers were now behind pay walls, but I was able to look at the BBC, Deutsche Welt, Al Jazeera, and a few other sources. Richard would know an international news stand at the railway station or

Fiumicino where he could get a selection in English and French.

While still at lunch, I thought that – in addition to pro-actively contacting the relevant offices of the Claims Conference, the World Jewish Congress, The Commission of Looted Art in Europe, the Holocaust Restitution Project, European Shoah Legacy Institute and others – the major national European art museums should be contacted. This outreach – as the Americans call it – would include an offer to send photos to authorised museum staff who requested it.

I called Giovanni and put it to him. He didn't like the idea, but when I noted that it could be cited as a sign that there would be no cover up, and that, internally, the position of the Vatican was that this would be proved not to be plunder, bribes or anything else.

"I don't know if I'm able to do that," he equivocated.

"What were Father Muldrew's instructions?"

"Make it happen," he said.

"I'll have to think about – "

"If you want to get in front of this, you cannot be reactive."

He was quiet for a while then asked me to email him an outline of my suggestions.

Apart from sending Richard to get the newspapers, there was nothing for me to do but continue going through the cardinal's mountains of papers. I had done two of four drawers and had not begun on the book shelves.

From what I could glean from the contents of the drawers, the cardinal was basically orderly if messy. The piles weren't neat, but they were pretty much in chronological order.

Lest anyone think I missed a TV detective trick, I emptied each drawer and inspected the bottom, sides, and the inside of the carcass of the secretary for panels and envelopes taped out of immediate sight. That is not to say there were not notes and the odd letter spilled over from the drawers. The bottom panel of the secretary had several receipts, bills from bookstores, and half a dozen paperclips and rubber bands.

Pasqualina came in with groceries while I was unpacking the third drawer.

"It is good news that you are staying a while longer," she said. "It's nice working here."

"You are good to me, Pasqualina," I said.

"You don't complain, you're not fussy, you don't tell me to get out of your way, you eat all my food, " she said, as she put things away. "And you don't ask questions."

"Did you work for Cardinal Mauro?"

She shook her head.

"He became unable to live here about a year after my husband died," she said. "By the time I was able to do anything, Father Mézard needed someone to keep an eye on the cardinal's apartment and dusted.

"Just before the lockdowns, the Polish students who were living in your apartment went back to Poland and I began cleaning this one, too," she said. "So, I never knew the occupants of either of the apartments. These could be very nice if they were modernised a little and had some comfortable furniture in them."

She looked around the cardinal's room.

"I'm sorry, I keep making a mess in here."

A cascade of laughter flowed from her.

"This is your work," she said.

While she was laughing, Richard came in. I told him to help himself to a coffee and that I was going to send him out again.

"I'd better start cooking," Pasqualina said, and began to leave.

"Can you stay for supper?" I asked Richard. "I'd like to review how things look like proceeding. There will be enough food, won't there, Pasqualina? There usually is."

"I'll make sure there is."

"Any progress?" Richard asked.

I shook my head.

"What are you hoping to find?"

"I wish I knew."

Almost immediately after Richard had left, another young man in black arrived.

"Sir Nigel?"

"Yes?"

"Father Castrini presents his compliments and asked me to give you this."

He opened a document case similar to one Bonardi had carried.

"These are the records of Giuseppe Cardinal Mauro," he said, handing them to me formally. "They are copies, so you can write on them, but they are confidential. When you are finished with them, give them to Father Muldrew for disposal.

"Please sign here."

After I had done so and handed them back, the young man said:

"Father Muldrew knows how many pages there are."

Chapter XXX

Tuesday

Like a magic trick explained, a mystery loses its intrigue when the truth is known. Some theologians have speculated that this disposition of Man to prefer the mystery to knowing the truth is part of the debris of The Fall. While I don't subscribe to that theory, the pheno-menon it describes does appear to have validity.

My father and uncle were World War II veterans which has imbued this project with personal interest. My father was an army officer and my uncle in the Royal Navy. Neither did anything heroic except survive, but they played a role in the defence of the realm. What I remember both of them saying throughout my child-hood and the remainder of their lives, was that while they were serving, there was no certainty that the allies would win.

I would watch the classic war films in the sure and certain knowledge that victory was assured, even at a tremendous price, but without that certainty would the enjoyment have been as great?

Throughout this project, I had only the pictures and small objects. In general terms, I recognised what they were, but had no idea what their being in Cardinal Mauro's apartment *meant*.

That is what is so hard to express after the fact.

I could see three possibilities:

First, that the cardinal, for whatever reason, had bought them. Against this theory was the fact that the pictures and objects were indifferent, ordinary. If the cardinal was a man of taste, would not the quality of them be more even? Would there not be something more than Judaica linking them?

Secondly, he had inherited them. Without knowing who the cardinal was or what he did, this was a blank. Was he a convert from Judaism? Was Mauro even his real name? And who might he have inherited them from? For all I knew, they could have been left in the apartment when he moved in.

Finally, there was the least attractive scenario, and that is the one the press was suggesting, if not baldly stating: that this was plunder; perhaps even extorted in exchange for protection of some sort.

I did not want to believe this last one but, like my father hoping we'd win the war, I did not know where – if anywhere – the search would lead. All I could do was go on.

I was working through the fourth and last drawer of the desk when Richard returned.

"Pour yourself a coffee or glass of wine," I said. "There are some sheets of paper, scissors and paste on the table. Can you cut out all the articles and paste them up and label them with the name of the newspaper and the date."

I finished the drawer without finding anything and put it back in place. Wearily, I sat down again at the table and opened the envelope with Cardinal Mauro's records.

Richard joined me, followed by Pasqualina carrying a tray with two glasses of wine and a plate of cheese and biscuits.

"I'm going now. Give dinner forty-five minutes at one hundred eighty. Ciao."

Richard had found eight English language newspapers from the US and UK.

"I went to the airport and talked to one of the people who cleans airplanes. They collect the newspapers and paperbacks left on the plane," he said. "They sell the paperbacks to second-hand book shops and the newspapers to various places for packing, *papier mâché* makers, language schools, and anyone else who'll give them some money."

"How much did you give them?" I asked, reaching for my wallet.

"Ten euros."

"You had the fares to and from the airport, too," I said, handing him fifty euros.

"That's not necessary, Sir Nigel," he protested. "Father Muldrew covers my expenses."

"You don't have to tell him that I paid you," I said.

Richard, tactfully, said nothing and put the money in his pocket.

I drank my wine as I watched him paste down the first clipping. He passed it to me. It made depressing and infuriating reading. Cleverly not saying anything definite, its implications were clear and renewed my determination to find evidence to combat the innuendoes.

I began reading through Cardinal Mauro's file.

"Where's Bevagna?" I asked Richard.

"I think it's in Umbria," he said. "It's supposed to be one of the most beautiful places in the country. It's where St Francis scolded the birds."

I laughed.

"A suitable place for a cardinal to be born."

I leafed through the pages. Giuseppe Mauro had been a cardinal since 1976, making him eligible to have been in the Conclaves for Paul VI and both John Pauls. By the time Benedict XVI was elected, Cardinal Mauro was over eighty and ineligible to vote.

At various times in his cardinalate, he had served in the Congregations for Catholic Education, the Bishops, and for the Mission as well as being assigned a range of daily administrative and active work. He appeared to have done much in distributing food and clothing to the needy in and around Rome.

The pages were not in chronological order, and I hoped that was not an indication that the file had been tampered with.

There were pages with comments on them in Italian or Latin dating from the fifties, sixties, seventies and eighties. While not outright performance reviews, from what I could gather they did relate to the projects he had worked on or was responsible for.

I then came to one of the things I'd been looking for. There was the Italian wartime ID card of a young man from Bevagna. It had his home address, a photograph, his occupation (student) and his address in Rome: Pontificia Università Urbaniana. A further note indicated that he'd only been there one year, having moved into Vatican City in September 1943.

This was worth a phone call.

Richard continued to clip the newspapers and glue down the articles as I telephoned Father Reynolds.

After impatient pleasantries, I asked him if he – or anyone at the college – knew about what happened to seminarians when the Germans moved into Rome.

He confirmed my suspicions that those who couldn't or didn't want to escape were accommodated in Vatican City and continued their instruction from whomever was available to do it.

This much I had guessed, but learning who he had studied with might open another door, but I had seen nothing. I found that he had been made a deacon in 1949 and ordained a priest in 1952. For his work in the Sacred Congregations, he had been created a titular bishop by Pope St John XXIII in 1960 and elevated to cardinal in 1976.

I was sure there was more that I didn't recognise, but this was more than I'd been able to winkle out in three weeks.

It was dark and we'd both been working by a poor overhead light before Richard fetched the standing LED lights from my apartment. The improved lighting gave us both second wind.

I returned to the final drawer. Everything there related to duties in the sixties.

I sighed.

"I think it's time to bring the bottle in here, Richard," I said, standing. "No, I'll get it. Could you slide that drawer back where it belongs."

He had done so when I returned with the wine and was looking at the large bookcase. It stood more than seven feet high and was about as wide, in two sections. It had shelves all the way to the floor and looked to be a piece of standard institutional furniture. How they got it up here was a mystery.

"Must have come flat-packed," Richard joked.

"Have you finished the cuttings?"

He nodded.

"The story they tell is remarkably similar."

"Probably just grabbed off the wires."

I poured him a glass and sat down.

"How did you get on?" he asked.

"I know where he's from, where he studied, when he was ordained and made a bishop and cardinal. Judging from all his notes, who he worked with and the offices he worked for, I would guess he was considered a safe pair of hands. A work horse, not a show horse."

Richard looked around.

"This is the apartment of someone serious about a modest life."

We sat quietly.

"Suppose you don't find anything?" he asked.

"Earlier, I was thinking that was unthinkable," I said. "Now that I am faced with the real possibility, it will just be another slander on the Church. Worse than some, less than others. The reality is that no matter what you tell some people, they will continue to believe what they want to believe."

"Ha! I never thought you were that cynical, Sir Nigel!"

I smiled it him.

"Like death, it comes to us all."

᪥

I cleared the table and went to the book case and removed the books from the top shelf left section and stacked them on the table. Before sitting down to go through them, I checked the back of the shelf to see if anything had fallen behind the books.

I flipped through each book, looked for inscriptions, addresses and dates, and loose bits of paper. It took about twenty seconds per book.

"Would you like me to help with that?" he asked.

I shook my head.

"Not to be a *prima donna*, but if someone misses something, I want it to be me," I said. "What you can do is get the next shelf down and stack it up, then put these back on the shelf. The order isn't critical. Check the back of the shelves, too."

We continued this way without finding anything significant in the books. Richard did find a collection of memorial cards behind the books and the odd funeral programme. I wondered what he did with the programmes to the installations of the popes and their funerals. They must be around somewhere.

"Perhaps he didn't feel he needed to keep them. There must be copies in all the libraries," Richard offered.

Richard put the memorial cards aside to look at later. They weren't all related to deaths. Some were for ordinations, consecrations, anniversaries and other occasions of celebration for the clergy.

When we'd cleared the whole left-hand section of the bookcase, I told Richard to turn the oven on. That put a forty-five-minute time limit on what we were doing.

I had come to a row of books on English saints. I'd seen no evidence of books or writings in English, but here there were books on St Thomas More, St Thomas Becket, a book on Bishop Lancelot Andrews by an American Jesuit, and a book about St John Fisher. These latter two looked like dissertations whereas the first two were more popular biographies.

The Lancelot Andrews book had nothing inside, though I noted it was published in 1955, by Loyola University in the U.S. The book on St John Fisher was published in 1943 by Pontificia Università Urbaniana.

Opening it, I saw a dedication: *"To Father Mauro" on his ordination, Owen. 1952.*

The book was by a Father Owen Snedden who obviously had some connection with the cardinal possibly reaching back to the university. Typical of a dissertation, there were no biographical details.

I showed Richard when he came back in.

"Have you looked him up on the web yet?" he asked, with interest. "This is the first name you've come across that could relate to the forties' period."

I turned my laptop towards him.

"Go ahead. I'm going to continue this."

I left the Fisher book out but returned the rest and unloaded the next stack and began going through them.

"Holy shit!" Richard exclaimed, then spent the next few minutes apologising.

It shocked me so much (coming from him; it is part of the vernacular of the art world) that I didn't reply.

"Owen Snedden was a New Zealander who later became the Auxiliary Bishop of Wellington."

"A cardinal and a bishop, not bad," I said.

Richard gave a short laugh.

"It's not the bishop who's important: it's the bishop's friend, the monsignor!"

He turned the computer back to himself and read:

"This is from a New Zealand historical magazine: 'Father Owen Snedden and fellow New Zealand priest, Father John Flanagan, during the Nazi occupation of Rome were part of the clandestine operations that protected thousands of Jews in the city headed by *Monsignor Hugh O'Flaherty!*'"

It took a moment to take this in.

"'The Scarlet Pimpernel of the Vatican,'" I whispered.

He had hidden thousands of Jews and allied soldiers around Rome during the German occupation, and kept them protected or helped them to escape.

I flopped back in the chair, my mind racing.

"That indicates a clear link with refugee Jews," I said. "But it doesn't get us much further with the pictures. It just shows that there was opportunity to take them."

"Perhaps," Richard said, soberly, "but you don't believe that."

"No," I said, standing up. "We'll keep digging."

And we went through the books on the next shelf, and the next. Only two more before we'd done.

Richard was restacking the shelves and taking books out of the antepenultimate shelf when he stopped.

"Hello."

He removed a large old envelope and handed it to me. It was heavy paper, gusseted and closed with a string washer. Richard quickly finished removing the rest of the books and sat with me to see what was in it.

There was an old-fashioned order book with printed lines, numbered sheets and carbon paper. The book was about half-used, but when I looked at the first carbon copy, I knew we were done.

Eva Gusman
Precedentemente di Via del Portico d'Ottavia, 16
Roma
Un ciondolo a forma di stella di Davide in argento
36 cm
Per la custodia.
15 Gennaio 1944

Then, Sra Gusman's signature and Father Snedden's. I recognised the writing from his brief inscription in the book.

"*Per la custodia*," Richard said, slowly. "For safe keeping. This was not plunder."

"No, it was not."

We went back to the first entry. It was dated October 1943, a month after the Germans moved in. It listed a painting of a Shabbat meal (*Cena di Shabbat con candele, pane e vino*) and gave its dimensions.

Most gratifying were the pages we'd come to that were crossed through with big "X"s and the words, "*Consegnato,*"or "*Raccolta,*" on them with dates and further addresses, some in distant lands like England, the United States and one to New Zealand.

We were both engrossed in these discoveries when the alarm for dinner went off. I went to set the table in my apartment and get the dishes out as well as a new bottle of wine which I felt we deserved.

Richard came in with the receipt book while I was doing this.

"Look," he said, enthusiastically, "All of the receipts were signed by Father Snedden, but the returns were all signed by Cardinal Mauro. Why do you suppose that was?"

"We'll have to check," I said.

Richard stood.

"Do you want me to get the laptop?"

"No," I said. "I want to enjoy this nice meal and talk about something else."

Pasqualina, as usual, had done us proud with a delightful salad and a lemon chicken dish on pasta with basil sauce. There's no doubt that I'd miss this on my return to London.

Hard though it was, once we started joking about the impossibility of time-travel and inaccuracy of science fiction "science," the power of good food and congeniality took over. We didn't rush our desserts, but we did take our coffees back to the cardinal's rooms and sat at the table. I was feeling weary in spite of the excitement of our discovery. Richard picked up the receipt book and slowly read the entries.

"What's the date of the first return?" I asked.

He flipped through some pages, turning forward and back to confirm.

"February 1947."

I sat up.

"When did Father Snedden leave Rome?"

Richard caught my train of thought and tapped the laptop, waking it up. The page we had read was still open. He scrolled down the screen.

"He was designated a military chaplain and left Italy in 1945 – hey! – he collected an OBE on the way home."

It all fit.

"The Germans surrendered in April but the fighting in Italy went on for another few weeks, though they had already begun to withdraw from Rome," Richard read from the laptop. "From about mid-May, people were able to move again."

If this led where I thought it would, so would I, I thought.

Richard looked at the remaining papers from the envelope.

"What do you suppose these are?" he asked. "Sir Nigel?"

I looked up.

"I'm sorry, Richard. Supper was too good, and I was *reflecting* on the possibilities."

"These letters?"

I shrugged, but then reached across the table and began to glance through them. Most were in Italian, but one was in English from the United States and said it all.

"Listen to this, Richard:"

Dear Father Mauro,

It is hard to believe that nearly three years have passed since the end of the horrors. Our lives here in Missouri are blissfully boring, the only excitement being when the President visits his hometown.

When one is used to thinking that normal life will never return, it is hard to accept it when it does – especially in a foreign land.

The return of our precious painting has closed that time of fear and made our new lives seem secure and complete. Thank you, Father, for restoring our personal heritage. . .

Epilogue

2 December

My exit from Rome was fast. The day after our discovery, I met with Father Muldrew and handed all the documents over with a synopsis of my conclusions. Giuseppe Bonardi was summoned to Father's office, given the information and told to put a statement together.

It would be weeks before it was approved. In the end, I didn't see anything apart from a small paragraph in *The Tablet*, that said that owners of the property, believed by some to have been looted from refugees, had been identified and efforts were being made to return it to the owners or their heirs.

Sophie was furious.

"After all your work! You must be seething," she said, outraged. "Apart from anything, it's a fabulous story about the commitment of the Vatican to protect property as well as people."

"The people in the Vatican know," I said, having argued her very points vociferously at the time.

"It's not enough!" she protested.

"Sometimes, it's enough that only the right people know."

I couldn't argue. I had tried to convince myself that it was enough that the Vatican knew, and that Cardinal Mauro's actions in this had been of the same high standard that it appeared to be in other aspects of his life and work.

While justice had been done, it hadn't been seen to be done. That was a mortal failing and nothing I could do anything about.

Sophie also wanted to know about the Polidoris and was unhappy with the little I had to tell her.

"You never knew where Stephano fit into all this?"

"No."

"And you never heard from Francesca again?" she tried again.

"No."

"Oh, you can be so infuriating!"

Wasn't it enough to have solved the riddle?

ᦊ

June

Since my arrival back in London, I had kept a low profile – at least until the Summer Exhibition at the Royal Academy opened. Critics and art writers who I never knew existed were writing about my supposed conversion into some Bible-beating evangelist churning out religious art.

After the third interview, I declined other requests. I pointed out that these weren't religious pictures *per se*, rather they were depictions of religious people – most of them not even saints. Being England, *Thomas More in His Cell* received the most attention and was widely reproduced in newspapers and magazines. People wanted to know who the model was for *Julian of Norwich*, and there was a great deal of speculation, much of it very amusing (to me at least).

As for *Galileo Building an Orrery with Alasandro Orsini and St Robert Cardinal Bellarmine*, no one appeared to get the joke – probably because no one knew what an orrery was. Several commented that the title was too long.

Speaking of jokes, despite the disparaging remarks about pseudo-religious art for a post-religious age, all three were sold by lunchtime on opening day.

"Was I doing any more religious paintings?" "Would I do more 'normal' portraits?" "Was I retiring?"

These questions were most asked. No one asked why I chose religious figures to paint let alone those people in particular. Regrettably, they probably didn't know enough to ask.

I had been, in fact, working on a few more. I'd thought of painting *Thomas á Becket Arguing with Henry II,* but didn't want to stir up any more Church and State turbulence. The idea of doing St George, St Andrew, St David and St Patrick separately had a flickering appeal, but that required a commitment I wasn't sure I could sustain. It would be like starting on the treadmill again, and I had enjoyed being off it.

Sophie was uncharacteristically quiet about all this. I think she was still in shock that I'd risen to her challenge at all and was afraid of setting a new one. She was also still surprised by the success of her play which looked like running for at least another year.

Shortly after the exhibition opened, I received a commission from the buyer of Sir Thomas More for a companion piece of Bishop John Fisher in his cell in the Tower. The idea appealed both as a project and as an homage to Bishop Snedden and Cardinal Mauro. I'd find a way of working a nod to both of them into the picture, and that would close the circle for me.

"You've got a full calendar of saints to run through," Sophie said one evening over a late dinner after a performance.

I'd made a *cacio e pepe* which had turned out reasonably well. With her schedule, the opportunities for dining were restricted.

We drank our wine slowly, and I had the feeling that something was on Sophie's mind. I'd noticed a hesitancy after the novelty of my return from Italy wore off. I'd put it down to us both becoming used to not seeing each other everyday. Then, I thought it might just be the creeping strain of a potentially long run. Tonight, I wondered about her health. It had occurred to me before, but my sense of it was now stronger.

"I have one of your favourite desserts," I said.

She looked up and smiled. In the candlelight, she was ageless and the smile reminded me of one of her first visits.

"What have you made?" she asked, with a little girl giggle.

"I'll give you a hint: I haven't made it yet."

She thought for about four seconds.

"*Zabaglione!*"

I smiled.

She gave a big smile and leaned forwards anxiously.

"You know me so well."

"Oh, spare me the clichés."

And she laughed again.

"I am going to make you work for it, though."

She nodded.

"What do you want?"

I took a deep breath.

"I want you to tell me what's bothering you. Are you all right?"

Her smile disappeared.

"You're an outstanding actress," I said, to give her time to decide how to answer, "but I can tell when you *are* acting."

She stood from her place at the end of the table and moved to the chair at right angles to me. She sat, composed herself, then faced me.

"We've been a curious pair for nearly two decades," she began. "I moved into your life deliberately because I felt you knew something of the real me. I still believe that.

"When I was alone here and you were in Italy, I was not expecting to miss you as much as I did. I thought hard about what it was that I missed, after all, I had endless fawning attention and didn't need to be alone a single night – but, of course, I had to be.

"Was it the familiarity I missed? Or, was it not having you there to recognise who and what I really am?"

She stopped and thought.

"More than anything, it's your quiet influence," she continued. "Being around you makes me a nicer person. When you weren't here – oh, don't worry, I behaved, and no one saw any change in me – but I was uncomfortable with myself. And like all people of a certain age, I went to see my doctor."

I instantly lost any enthusiasm for *zabaglione*.

She reached back to her place for her wine glass.

"The play looks set to run and the audiences appear to like. . ."

It was at moments like this that I was glad she lived across Rope Walk.

"Nigel? Are you all right? You look dreadful!"

She started to stand.

"*You went to see the doctor. . .*"

"Yes. I'm fine. He gave me some iron tablets," she said, casually. "But you – "

"I'm – I'm fine now," I managed to say. "You frightened me."

Sophie sighed.

"*If you let me finish*," she said, sounding genuinely peeved. "The play looks set to run and the audiences appear to enjoy it, so we should make it into a second year.

"My contract runs until the end of August, and I'm tired. I mean long-term tired. I've been performing almost non-stop for nearly forty years. I've been blessed and haven't had long periods resting, but I haven't had many real holidays, either."

I was so relieved that I missed her next few sentences but it was an abbreviated chronology of her career.

"I loved our break in Rome," she was saying when I tuned back in. "I think I'd like to go again, but live there, not in a hotel. We'd have to find two apartments near each other. It wouldn't do for you to be shacked up on the doorstep of the Vatican."

I was laughing now.

"You said the apartment you were living in and the cardinal's were being renovated. Do you think they'll be done by then?"

She kept up her stream of enthusiasm as I prepared the *zabaglione*.

Over the next few weeks, more pieces came together that made this mad idea more plausible.

I had an email from Father Reynolds saying that Father Muldrew was named a cardinal by His Holiness. It was unusual for someone who was not an archbishop, or at least a bishop, to be elevated, but this pope was one for surprises, though I suspect Father Muldrew had well earned his elevation. The ceremony would be in St Peter's in early September.

Also in September, according to Sophie, would be the premier of Gaetano Minetti's film, now called *L'amore riccordato*, and, of course, Sophie was invited.

Richard's ordination might also fall into that timeframe.

Sophie wanted to stay in Rome for six months and use it as a base for touring Italy. Not being a stage or film star, I would have to continue to work and had calculated how many pictures I'd have to sell to keep both the Albany set and Southwark studio.

One Sunday evening, when there was no performance, Sophie came in and made herself a gin and tonic. She found me looking at online property listings.

"That's not Rome," she said, looking over my shoulder.

"No. I'm trying to get an idea how much I could get for my studio," I said. "It's gone up a bit since I bought it forty years ago."

"What do you want to sell it for? It's your *studio*! You'll be coming back," she said, sounding horrified that I'd think of selling it.

"I know you don't think of such things, but three apartments don't pay for themselves," I said.

"So, how many paintings do you reckon it will cost to stay in Rome for six months?"

"Half a dozen?"

"And how many can you paint in six months, given that you now don't have to rely on commissions?"

I burst out laughing.

"So, this is a holiday for you, but I've got to keep working? I see."

"Oh, stop worrying!" she said, dismissively, setting down her empty glass. "What was it you told me? 'And all shall be well, and all shall be well, and all manner of things shall be well.'

"Now, put that away and let's go find someplace for supper."

Notes & Acknowledgements

A number of liberties have been taken in this story. The first significant one is that due to the closing of a rail tunnel, the sleeper service described was not running between Paris and Rome at the time of the story. I have used a pastiche of Thello and Frescarossa services as they had run prior to the landslide.

While the Roman Forum has several entrances and exits, only the one near the Colosseum can be counted on to be open. A further reason not to take this novel as a guidebook is that the frequency of Roman buses, trams and subways is not as reliable as might be inferred.

The quotation on p. 39, like that on page v, is from Josephine Tey's enduring historical detective novel, *The Daughter of Time*, and the man described was Richard III.

Scott Erikson's YouTube videos, including the one referred to in Chapter V, "Why the Church Needs Art," are thought-provoking and accessible.

The detective story mentioned in Chapter XVII is by Lisa Scottoline

The money collected from the Trevi Fountain belongs to the Catholic Church and is spent, through the charity, Caritas, to feed and house the poor.

The painter referred to on page 223 is Darren Thompson.

The Hilaire Belloc quote is taken from Robert Speaight's excellent biography published in 1957.

Of the clergy mentioned, Monsignors Michele Basso, and Hugh O'Flaherty and Bishop Owen Snedden and Father John Flanagan were real and so are the remarkable things they did.

Reservations and getting tickets for the Galleria Borghese and other museums and sites in Rome can be expensive and frustrating. However, when one realises the reasons, it's forgivable. It's not about exclusivity, though this is a by-product, it's about self-preservation, and only those who are genuinely interested will persist.

I acknowledge the allusion (p. 269) to Garrison Keillor's delightful line about dining in a Midwestern Lutheran family in *A Prairie Home Companion*, "Food was not fuel but ballast; we ate and then sank like rocks."

Additionally, Adelina (p. 270) was Inspector Montalbano's devoted housekeeper throughout the series, but notably in Andrea Camilleri's story, "Gli arancini di Montalbano" ("Montalbano's Croquettes").

Those interested in the clandestine activities of the Roman Catholic Church during World War II should read Mark Riebling's *A Church of Spies*, and listen to Hugh Costello's radio play for the BBC, *My Dear Children of the Whole World*.

Thanks to London-based portrait painter, Phyllis Dupuy, for sharing her technical expertise; Ian Thomson, author, for his arcane information on language and rhetoric; Dr Jan Wubbena and Mlle A. Smith for their musical expertise, and Cristina Rossi for help with Italian. Thanks also to Julie Dexter who helped me through another book.

By the same author:

Other Novels

Ardmore Endings
The Rock Pool
Lost Lady
The Countess Comes Home
Entrusted in Confidence
Portland Place: A novel of the time of Jane Austen
The Camels of the Qur'an
Wachusett
Nantucket Summer

Lattimer & Co.

Lattimer & Co. was established in Philadelphia in 1870 by "Colonel" Jonas Lattimer. The company now includes the imprints of Defarge Frères and Éditions Chaillot, both of Paris.

Printed in Great Britain
by Amazon

43059199R00219